Rand pulled  **into a garage the parking lot of her apartment complex.**

He shifted the transmission into park and turned to her. "Please listen to me. I'm not saying anything disparaging about Adam. It's my uncle's reaction that I'm concerned about."

"I hate this whole thing," she said bitterly. "I hate it! Do you understand?"

He reached for her and she yanked free. "Don't. I detest you, too."

"You're getting much better at this, aren't you?"

"I beg your pardon?"

"The lying—it's starting to roll freely from your tongue."

"I am not lying."

"Yes, you are."

"Oh, believe me. I do detest you."

"No, you don't." His voice was a tease.

Taken aback by his arrogance she stared at him, wide-eyed and speechless.

"I hate your guts. How's that?"

Rand leaned in dangerously close to her. She could see his eyes alive with amusement in his dimly lit car's interior. She held her breath.

"You may hate my guts, madam, but you're rather fond of my lips."

Daisy bolted from the car and slammed the door. She could hear his laughter as she stormed to her front entrance. Fumbling with her key, she cursed it for not cooperating. Finally her door opened. She locked it behind her, turning the deadbolt with a flourish.

Reviews of M. Kate Quinn's
The Perennials series:

"A mother's love, an uncle's fortunes, a tangled web of deception all lead to love in M. Kate Quinn's latest release, *BROOKSIDE DAISY*. Daisy and Rand, along with a delicious cast of secondary characters, make *BROOKSIDE DAISY* as scrumptious as any NJ diner's bakery section. (All cooking done on the premises, of course.)"

~Shirley Hailstock, award-winning author, current president New Jersey Romance Writers, past president Romance Writers of America

~*~

"*MOONLIGHT AND VIOLET* is a beautifully written novel about family relationships and second chances at love. Strong character development, an appealing storyline and amusing dialogue engage the reader and keep *MOONLIGHT AND VIOLET* at a fast pace. M. Kate Quinn tugs at the heartstrings and delivers a story that will bring laughter as well as tears. *MOONLIGHT AND VIOLET* is a rare treat!"

~Long and Short Reviews, Top 500 Reviews

~*~

SUMMER IRIS: "A remarkable talent for creating realistic characters, secondary characters are as well developed as the main characters. One thing is for sure, M. Kate Quinn is definitely an author to keep your eye on!"

~Detra Fitch, Huntress Reviews

~*~

SUMMER IRIS, Book One of the Perennials Series, is a finalist in the Golden Quill Awards 2011, Best First Book Category.

Brookside Daisy

The Perennials, Book Three

by

M. Kate Quinn

Dear Kelly,
Happy Birthday!
Best
M. Kate Quinn

Brookside Daisy: The Perennials, Book Three

COPYRIGHT © 2012 by M. Kate Quinn

Cover Art by *Kim Mendoza*

The Wild Rose Press
PO Box 708
Adams Basin, NY 14410-0706
Visit us at www.thewildrosepress.com

Publishing History
First *Last Rose of Summer* Edition, 2012
Print ISBN 978-1-61217-009-1

Published in the United States of America

Dedication

To my champion, my daughter
Melanie Rose Hemsey,
and her husband, Emil Hemsey,
on this, the year of your wedding.

All the blessings for all your lives.

Chapter One

It was half past Saturday and his Rolex was ticking. J. Randolph Press, Jr. yanked open the door to the smarmy little office of Uncle William's attorney and charged into the room. Max Willoughby's reception area was an ice box. It was dark and dead silent, like a tomb.

Sure, Rand thought angrily, *the whole damned staff is out enjoying their weekend while I've been all but summoned here to overcrowded downtown Morristown on a perfect September day. Is everybody in northern New Jersey shopping here today, for crying out loud? This better be good.*

"Max?" Rand barked. The bitterness in his tone was satisfying to his ears.

"Randolph, come in." The familiar whine called out from down the corridor where a beam of light streamed out of the back office.

Rand made a beeline down the carpeted walkway and strode across the room. He sat hard onto what had to be the latest addition to the attorney's collection of ostentation, a tapestry-covered Louis XIV arm chair. Uncle paid this clown a fortune.

Max, a little, nervous, weasel-looking man with his beady eyes and pointy nose, leaned forward on his desk. The mahogany edifice was so immense the twerp looked even more absurd. A file folder sat open in front of him. "Thank you for coming, Randolph. Your uncle—"

"Cut to the chase, Max. What's up?"

Max cleared his throat, his pinched look soured.

Too bad. Rand stared him down. "Just spill it. I've got things to do."

One of *those things* involved a certain blonde flight attendant that he'd met on the trip back from Vegas. Now there was no way he'd have time to meet with her before her next take-off. No great loss, but still.

"Your uncle has taken a turn for the worse."

"Since when?" Now Rand was more annoyed. Why hadn't Florence called him to report that his only relative's health was failing? Why had the old guy's caretaker sidestepped him and called this shyster first?

"I'm not sure," Max continued. "You can find out the details of William's condition from his doctors or from his in-home, Florence Harvinger."

"So then why am I here?"

Max fingered the file in front of him, thumbed through the top pages. "William has changed his will, I'm afraid."

Rand gripped the arms of the chair he sat in, tight enough for the old wood to creek in protest. He took a deep breath. "Be specific."

"All right, Randolph. Here it is, in a nutshell. William has had some concerns about how you've handled your inheritance from your parents' estate. And, I'm afraid he's convinced the pattern would continue with his holdings once he's departed."

It was true that his parents' money was all but gone, and that his existence depended on the rest of the Press fortune. But he wasn't going to let this punk think he was nervous.

Rand was adept at bluffing. His recent success at the Bellagio's craps tables were a testament to his ability. But right now he felt a tremor rise up from the pit of his gut, climbing like a vine to strangle him.

"So, what's that mean, Max? I'm out?"

"No, not exactly."

"Then what?"

"William's stated that he intends to leave all his worldly goods to charity unless you can show distinctly that you have"—Max paused to clear his throat, lifted the top corner of the page in his folder, and recited from the text—"'turned a new leaf with your conduct.'" Max looked up from the paper, and waited.

Too stunned to comment, Rand nodded his head as though sizing up the new deal. But what he was really doing was trying to process the bullshit that Max had just spewed.

Max looked down again at the paperwork. "William would like to see that you've become settled, Randolph. That you're living a more stable existence."

"For God's sake, Max. What's he want from me?"

"Apparently marriage."

The words struck him funny, like an earthquake had tickled him in the ribs. Rand released a loud, harsh crack of laughter. "That's absurd."

Max shrugged his narrow shoulders. "That's his stipulation. He's stated here that if you don't have a wife by your fortieth birthday...well, the fortune goes to charity."

His fortieth birthday—that was just over three months from now! *How the hell am I supposed to do that? That's ludicrous. Maybe the old guy's lost his marbles. Yeah, that's what it is. Uncle William's off his rocker.*

Rand could feel the familiar curve of his signature charming grin sprouting onto his lips. "Now, does that sound rational to you, Max? I mean...come on."

"William has all his faculties, Randolph. I assure you he's not delusional or anything close to it. He's as sound as he's ever been. His ticker's giving out, but his mind's quite fine."

Rand tasted his own blood. He hadn't been aware at just how hard he had bit the inside of his mouth. He wanted some water, but he knew that asking would reveal his angst. He wasn't giving up his hand. Instead, he crossed his legs, placed his elbows on the arms of his chair, and folded his hands in his lap like a ticket-holder patiently awaiting his goddamned train.

"Is that all?"

"He's unhappy with your idleness, Randolph— and your playboy exploits. He won't see his fortune go toward paying off more women whom you've scorned."

Rand knew better than to deny the allegation. Uncle William had come through for him with the last two women who had declared Rand had ruined their lives. He'd alienated affection, blah, blah, blah—it was always the same. The ladies had dried their eyes with a big fat check to soothe their so-called pain.

Each time he had assured his uncle that it was the end. But, then another beauty would pop into his line of vision and, well, it would start again.

He looked out the window, beyond Max's baseball of a head. The sky was a cloudless expanse of startling blue. He could have been taking a country drive through the hills of northern Jersey with the pretty flight attendant, Debbie—or was it Donna?—charming her into staying at an inn, perhaps. Rand shook his head, throwing that image right out the window.

I'll be damned if anyone is going to cut me off, especially for such preposterous, controlling bullshit delivered by this little squirrel of a lawyer.

He cleared his throat and blurted out the first thing that came to mind. "Lucky for me, I guess, that my lady and I are ring shopping. Please relay the good news to Uncle."

Max's mouth pressed into a seamless line, his eyebrows waving at Rand like imbecilic caterpillars. "Randolph, I'm sure you know that your Uncle has ways to verify this...uh, news."

Rand gave a nonchalant shrug. "That's not a problem, Max. But, please don't have Uncle delve into my personal life just yet. I'm planning a surprise and I wouldn't want his bloodhounds to blow the big moment for her."

"I see," Max said, eyeing Rand with his black-pebble eyes. "But, just so you're aware...William will not hold off long. My guess is that he'll want to meet your, um, your..."

"Fiancée, Max. You can say it." Rand was incredulous as he kept digging the hole. He staged a chuckle. "I'm still getting used to it myself."

"What's your fiancée's name? Your uncle will want to know."

Rand wagged a finger at the little rodent. "Not yet, Max. It's a surprise."

Max slapped the file folder closed and laced his girlie-looking hands on top of it. "Do you have a proposal date, Randolph? Or is this some nebulous plan?"

"Of course I do," Randolph said with just the right amount of indignity in his tone.

Max reached a hand to his desk calendar and flipped a page. "And what is that date?"

"Uh-uh. Not yet, Max." Rand feigned amusement to cover his itch to punch this guy.

They locked eyes for a long moment before Max spoke. "Then what date shall I tell your anxious uncle that he can meet your bride-to-be?"

Bride-to-be! Okay, those words almost blew his chicanery. Randolph felt the floor beneath his feet tip like a funhouse. Only there was nothing fun about any of this.

5

With everything he had in him Randolph lifted a steady hand into his inside jacket pocket and grabbed his Blackberry. He pretended to consult his calendar, and paused just enough to appear to be calculating a good time for his crackpot uncle to meet this made-up fiancée *after* the non-existent proposal. He needed to stall this nightmare. "How's Thanksgiving?"

"William may not have that long, Randolph. And, if he's not satisfied with your *improved lifestyle*, I'm afraid he may decide to go forward with the charity endowment."

Rand stared at his hand-held screen some more, then lifted his head. "Okay, how about October first?"

Max twisted his mouth. "If you're willing to risk losing your inheritance...fine. If not, I suggest you move it up, son. Or you and your, uh, new bride may find yourselves penniless."

"How soon would you suggest then, Max?" Rand knew when to fold them. He was out of cards.

The lawyer rustled the pages of his calendar, flipped back and forth, making a racket.

Randolph steeled himself for the response that he was sure Max was delaying for dramatic effect. How he'd love to serve the weasel that calendar for lunch.

"I'm assuming you'll need a little time to make arrangements. How's next Friday?"

Six days! How on earth am I supposed to pull this off in six little days?

Randolph pulled air into his lungs, forcing the tension in his chest to release. He smiled at the man who held all the cards in his pasty little hands. "Next Friday would be fine."

Max grinned in return, a disingenuous curve of his lips, a victor's smile. "I'll let your uncle know the wonderful news.

"Thank you." Rand stood on legs that no one would ever guess were wobbly enough to collapse.

"I'll call you on your cell to give you his response."

"Wonderful," Rand said. He reached across the desk and shook the man's clammy little paw.

Striding through the interior, he elbowed open the front door and padded down the steps to his Jaguar XF. A parking ticket graced its windshield. Randolph flipped the card onto his passenger seat, poked the keyless start button, and shifted into reverse. He turned out onto the thoroughfare and floored it the minute the road opened up. He zipped over the Algonquin Bridge with no thought to his destination. He would look back upon this move as fate.

Chapter Two

Daisy Cameron looked up from the stack of receipts, losing her train of thought as she tallied. She eyed the Brookside Café's bank of windows, grateful for the empty parking lot beyond. It had been a long Saturday and all she wanted to do was finish closing up the little diner so she could get in her car and go the hell home.

Her friend Candy broke into Daisy's thoughts. "I'm almost done with these things."

Candy stood at the counter with a lineup of salt and pepper shakers, their chrome toppers removed. She decanted white granules into some of the glass receptacles and tapped black powder into others. She reminded Daisy of a mad scientist with her pinch-browed concentration.

Daisy looked back at her fistful of tickets. "I lost count again."

"I've got to get out of here. I have to drive Little Bruno to his friend's birthday party."

Daisy looked up at the clock over the register. "I know. I've got to get home, too. I want to go over Adam's paperwork from Pratt Institute before he goes out with his buddies."

"Daisy, not for nothing, honey, but you sure you want to do that?"

"Do what?" Daisy looked up and regarded her friend.

Candy stood with hands on her ample hips, doubt contorting her pretty, cherubic face. "I just don't want you to get your kid's hopes up—or yours either—if, you know, you can't swing the tuition."

"I'll figure it out. I'm not worried." Daisy turned back to her task, punching keys on her calculator. She wondered how many times she'd need to say that in order to actually believe it.

"I learned a long time ago that there's the *haves* and the *have-nots*. You just have to, you know, embrace whichever team you're on." Candy shrugged and wiped up the grains from her endeavor.

"Well, then, Adam's going to be a 'have'."

"Okay, Daisy-girl, I believe you." Candy smiled affectionately. "You almost done?"

"Five minutes and we'll lock up."

Only, that was five minutes too late. The front door to the café opened wide. The bell above the door rattled as if protesting the intrusion.

A tall, well-dressed man stood on the welcome mat, covering most of the letters with his shiny alligator loafers, the only letters still visible spelled "me."

Daisy eyed the man, catching the scowl on his lips and the crease in his brow. He strode to the far end of the counter, a folded newspaper tucked tight under his arm, without so much as acknowledging the two women in the small interior of the luncheonette. He mounted a stool as if he owned it.

"Crap," Candy whispered. She clicked her cherry Lifesaver on her teeth.

"Yeah."

"He's all yours." Candy said.

"What? Why me?"

"You have your kid's college to pay for. He looks like a big tipper."

Daisy smirked at her friend. "He looks like an ass."

"Come on, please? I really have to get Little Bruno to his party. Be a pal."

Daisy sighed and looked over at the stranger again. "Fine."

Candy gave Daisy's shoulder a little squeeze. "You're the best."

He opened his newspaper onto the surface of the counter and quickly jerked it up with a snap.

"This counter's wet," he said with all the authority of the lord of a manor. Daisy and Candy exchanged a look that said the two comrades had pegged him right.

Daisy's jaw tightened. She had a particularly keen distaste for pomposity. This guy reeked of it. Candy knew Daisy had a tough time tolerating such behavior. Amusement danced in her dark brown eyes.

"Down girl," Candy said in a hushed tone. She giggled.

"Excuse me. Can one of you dry this off?" His tone was absent of courtesy, more of an order. "And, I'd like some coffee, please."

Daisy grabbed the glass pot from the burner and turned to her friend. She whispered, "you owe me."

She needed this like she needed another blister on her feet. She made her way toward the end of the counter, ever professional. Daisy smiled as she approached and kept that curve on her mouth although he eyed her with a narrowed gaze. The sides of his mouth were pressed down. *Get over yourself,* she thought.

She was suddenly glad that the dark brown liquid hovering at the bottom of the carafe had to be over-heated and nearly stale. It would probably taste good and bitter.

After running a paper towel over the surface of the counter, she grabbed a ceramic mug and saucer from the shelf and poured the too-dark liquid into it. She pushed the sugar jar in front of him and pulled a few creamers into her palm. "Cream?"

He held her gaze, making her squirm. She loathed arrogance. French cuffs studded by diamond links didn't necessarily mean somebody was a pompous ass. It was the look in his eyes—dark green orbs filled with some self-imposed clout—and the way he looked down the length of his aristocratic nose that bespoke snobbery.

Daisy had seen plenty of snobbery in her day. It still amazed her that after all these years the sting of being shunned by this echelon managed to surface.

"Yes," he said, using just one side of his mouth. "I'll take cream. Thank you."

She placed three little plastic cups on the counter. "Enough?

"Fine," he said. A glint was now forming in his eyes, a spark of amusement that annoyed her further. "However, I could use a spoon."

Daisy reached into the silverware tray on the shelf below the counter without looking. She fingered through the objects, making a louder racket than necessary, then pulled a spoon into her grasp.

"Unless you'd like me to use my finger." His mouth curved in a smirk that cut into his cheek.

Daisy placed the spoon onto a napkin. She smiled as if his comment had been funny, or cute, or anything other than arrogant. Her eyes held his gaze. She hoped that telepathically he was getting her message that she had a finger of her own she'd like to use.

"Thank you."

"You're welcome." She turned on her heel. She caught Candy's eye as she headed back to the coffee station with the empty carafe. Daisy crossed her eyes and poked her tongue out of her lips. Candy chuckled behind a hand.

"Oh, uh..." he called to her.

Daisy turned in his direction. "Yes?"

"I'm feeling like a little bite."

Daisy heard her coworker stifle another giggle.

11

A stream of seething swirled around her head like a misguided halo. Daisy took a breath and then closed her eyes to regroup. This guy meant nothing to her. His attitude was just a momentary annoyance, a mosquito bite, a run in dime-store hose. No biggie.

There was no sense in letting old wounds surface just because some first class ass reminded her of the old days, the old wounds. Besides, she was nicer than this and she was a professional.

Since coming back to her hometown in Hanover Heights, New Jersey, she had been grateful for her job as bookkeeper for Ima and Pete. And she was a decent Saturday waitress in their beloved little café. She owed it to them to tolerate the itchiness of this customer's behavior, although part of her wanted to tell him to go scratch.

"What's good?" he asked.

"I'm sorry, but the grill's closed for the day," Daisy said with renewed congeniality. "But, I can offer you something from our dessert menu, if you'd like."

"What's that?" He pointed to a dome-covered cake pedestal. In it was a half of Ima's specialty—homemade double-dutch chocolate mocha cake.

"Chocolate mocha cake," Daisy said.

"Is it good?"

"Ima made it fresh this morning."

"Well, then I guess I should have some."

As Daisy sliced into the thick, rich cake, Candy sidled up to her and whispered. "Maybe I better not leave you here alone with this guy."

"I'll be fine."

"I'm not worried about *you*, honey. I'm worried about what you might do to *him*."

Daisy cracked a smile. "I promise to keep the sacred 'no harming the customers' oath."

"Good girl," Candy said, giving Daisy's shoulder

a pat. "They can't tip you if you kill them."

"Ha. Ha. I thought you were leaving."

"I am. Promise to call me when you get home?" She reached for the top button on Daisy's uniform. "Loosen up, cookie," Candy offered in a cherry-scented whisper. "They tip better that way."

Daisy swatted her friend's hand, and clucked her tongue. "Will you stop?"

"Call me," Candy said. "Okay?"

"Yes, yes."

Candy planted a quick kiss onto Daisy's cheek, grabbed her purse and sweater, and headed toward the door. She stopped with her hand on the knob. "Come over to our house tonight for pizza."

Daisy offered a tired grin. "I'll take a rain check. But, thanks."

"What have you got cooking tonight?"

"Going to review that financial aid paperwork."

"Now *there's* a hot time." Candy's mouth had a disapproving twist. "Honey, if I was single that's the last way I'd spend my Saturday night."

Daisy shot her friend a look and motioned her head toward the guy at the end of the counter. She willed her friend to zip her lip. "Don't you have a kid waiting for a ride to a party?"

"Crap!" Candy opened the door and dashed outside offering a final "call me!" in her wake.

Daisy gingerly transferred the wedge of cake onto a plate and carried it over to her customer wondering how much of that exchange he may have heard.

As she placed it in front of him, he said, "That does look good. Homemade, huh?"

She retrieved a fork and slid it onto the dish. "It is."

He sunk the tines of his fork into the confection and as he ate his cake with agonizing slowness, Daisy finished her end-of-day routine.

She keyed in his check then printed out the day's totals from the register. Maybe, with luck, he'd get the message that it was closing time. She consulted the clock on the wall again.

She knew Adam would wonder where she was, especially since she specifically told him to delay his departure until she was home. Daisy grabbed her cell phone out of her purse and hit the speed dial. Adam answered on the first ring.

"Ma?"

"Hi Adam," she said into the phone, deliberately keeping her back to the man at the counter. "Just wanted to let you know I'm running a little late."

"Mom, come on. You know the guys are waiting for me," he protested.

"I know, I know. There's one customer left and…"

"A customer? It's almost four o'clock."

"He's just about done. And, then I'm out the door."

Adam breathed loudly into the phone. "Okay. I'll hold the guys off."

"Sorry, kiddo. I really want to go over some of the stuff from Pratt before you go out tonight. We have to get that paperwork in."

"I know, Mom. It's just that, you know, I—"

"Adam, remember our promise. No negative thoughts, right? Pratt is in your future."

She heard the whoosh of her son's breath. "Mom, listen. I took a look at the package they sent. They've included the new tuition numbers, and—"

"Did the tuition go up again?"

"Ready?" Adam chuckled into the phone but Daisy detected no humor.

"Shoot."

"Thirty-three."

In spite of her resolve to keep positive—no matter what—Daisy felt a jab in her gut as though a

14

fist had walloped her. "Thirty-three thousand dollars?" Her incredulity elevated her pitch.

"Per year."

"Per year," she repeated. She stopped dead. After all, what else was there to say?

"I'll see you when you get home, Mom," Adam said. "It might be time for a new game plan."

After the call ended, Daisy let her hand slide over the money in her pocket. She had become adept at judging a day's take just by the size of the wad of bills and the weight of the coins. She squeezed the lump. It felt extra abundant today, ninety bucks easy. But, even a string of extra good tip days like today wouldn't get Adam to Pratt.

She thought of the last time she and her son had discussed an alternate game plan. Adam had brought it up over dinner, mentioning that their local community college had—what he termed—a pretty decent art department.

But Daisy wanted better for him. His talent deserved a top school. If she could do anything, she would make certain that her only child had the best possible chance in life, realized his dreams, and received the respect he deserved.

Respect—the word sparked an image in her brain. She saw herself as she'd been, a young college girl of twenty, pregnant and scared.

She and David had sat in the grand living room of his family's home. He and his parents were positioned on one side of the room while she was isolated in a stiff high-backed chair on the opposite side. She endured their angry whispers as their icy glances scrutinized her like a used Chevy.

The burning, buried humiliation rushed to the front of her mind like a greedy pigeon securing a bread crumb. She closed her eyes to dash the memory and the pain it evoked. When she opened her eyes, the only thought in her mind was the important one: Adam would have the best opportunities, and it was her job to make that happen.

****

The longer he dawdled with the slice of decadence—admittedly pretty damned good cake—the longer Rand could ignore the fact that his life was in ruins.

He shook his head. He was J. Randolph Press, Jr. for heaven's sake. Life was his oyster—or at least that's how it had been. Now, thanks to Uncle William's ridiculous decision, he was out of options, a desperate slug.

Rand took one last sip from his poor excuse for coffee and grimaced at the muddy consistency. He went for another forkful of cake hoping its flavor might erase the taste of that battery acid this place called "fresh brewed."

He scanned the page of the paper open on the counter in front of him as though an answer to his problem would be typeset on the page. Oddly enough, it was the Opinion Page of the Record. Everybody who was nobody had their view on the current state of health care, the Middle East, and the price of oil.

There were no insights on his dilemma. No one offered advice on how to produce a pretend fiancée to fool the dying uncle holding the purse strings of his very existence.

Rand sighed loud enough to ruffle the page. Feeling desperate had never been something that plagued him. He detested it now.

The waitress was back in front of him with a hand on her hip. This chick wanted out of here. That was apparent. But, she was stuck as long as he lingered in the little dive. A tinge of satisfaction poked at him, a pathetic reaction to still having some piece of power, even if it was over this grumpyassed waitress.

Maybe he'd ask for another hunk of cake and eat that one just as slowly as the first. That might make her head spin off her neck. He smiled at her. That might be worth seeing.

"Anything else I can get you?"

He looked at her for a long moment. Her eyes were sad, he decided, and he almost felt bad for delaying her exit. Truthfully Rand had to give the girl credit. He could tell she was trying her best to be courteous. But, he wasn't fooled by the façade. He knew annoyance when he saw it. After all, he was its aficionado.

"No, thank you," he said watching as her hand slipped into her pocket. His gaze slid over the curve of her hip. The fabric of her uniform stretched over her shape just enough to be provocative, yet not cheap. "I think I'll just take the check."

She smiled, relief in her powder blue eyes—pretty eyes, really. He liked the way her thick, black lashes bordered her cerulean eyes like a picture frame. If he wasn't so deep in his own problems, he might even flirt with her just for the hell of it.

She handed him his check—five dollars and eighty-three cents. She'd had to wait around for him for a measly tip of what, a buck or two?

He had overheard her on the phone about the cost of Pratt in New York. He'd heard of the school and knew it was pricey. Tips in this joint weren't going to get her or her kid anywhere—particularly to a big-name art school—especially since he'd overheard earlier that she was a single parent. Now, *that* was desperation.

And that's when it hit him.

Chapter Three

Rand couldn't believe his own thoughts. But he couldn't believe anything about this damned day, so this was just icing on the cake.

He gazed over to the glass dome displayed on the counter. One good thing was this waitress could bake, too. Hadn't she said she made the cake this morning? At least that's what he thought she said.

Maybe the fact that she was a baker *and* a looker would fool Uncle William. Maybe the man's raging sweet tooth would cloud the façade. Okay, it was a long shot, but at least it was something.

He scrutinized her as she fussed about. Uncle knew his penchant for blondes. Her hair was a nice golden blonde that looked natural. It had to be. After all, any salon that produced a color that realistic would be one pricey place. A waitress couldn't afford that.

He let out a sigh. *She's a waitress, for God's sake.* She couldn't possibly play the role well enough to convince his discerning uncle that this was legit. Could she?

He surveyed her moves, efficient, yet graceful. Her face was concentrated as she performed her tasks. Not a stunning beauty, true.

She sure as hell wasn't another of his typical glitzy trust-fund airheads, or one of those stuck-up posh socialites. Maybe she had something better. He felt the stir of hope brush over his skin like a feather.

She could present as someone real, less than perfect, minus the fashion-doll beauty. He tossed a twenty dollar bill on top of the check with a sense of purpose, a spider ready to weave.

She approached him again. "I'll get your change."

"Keep it."

She gave him a long look. Yeah, it was a generous tip for just a hunk of cake and a cup of mud. Her look said something other than gratitude. It had a challenge in it, or an awareness perhaps—as though she knew he thought he was better than her.

Those mocking powder blues of hers were telling him he was wrong. Oddly, it stimulated his curiosity. Maybe this pretty little baker with a desperation of her own *could* really help solve his problem.

Maybe he could pull off the whole damned thing. It was like the dice were back in his hands and he was on a streak again at the Bellagio.

Rand stood from the counter stool and met her eyes, working his lips into a curve that he hoped looked impish.

"Pardon me, may I tell you something?"

She put a hand on her hip. *Attractive—not too narrow, not too curvy.* With that cool look in her eyes, she wasn't going to be an easy sell. But that could be a good thing. Stubborn women had backbone, and this charade would require it.

When she continued to stand there, not responding, he cleared his throat and began. "I couldn't help but overhear your telephone conversation a few minutes ago."

She cocked her head. "I beg your pardon?"

Rand laughed softly, tucking his chin in the way that women told him was adorable, and better yet, irresistible. "I couldn't help it. Sorry."

"Look..."

"No, no, wait." Rand held up his hands. "I only heard you mention Pratt, that's all. I know the

19

school well."

Lie number one. All he knew was that one of the artists that had come up with the promotional package for the launch of his Uncle's new apartment complex had gone to that particular art school. Apparently, it was enough. Rand had her attention now. He could see her body relax. She continued to wait for him to elaborate.

"It's a great school."

"Yes." There was a wariness still in her gaze.

"Someone you know trying to get in?"

"My son."

That was another thing. How old could she be if she had a son going to college? Maybe she got pregnant in high school or something. There was only one way to find out.

"Your son?" He sounded purposely incredulous. "What? Did you have him when you were twelve?"

The waitress pursed her lips as though onto a poor excuse for a come-on. "Yeah," she said, turning away from him. "It was a seventh-grade science project, and I got an A."

In spite of himself he laughed. She was feisty. He liked that.

"If there's nothing else..." She deliberately looked at her watch.

"I know what tuition is like at a school like Pratt. And, I know how tough it can be to come up with the funds. I may be able to help."

She turned around to face him. Her pretty eyes narrowed and her full mouth pursed into a pink bow.

****

Daisy had heard enough. Now this guy was scaring her.

She was alone with this stranger and he was making offers. She didn't like him—didn't like that leer of his, and her gut was telling her to make a beeline. She fingered the car key in her pocket.

"Maybe I should explain."

"No," she said firmly. "Sir, we're closed, I'm about to lock the door. I have an appointment to get to. So..."

He reached into his inside jacket pocket and withdrew a business card. He extended it like a cigarette wedged between two fingers. His wide smile reminded Daisy of a painted mask.

When she didn't move to take his card he waved it in the air at her.

"Please," he said. "Take my card. Maybe we could meet for a drink or something. My intentions are honorable, truly they are. I have a sort of *position* to fill, and I think you might do well in it. It's just temporary but quite lucrative. My name is Rand, by the way, short for Randolph. I'm J. Randolph Press, Jr."

He recited his name as though it should mean something to her. She had known guys with names that started with a lone letter. Experience told her that everything about this one's J stood for Jerk.

"Google me," he said, his tone sugary. "You'll see I'm quite harmless. I'm an honest man with an honest offer. Please take the card."

"And, you've decided I'm a candidate for this *temporary position*, why? Because of the way I wipe down a counter? Pour a cup of Joe?"

He laughed. "I know how this sounds. It's sort of a PR position. You relate to the public every day. I have a feeling this could be just what you're looking for."

"I'm not *looking* for anything. But thank you anyway."

"At least take my card in case you change your mind."

"I won't change my mind."

"It's a lucrative opportunity that could help you with that college tuition."

Daisy reached for the card and snapped it into her hand. She knew that the second she was in her car, with the doors locked, she was going to tear it to pieces.

"Thank you," he said. "Don't forget. Look up Press Industries. You'll see that we're in the middle of a huge expansion project in downtown Morristown."

Daisy grabbed her jacket from the rack by the door. She withdrew the car key from her pocket and reached for the light switch. She stared at J. Randolph Press, Jr.

He extended his hand. "I'm sorry to have delayed your leaving. Really."

Against her better judgment, she shook his hand. He had large, strong hands—built for work. But the skin was smooth. There were no calluses, no toughness. These hands knew no labor. She pulled away from his grasp. Once upon a time her hands had been the same as his—smooth, elite. Now, she couldn't remember the last time she'd had a manicure.

"I hope to hear from you...I'm sorry, what's your name?"

"Daisy," she heard herself say, baffled by her revelation.

She saw his eyes flash with something that she couldn't decipher. It was gone just as quickly.

"Pleased to meet you, Daisy."

She gave him a quick nod and then doused the light behind her. Pulling the door closed, she waited for the lock's click. She dashed to her car thinking J. Randolph Press, Jr. had to be one rich dope if he thought for a second that she'd contact him.

The minute she got home, Daisy kicked off her shoes and flopped on the sofa.

Adam was in a mood. He sat quietly at the other end of the couch, raking his fingers through his black hair with swift, jerky moves as though trying to punish the locks for adorning his head.

She reached over and grabbed his wrist feeling the sharpness of the metal studs of his leather bracelet. "What time are your friends coming?"

"They're not."

"What do you mean, Adam? I thought they were waiting for you."

"They waited long enough, I guess," he said with a shrug and a droop to his mouth. Although it was easy enough for Daisy to recognize the gestures, today it was tough not to succumb to them.

"Sorry, honey. That last customer just wouldn't leave."

"No big deal," he said, unconvincingly. She knew her kid and he was doing his best not to make her feel guilty, but it tugged at her.

Being a single parent all these years carried its weight on her heart. There had been too many times when she had had to work and had missed too many of the little things that did add up to big deals. Maybe she knew what she had given up along the way, but what wounded her heart was what Adam had had to sacrifice.

"Take my car."

"Huh?" A smile fought with the frown he had plastered on his face. "Really?"

"It's the weekend. I don't have any plans. Take the car tonight."

"Are you sure?"

Daisy let out a long breath and put her feet up on top of a toss pillow propped on the cocktail table. "Trust me, kiddo, I'm not going anywhere. These puppies are screaming." She wiggled her toes. Eying their chipped polish, she envisioned them with a pretty French pedicure.

Suddenly J. Randolph Press, Jr. popped into her head. She dismissed it the same way she had conditioned herself to forget the days she had been in college keeping up with the campus debutants and preppies—the way it had unraveled, the betrayal.

"I'm going to stay in and do my toes."

"Thanks, Mom." Adam's voice was nearly back to normal. Daisy saw the light return to his eyes, the same blue as her own. "What are you going to do about dinner?"

She shrugged. "There's leftovers from last night in the fridge."

"I could get you something, you know, before I meet the guys."

"No way." She crossed one outstretched leg over the other, enjoying the softness of the pillow under her feet. "I'm fine with yesterday's chicken parm. And, I've got reading to do, remember? Where's the stuff from Pratt?"

"Under your feet," he said with affection.

Daisy sat up, sending the pillow to the floor which took a stack of papers with it. She reached down to retrieve them. The familiar Pratt logo at the top of an envelope beckoned her. "You've read through all of this, I hope."

Adam let out a sigh, shook his head at his mother. "Yes, I read it."

"Take that look off your face," she said. "We're going to review all this in the morning. Now, go have fun tonight. Deal?"

"Fine as long as you let me make you breakfast. We have eggs?"

"We have eggs," she said warmly. "The key's in the tray by the door. Now go. Oh, and, the tank's full."

"I won't be late," he announced as he sprang up from the couch.

"That's right, you won't," Daisy warned playfully. "Curfew's still in place until you're a college man."

Adam trotted off to his room, and emerged donning his black leather biker jacket, the collar turned up Elvis-style. She didn't flinch like she used to. She'd gotten accustomed to his appearance. Adam was an artistic kid, a passionate person. He expressed himself in many ways, his appearance among them—the tight pencil-leg jeans, the black combat boots, the thick silver chain around his neck.

All of this might scare some parents. She bristled at the memory of a neighborhood parent's words of caution about what her son might be into. But, Daisy knew better. Adam had a good head on his leather-clad shoulders.

She saw him fish into his back pocket. "You need some money?"

"Nah, I'm good."

Adam's after-school job, covering the front desk at the local YMCA, didn't pay him much. His spending cash never seemed to go far. "You sure?"

He gave her a quick nod and she acquiesced. "Okay, Rockefeller, have a good time."

Adam leaned down and kissed the top of Daisy's head as he passed behind the couch and headed toward the door.

After he was gone, she heated up a plate of chicken, deciding she needed fuel in her stomach before tackling the daunting task of reading through the school papers.

The tuition figures were there among the pages and even though she already knew what the numbers were, she just didn't want to see them in print. Somehow that was worse.

She poured herself a glass of red wine and sat back on the sofa with her reheated feast. Turning on the TV, she flipped through the channels. Maybe she'd find some juicy chick flick on the women's channel.

Nights when Adam was home they had to compromise on which shows to watch. It was better to sit through a crime drama with her son than for each of them to watch their own preference in different rooms.

Her eyes found the stack of papers. There was no avoiding them.

Daisy put her plate on the table and grabbed her wine. She pulled the information from Pratt into her hand and dug in. It was just the school her boy needed, that was for sure. The world couldn't help but respect him and his art with these credentials under his studded belt.

Realistically, it was just too damned expensive. Even with student loans and maybe a parent loan, the cost would cripple their finances. For someone who spent her work week making sure the café's debits and credits were in order, she knew an imbalance when she saw one. This one broke the scales.

The movie wasn't more than a half-hour in and her ruby-colored toenails were still wet when the doorbell rang. Daisy stared at the wads of cotton wedged between her drying toes; a perfect application of polish that she knew would probably not survive the trip to the door. Reluctantly she swung her feet from their propped position and carefully waddled toward the door on her heels.

"Who is it?" she asked the closed door.

"Room service," a voice said.

Daisy smirked at the sound of her friend. She opened the door to find Candy poised with a pizza box atop one upturned hand.

"Half plain, half mushroom," she announced.

"Candy, why did you do this?" Daisy was suddenly grateful for the company she thought she didn't want tonight.

"Because I left you alone with that guy and you

were supposed to call me." She breezed into the room on a waft of oregano-scented air. "I had to make sure there wasn't a murder at the Brookside tonight."

Daisy shook her head. "As you can see, my friend, I'm fine."

"Oh, I wasn't worried about you, Daisy-girl. I was afraid you might have hauled off and punched that *pompous ass* in the kisser."

"Trust me, I was tempted." Daisy made room on the coffee table for the pizza box, gathering the college papers into a stack and placing them aside.

"Is that the dreaded reading material you're torturing yourself with?" Candy motioned toward the pages.

"That's them," Daisy said sullenly. "Want some red?" She lifted her wine glass and gave the liquid a deliberate twirl.

"Sure, but just a little." Candy pulled a couple of paper plates and napkins from a brown paper bag.

Daisy went into the kitchen to retrieve another glass. Candy called in to her. "Bring the red pepper flakes, too. Whoa, are these numbers legit?" Candy whistled low. "Crap. Are they serious?"

Daisy poured her some wine then put a topper on her own portion. "That's the cost...and yes, they're serious."

"How on earth do you plan to pull this off, girl? You can't come up with this kind of dough on your salary."

Candy let out a whoosh of air. "You better be getting more tips than I do. Hey, what'd the pompous ass give you?"

"You mean besides a job offer?"

"What?" The word popped out of Candy's mouth like a hair ball.

"Turns out he's some big rich guy. At least that's what he said, anyway. And, he said he's got some temporary 'position' I'd be well-suited for."

"What kind of position? Missionary?"

Daisy laughed out loud. "I know. Right?"

They settled onto the sofa and Daisy pulled a gooey wedge of pizza onto a flimsy plate. She handed it to Candy who sat staring, her eyes big brown spotlights.

"What's his name?"

"J. Randolph Press, Jr.," Daisy recited. "La Dee Dah!"

"Sounds familiar, but I'm not sure where I've heard it." Candy accepted the plate and bit off the tip of the pizza slice. "He's probably a famous criminal I've seen on *America's Most Wanted* or something."

"Whatever." Daisy sampled her own slice. "I'm not interested. That's for sure."

"Eat up, girlie," Candy said. "After we're done, we're going surfing."

"Huh?"

"Web surfing."

"For what?"

"J. Randolph Press, Jr."

Chapter Four

They sat side by side on the sofa, laptop positioned in front of them on Daisy's coffee table. Candy clicked the mouse.

The website for Press Industries opened onto the screen. Apparently, the Press family consisted of a long line of real estate moguls, their conglomerate owning the biggest and most prestigious apartment buildings in the greater Morristown area. The company was responsible for the upgraded downtown area that included the new shopping mall on the ground level of the newly renovated Colonial Arms Hotel just off the town square.

"Are you seeing what I'm seeing?" Candy asked.

"They're northern Jersey's answer to the Trumps, for crying out loud."

"Wait." Anticipation was bright in Candy's eyes. She hit the "Officers" tab at the upper left corner of the screen and nudged Daisy. "Let's see what it says about your pompous ass."

Daisy put the rim of her wine glass to her lips, but was too riveted to the screen to take a sip. His image popped up on the screen. J. Randolph Press appeared professional, serious, and—if Daisy were completely honest—dashingly handsome. Yet, there was that mocking look in his green eyes—the one that she remembered seeing while he seemed to study her from his seat at the counter at The Brookside. Something about his aura unnerved her.

"What do you think?" Candy asked. She turned from the screen and faced Daisy. "This guy wasn't kidding. He's as rich as they come in these parts."

"Yeah, so?"

"So, his job offer might be worth investigating."

"Don't be ridiculous, Candy. I don't even know this guy."

"Who cares? He's part of Press Industries. They're huge. And, there's some job in that big fat company with your name on it."

Daisy gnawed on a strip of crust, working her jaw feverishly. This was crazy, she knew. But the idea did intrigue her. This guy was indeed legitimate. But was his offer?

"Candy, let's be serious for a moment here," Daisy said. "A man comes into a diner, orders a piece of cake and tells the waitress he's got a job for her. I mean, come on. Don't you ever watch crime shows?"

"I'd be with you on that, Daisy. You know me, I can be as skeptical as you. But why on earth would somebody so prominent go out on a limb like this unless he was serious?"

"Maybe because he's nuts." Daisy angled the laptop toward herself. "Sure the company website makes him seem on the *up and up*, but let's see what else is out there on him."

Daisy hit the undo tab at the top of the screen again and again until she was back to square one of their search. She scrolled down until she saw something that caught her eye. She took her finger off the mouse. "Ah-ha!"

Candy leaned in closer. "Ah-ha, what?"

"Our real estate mogul's made it to *Page Six*."

Candy squealed, clapping her hands together like a school girl at her own birthday party. "If you make it to the *New York Post's* gossip page, you're big."

Daisy pursed her lips and shook her head at Candy's ridiculous rationale. She clicked on the link and the *Post's* home page opened on the screen. She navigated to the icon for *Page Six* and did a search for his name.

J. Randolph Press, Jr. had been a busy boy—a very busy boy. And, according to the popular paper's gossip column, it didn't have much to do with real estate or the man's fortune, but rather to a string of affluent female liaisons a mile long.

"This guy's a slut," Candy said, reading the text over Daisy's shoulder.

"You think?" Daisy asked sarcastically. "Holy smokes, look at this. He's been involved with Jada Jeffries. *Jada Jeffries!* She's the biggest soap opera queen on the planet, isn't she? It says here that 'insiders speculated that Randolph Press was the reason she went on hiatus from *Bridges Crossing.*'"

"Yeah," Candy said. "I remember that. It was a couple of years ago. When she came back to the show she had lost so much weight people were saying she had an eating disorder."

"Maybe what she had was a man-choosing disorder," Daisy said.

"I remember they wrote her emaciated look into the script. Made her kidnapped and imprisoned in the bottom of a well."

Daisy turned slowly to face her friend. "Do you actually watch that stuff?"

"When they threw her in the well she fell right on top of her long-lost twin sister."

"You need serious help."

Candy gave her shoulders a small noncommittal shrug, but her eyes danced with delight.

Daisy shook her head then turned back to the screen. She rolled her index finger over the mouse. "Okay, look at this one. Some model accused him of reneging on a plan to marry her. 'Not long afterward photographers took these pictures of her outside a newly acquired beachfront condo on Maui.'"

"Paid her off."

"Yup." Daisy looked to her friend. "The guy's a

dog."

"But a really rich dog."

"I wouldn't go near him with a ten-foot biscuit."

****

Rand was going nuts. He paced around his living room as though enough laps would produce a result. He was getting nowhere and time was of the essence.

He strode over to the glass doors at the end of the room and opened them. Stepping out onto his balcony, he pulled in a chest-full of crisp evening air. He let it expel as he rested his hands on the wrought iron railing.

He took in the view. The downtown lights were lit up like a holiday. In the distance he could see the pinpoints of light dotting the night sky in some other town, Livingston probably. He closed his eyes. That world out there belonged to him. It did. He needed to keep it that way.

Randolph had spent the evening looking through his address log. He thought again of the waitress at the Brookside. *Daisy...of all names.* It reminded him of some backwoods type, a name for Ellie May Clampett's best friend. He swore out loud to no one's ear but his own. Every hour that passed intensified his doubt that she'd actually call.

He darted back inside and grabbed the leather-bound book again. He flipped through his list of names turning the pages with an angry hand. Maybe there had been some woman he'd dated but hadn't pissed off so much that he could still contact her with the proposition—but who?

Every female he'd entertained in the past two years, the years following the Jada Jeffries debacle, had a drawback. Either they were already paid off because of his so-called alienation-of-affection-type exits, were married already, or the dalliance was so insignificant that he failed to recall their faces.

Anger chased the fear through his veins like a couple of Indy cars on a track. Anger won. He threw the book hard against the sliding doors behind him. The glass rattled at the assault.

Screw it! Screw the doors, this whole place, and this whole goddamned mess!

He thought of selling off everything that he owned out-and-out and living on the proceeds. Yeah, that would render him free of his Uncle's clutches and the old man's condescending demands... But it would also leave him, well, common. Rand winced.

It was the one word his uncle had cautioned him against all his life: *common*. Be ruthless, be cagey, be smart, but never, ever, be common.

Commoners were not in the Press family league. It is what Uncle William said had plagued Randolph's parents like a disease—and the one true reason for their demise.

As harsh as the words had been, Randolph grew to understand and embrace them. After all, if his parents hadn't died when he was twelve, he would have been raised with their far-too-ordinary, lackluster lifestyle unbefitting a Press. Perhaps he, himself, would have grown to seek a world beyond the money and prestige as his parents had.

Rand poured more vodka into his glass and took a deep pull of the clear, potent import. He was not common. He had been reared and groomed by Uncle William, the embodiment of what their lineage meant. His blood was blue.

Yes, Rand was angry. But suddenly he remembered that nothing and no one had ever stood in his way before. And, nobody would now either, especially a crotchety old dictator about to make his grand exit.

Randolph felt a chill rise up his spine, like an icy finger had dragged along the string of vertebrae one by one, leaving behind a trail of shame. As mad as he was, Randolph recognized that the old guy—now on his deathbed—was the one person who took him in when he'd been orphaned.

And, it also occurred to him that he had not even called to find out firsthand about Uncle Will's condition. "Shit." He muttered and picked up the cordless beside the leather sofa. He dialed his uncle's housekeeper's personal number. After three rings he heard her wispy voice.

"Florence,"—he downed the remainder of Grey Goose in his glass—"it's Rand."

"Yes, hello. I've been waiting for your call."

"How is he?"

"Sleeping. The doctor gave him a sedative."

"Is he in pain?" Randolph felt something stir inside his chest.

"Why don't you stop by to see him in the morning?" Florence's voice was filled with familiar affection. Randolph knew that Uncle Will's long-time employee felt a kinship to the old man.

He also knew she had a soft spot for him, too. As a kid he had capitalized on it when he needed a favor, but he wouldn't do so now. He couldn't charm his way out of the situation Uncle had put him in.

"Be honest with me, Flo. Is he dying?"

"I guess that depends on how you define the word."

"Max Willoughby told me this afternoon that Uncle's at death's door."

"And it took until now for you to call to find out? Randolph."

The way Florence said his name took him right back to his childhood. Suddenly he felt like the kid that had filled the beleaguered woman's days with his teenage antics. She always had a way of making him feel like shit without saying anything but his name. It surprised him to see that it still worked.

"I'm sorry, Flo. Really. Should I come now?"

"No, he's not going anywhere just yet. But, you do need to see him."

"I'll be there in the morning."

"Good. Bring something for his sweet tooth. He'll like that."

When Randolph hung up the phone he knew with certainty that tomorrow morning he would make a stop first to the Brookside Café to get a hunk of that chocolate mocha cake for his uncle. And with any luck he'd snag himself a pretty little pretend fiancée that had baked it.

Chapter Five

"So, what do you think?" Candy cradled a mug of tea between her hands. "What have you got to lose?"

"Candy, I'm not calling him."

"Aren't you even a little curious? I mean this could be a dream come true."

Daisy laughed. Curious wasn't the word, she felt something more like a warning. Every red flag she could imagine had popped up around her head like the spikes of the Statue of Liberty's crown.

She'd been fooled big-time by a man before. Even though that had been years ago, the lesson was etched in her heart in concrete. If it seemed too good to be true, well...life had taught her that it was.

"I have a better idea. How about you call him?" Daisy suggested.

"Why are you so impossible?"

"I'm not impossible. I just don't believe in fairy tales."

"You're a cynic."

"I'm a realist."

"Really? A realist? Adam's going to get into that fancy art school how? There's no fairy tale about that one...for sure."

Daisy bit her lip. "Don't."

"Honey, listen," Candy softened. "I'm on your side. I hope that one happens because it's so important to you."

"It's not for me, Candy. It's for Adam's future. He's got to go to Pratt. No option."

"Then call Mr. Press." Candy sipped from her mug. She grimaced. "I can't believe you drink this stuff. Tastes like lawn clippings."

"It's a blend that's supposed to uplift the spirit and open your senses to possibilities."

"And *you're* the realist. Okay, reality girl, drink boiled shrubs, but don't call the gazillionaire that's offered you a job. Makes total sense."

Daisy took a sip of her tea and let it bathe her throat and warm a trail down into her body. She hated the truth in her friend's words. No herbal blend would wash that away.

"Just because some jerk you knew a thousand years ago turned out to be a lying sack of crap doesn't mean every man on the planet is the same." Candy shuddered and put the mug down onto the table. "My stomach's not used to fertilizer."

"I'm not continuing this subject." Daisy sighed and leaned back onto the sofa cushion.

"Adam's sperm donor was a coward." Candy went on as though she hadn't heard Daisy's protest. "A one-dimensional louse that just so happened to have a daddy with a big old bank account. Honestly, if you had put your pride aside and taken that money he offered you—"

"Candy, not tonight, please. I'm too tired."

"Okay, I'll get off the soap box, but only if you promise me something."

"Depends," Daisy smirked.

"Promise that you'll open your mind to the philosophy of these boiled sticks you drink. Me? I'd rather go to church and make a novena. But, you believe in that stuff. So, just promise me that you'll entertain the idea that maybe this opportunity could be a positive one."

Debating it now would leave the door open for Candy to keep talking about the other rich man that had offered Daisy money eighteen years ago. Then it had been a bribe for her to simply go away...vanish. She had, but she'd walked away from her college boyfriend, David Babbage without a single dime of his parents' filthy money.

"Sure. I'll think about it."

"Promise."

To promise would be a bold-faced lie. Daisy had precious few things over which she had control and honesty was one of them. She opened her mouth to speak but stopped at the sound of the telephone's ring.

She grabbed the receiver, grateful for the intrusion.

"Hello?" Daisy said absently. She heard a siren in the background and her heart stalled in her chest. "Hello?"

"Mrs. Cameron?" a male voice inquired.

"Yes?"

"This is Officer Dean Alexander with the Hanover Heights police. There's been an accident involving your son, Adam."

Chapter Six

Daisy felt the world sway as she watched the ceiling and the floor trade places. She held onto the end table to steady herself. She let out a cry. "Oh, God."

Instantly Candy was at her side. She stood silently as Daisy continued to speak into the mouthpiece. "Is he hurt?"

"Hanover Heights First Aid Squad is transporting him and his passengers to the emergency room of Morristown Memorial. I'm following the ambulance. I'll meet you there."

"The hospital? What happened?" she pleaded. "Please, tell me."

"Mrs. Cameron, apparently the boys had been drinking. Your son ran through a red light and hit a tree."

"Oh, God."

"They'll be able to answer your questions in the ER."

"Yes," Daisy said. "I'll be right there."

She clicked the phone off and dropped it onto the floor.

"Come on," Candy said, reaching for her purse. "Get your pocketbook. Do you have your insurance information in there?"

"Yes."

"Okay, then, let's go. I'll drive you."

They sped down the stairs from Daisy's condo and sprinted to Candy's Camry in the parking lot. "Put your belt on." Candy ordered like a parent. Daisy reached with a leaden hand and pulled the metal buckle across her body. She felt doom closing in on her.

She watched out the windshield as the familiar nighttime surroundings whizzed by with Candy breaking the speed limit racing down Ridgedale Avenue. Houselights blurred before her like a comet shooting across the night. Her mind was stuck on one word, a relentless chant that thrummed in her heart and pulsed to her every cell. *Adam, Adam, Adam...*

****

Daisy could barely recite her own name to the woman at the intake desk. Nausea roiled inside her stomach and she thought she might lose her dinner. She thought she'd go mad if they didn't take her to her son.

The young woman in scrubs lackadaisically tapped at her keyboard. Her tone unfazed, she finally said, "You can go right in."

Daisy wondered how someone so young, someone who wore kitten-patterned scrubs, could have achieved such immunity to the frenzy in the air of the emergency room. To Daisy, the feeling of doom was as palpable as the assault of antiseptic to her nostrils. "Push that big red button and the doors will let you in."

"Thank you," Daisy said.

Just then Candy darted in through the entry, hair askew and eyes wide. "Is the whole world here tonight? I had to park in East Jabib."

Daisy went to the wall with the designated button. "I'm going in."

"I'm coming with you."

"Excuse me," the benign kitty cat girl said. "Are you a relative?"

"Yes I am," Candy lied. "I'm his aunt."

The girl said nothing but continued to stare at them. Candy put her arm around Daisy's shoulders.

"I'm his aunt *and* his godmother," she said.

The girl pursed her lips and said, "Go in."

A nurse holding a clipboard informed them Adam was in the cubicle at the end of the corridor.

As they passed by the harsh-yellow curtained areas Daisy saw the parents of Adam's friend, Jacob, huddled outside a closed cubicle. Jake's mother was crying, the father ashen.

She went to them. "Is Jake all right?" Daisy asked, touching the mother's arm. The mother looked at her with unfocused eyes. Then she turned her gaze to her husband. Daisy did the same.

"They're pumping his stomach. He's going to be fine, thank God."

Daisy's heart squeezed. "Pumping?"

"He's drunk," the father said with the solemnity of a bad test result. "Twice the legal limit, apparently."

"Oh, God."

"Adam was driving."

"Was he...?" Daisy couldn't get the word *drunk* to form on her lips.

The father shook his head and reached to Daisy's shoulder. "Adam was driving them home from Paulie's house. Michael Bower was in the car, too. His parents have taken him home already. Adam was the only one sober."

"He was the designated driver," the mother offered just before she clamped a wad of limp tissues to her mouth.

Relief washed over Daisy, but not enough to quell the panic zinging through her system. She needed to see Adam. Daisy and Candy hurried down the glossy-tiled corridor to the last cubicle. The curtain was partially pulled back. Daisy recognized her son's black combat booted-feet dangling off the side of the gurney. She yanked open the curtain.

"Adam." A sob caught in her throat.

Sitting with his head in his hands, he looked up when he heard his mother's voice. His eyes were filled with fear and his mouth pulled down at the corners.

"I'm sorry, Mom."

She rushed to pull him into her embrace. He smelled of smoke and something rancid, stale. Puke maybe.

"Oh, Adam."

"They towed your car to the gas station. I blew a tire and maybe bent the front axle. I'll pay for it, Mom. I'm so sorry."

"What station?" Candy startled mother and son with her presence. Daisy had completely forgotten that her friend brought her here. "I'll call Bruno and tell him to pick it up in the morning. Bruno and his guys will take care of it."

"Thanks, Mrs. Martino. I think my mom's going to have to see what the insurance company says." Adam raked his fingers through his already tousled hair.

"You're okay, honey?" Daisy pulled away to arm's length to survey him.

Adam nodded.

"Do they have to examine you? What are we waiting for?"

"They're just waiting for you to sign the release. The intern was just in here. She's the one with the long braid out at the desk."

"They're not doing any tests on you or anything?"

"No. The cop did a breathalyzer on me. I wasn't drinking."

"You ran a red light? Why would you do that?" She felt a bitter morsel of anger on her tongue.

"Yeah," he sighed. "The cop gave me a ticket."

"I think that's three points, kid," Candy added with a grimace.

"I don't understand, Adam," Daisy said. "How could you be so careless?"

"Jake was puking his guts out. I was freaking and took my eyes off the road."

"He threw up in my car?" She couldn't swallow her anger now. "Are you kidding me, Adam? This is so negligent."

Just then the intern Adam spoke of waltzed into the space. Her long white coat made her look like a kid playing doctor. Daisy wondered how old she was. Were doctors allowed to look that young? Her nametag said "Dr. Anne Fox".

"You must be Mrs. Cameron," she said genially. "Adam looks just like you, you know, except for the hair."

Arms folded across herself, Daisy felt the movement of her chest as she took deep breaths. The effort did not calm her down.

"He's a lucky young man," Dr. Fox said. Her mouth turned into a pretty smile. "The officer at the scene is outside in the waiting room. He just wants to go over a couple of things with you. First, we'll need you to read over the release form and sign it. I'll be back in a few."

Adam turned to Candy when the intern left. "Thanks, Mrs. Martino, for...bringing my mom here. I'm surprised they let you in back here, though. They seem pretty strict."

Daisy knew her kid. He was looking for a friend in the room. She clucked her tongue.

"I told them I was your aunt."

"You did?" A slow smile curved on Adam's lips.

"Really, Candy! Lying?" Daisy was now mad at her, too. Why not? Her son had acted irresponsibly. Her car was full of puke. She was pissed at the world.

"I wasn't taking a chance of them kicking me out of here. Besides, it's just a white lie. No harm, no foul."

Daisy narrowed her eyes at Candy and shook her head. Spying a jar of tongue depressors on the counter of the cubicle, she wondered how many it would take to silence her friend.

"How young do you think that intern is? Jeez, I think my pocketbook is older than she is."

Daisy refused to react.

"Where do you think she got her degree? Gray's Anatomy?" Candy was babbling now.

She put an arm around Daisy's shoulders and gave her a gentle squeeze. "Come on, girlfriend. Relax. Your son's okay. We'll get your car fixed. They'll fumigate it for you. Stuff like this happens all the time."

"Not to us, it doesn't." Daisy eyed her son. "This isn't how Adam behaves."

"Mom, I said I was sorry..."

Dr. Fox returned for the signed paperwork. She reminded Adam that ibuprofen would be fine for any aches or pains, and said goodbye.

They made their way back through the area and noticed that Jacob's curtain was wide open, the compartment empty.

The officer that had contacted Daisy stood in the anteroom talking with an EMT. "All set to go home, Adam?" the officer said. "Hello, Mrs. Cameron. I'm Officer Alexander."

"Hello."

"How are you doing? Okay?"

"Yes," Daisy said with a sigh. "I'm just glad that they're all okay."

"You'll have to contact your insurance carrier with the accident report. I'm sure your son has told you that he was issued a ticket for running the red light."

Daisy merely nodded.

"This is so unlike him," she whispered.

"Really?" The officer looked up from the paperwork in his hand.

She bristled. "Yes, really. Adam's usually very responsible."

He let his gaze slide over Adam's form. "Good to hear. I wouldn't have pegged him for the sober one." He shook his head abruptly. "The other kids in the car are"—he paused, changing gears—"their families are prominent in town. Goes to show you never know."

He handed her the paper. "If you have any questions, call the precinct. I'm on all day tomorrow."

"Thank you." She gripped the paper firmly, wrinkling it.

It was almost two in the morning when Candy drove them home. Suddenly the weight of the night was more than Daisy could bear. She hadn't given herself time to think about the repercussions of the accident.

She was without transportation now. The reality of that circumstance pressed heavily into her thoughts that now included the insurance company, the cost for the tow, the repair, her deductible, her premiums.

As glad as she was that everyone involved was not hurt, the pain of this event was not over.

She detested the officer's implications and presumptions about Adam. Her jaw was tight. She could not allow anyone to inflict her son with a stereotype he did not deserve. She knew that pain and wanted to shield Adam from it.

He had to have heard the cop's words. Did they sting? Would the man's comments make Adam vow to prove him wrong?

It was as though her thoughts were pouring out of her head like words on a page. She saw her son watching her, reading her with his adept ability. She offered him a feeble, tired grin. There was no fooling him.

"I screwed up big, Mom. This is going to cost a ton, isn't it? I've been saving some money. I can at least help with this."

She shrugged, too tired to say the words. She dropped onto the sofa, sitting on the materials from Pratt. She tugged them out from under herself and laid them on the coffee table.

"I can kiss Pratt goodbye." Adam sat beside her. "I already know that much. But, you know what, Ma? Maybe this decides it for us. County College has a good art program. A guy at my school, his sister goes there, and—"

"Adam, let's worry about that later, okay? You're fine. Your friends are fine. This accident was just that—an accident. We'll figure out the other stuff another time."

"I wasn't even supposed to be the designated driver tonight. Jake was. But by the time I got to Paulie's he was already on his way to wasted."

"Yes, by the way, where were Paulie's parents?"

"In Pennsylvania at his sister's soccer tournament."

Daisy shook her head. "Tomorrow, when we can think straight, we're going to discuss this further. Needless to say I'm extremely disappointed, Adam. Get some sleep."

Adam gave a sullen nod. "Yeah, right."

Daisy didn't even turn on a light in her room. She plopped onto the foot of the bed and just stared out the window.

The night was black, stars were few. Most of the lights she had seen earlier were off now. The whole town was at rest.

But Daisy knew rest would not come easily for her. There was just too much to consider—the expenses of this mess, the possible repercussions to

Adam's acceptance into Pratt.

Sitting in that darkness, the only light that Daisy could see was a single ray of hope that had popped into her mind. Tomorrow she had a phone call to make.

Chapter Seven

The minute Rand entered the little diner that Sunday morning his eyes scanned for Daisy. The waitress at the counter was an older woman. Her mousy brown, streaked-with-gray hair was pulled back in a barrette at the nape of her neck. She looked up at him and smiled.

"Good morning. Coffee?" She asked, reaching for the carafe.

Rand was quick to tell her no. No mud for him, thanks. He was here for two things. Cake and a waitress named Daisy.

He eyed the name tag pinned over the pocket of her blouse. "Good morning, Ima," he said, reciting her name. *What the hell kind of name is Ima? What's it short for? Ima waitress?*

"I'd just like a piece of that mocha cake to go, please." He punctuated his words with warmth. He needed Ima Waitress to give him some information. "I was hoping to see Daisy here this morning. Is it her day off?"

"Yes, she's only here on Saturdays."

"Oh." *Now what?*

"Well, I should say, she only *waitresses* on Saturdays. She's here all week in the office if you need her for something."

Rand's mind raced as he watched her cradle a slice of cake into a disposable Styrofoam container. She handed it to him. "They'll ring you up at the register. Want me to tell Daisy you were here?"

He wasn't sure that was a good idea. It would have been perfect if he happened upon her today while he had a legitimate enough cake-to-go excuse. He didn't want to risk appearing like a stalker. *Shit.* Even though time was limited, first thing Monday morning would have to do.

"No, that's okay. I'll stop by again, maybe tomorrow." *I say that as if I have all the goddamned time in the world.*

Ima pulled her lips in on themselves and angled her head at a contemplative slant. "Try calling first before you make the trip. I'm not sure she'll be in tomorrow."

"Is she sick?"

"No. Her son cracked up her car last night. Oh, he's okay and everything, but I think she's got some stuff to handle." The waitress clucked her tongue. "Kids! Right?" She shook her head.

"I'm sorry to hear that," he said. *Bad enough she's got a teenager, but maybe he's trouble to boot—a possible roadblock.* Hope drained from his veins like a puncture wound.

As he walked away, Ima called, "Like I said, call first."

****

He drove toward his uncle's house with new ideas bouncing in his head. He needed another plan and fast. Everything that came to mind was riddled with holes. The smoothest answer would be to find an alternate believable accomplice. *But who? Shit.*

Rand was a half mile from his uncle's driveway when his Bluetooth sounded. He pushed the phone button on his steering wheel to receive the incoming call. "Press," he said.

"Um..." a female voice began. He turned down the air conditioning fan to listen more closely. "Mr. Press?"

"Yes."

"This is Daisy Cameron. We, uh, met at the Brookside Café last night."

He pulled his car into a graveled shoulder area and thrust the gear into park. It was only then that he allowed himself to take a deep enough breath to keep his voice steady.

"Yes, I remember." His practiced nonchalance was like honey oozing from its dipper.

She laughed softly. "Honestly, I never thought I'd be making this call."

"I'm glad you did," he said. *If only you knew how glad.*

"So, can you tell me a little about the job?"

He hesitated. *Steady, boy. Reel her in slowly.* "I'd like to discuss it with you, Daisy." He spoke evenly though his mind was zooming. "I'm heading to an appointment now. Could we meet for a drink, say around four?"

As he waited for her to respond, his heartbeat thrummed in his chest. She was on his line now and he needed to finesse the reel, maneuver easily, not too fast, give it a little slack.

"You're familiar with Bradigan's in the Colonial Arms?" he prompted.

"The Irish pub. Yes, but perhaps we could meet in your office during the week?"

"The office will be fine, Daisy, for finalizing of the details, but first, if you don't mind, I'd like to discuss the position. Let's meet at Bradigan's. You understand, I'm sure." He waited, eyes shut.

The line was quiet for an agonizingly long time. If it weren't for the fact that he heard her breath, he'd have thought she had disconnected the call. Before he had a chance to come up with another strategy he heard her voice. "Okay," she said at last. "Yes. Four o'clock would be fine."

When Randolph drove up his uncle's long winding driveway he was prepared to begin with his plan. Although it would be hours before he would meet Daisy Cameron to divulge the part she'd play, he felt strongly that she was on board. Though he barely knew her, he was sure that her picking up the phone and calling him was the major chasm he needed her to cross. The rest of it, if he played his cards right, would be a walk in the park.

Florence met him in the foyer. While her hair had gone to a pleasant tone of dove gray and her face was lined with age, the woman was still attractive. A surge of affection poured over him. He leaned in to plant a kiss on her cheek.

"Randolph."

"Hi gorgeous."

"Don't be trying your charm on me, young man. It didn't work when you were twelve and it won't work now. What took you so long to get here? William's been anxious to see you."

I'll bet, Randolph thought. He shrugged the thought. There was no need to brace himself for a confrontation with his uncle. Rand had the right card in his hand—a pretty little blonde willing to play queen of hearts.

"Well, I'm here now, Flo. And look what I've brought." He waved the small Styrofoam container under her nose. "Chocolate mocha."

"He'll enjoy that, I'm sure. And, he'll be glad to see you."

"Shall I go up?"

Florence motioned toward the winding staircase with a sweep of her graceful arm. Randolph trotted up each step with the confidence of a winner.

****

Braced against the cluster of enormous pillows in crisp white cases, Uncle William appeared lost among the starchy bedclothes backed by the massive wooden headboard. The coverlet draped over the man's legs, outlining their spindly frailty.

"Well, well..." the old man croaked. "Look who's here." He cleared his throat. "Come in."

"How are you, Uncle?" Randolph forced a smile he did not feel. He was baffled by his physical response to the decrepit tyrant's appearance, confused by the lump that had lodged itself in his throat threatening to cut off his air. He, too, cleared his throat. "How are you feeling?"

William smirked. His face was a macabre mask, his bilious pallor a stark contrast to the bright white fabric of his pajamas. His eyes, rheumy drab stones that sat in sagged sockets, studied Randolph. For the briefest of moments Rand thought he'd seen a flash of the man's former fire.

"You touch me with your concern, my boy." William then erupted in a sardonic chuckle.

Rand placed the foam container onto the bedside tray. "I brought you a treat." He sat in a nearby chair.

"What have you brought me?" The old man's tone was flat.

"Something for your sweet tooth."

"The doctor said I'm to cut back on my sweets. Triglycerides or some such nonsense. Sugar, apparently, is lethal. You're not trying to kill me are you, Randolph?"

Randolph met the old man's gaze. There it was again—a spark that poor health and advanced age would never quell. He was eighty-four years old and he still got a jolt from a good spar. That was one thing they had in common. A joust was folly when you were well-armed. What Uncle William didn't know yet was that Randolph had acquired his ammunition.

"Uncle," Rand said genially. "I brought you a sample of a wonderful homemade chocolate mocha cake. Florence said it would be all right for you to have a sweet."

Rand squeezed the foamy sides of the container and the lid sprung open, exposing the rich, dark confection. "I'll buzz Florence to bring you a fork. Just take a little taste."

"Mocha, huh?" William asked with interest as he eyed the offering. "Looks like devil's food. Is that what this is, Randolph? Have you brought me devil's food?"

Rand ignored the reference, but noted the sly tone of the innuendo. Fortunately, the comment was a perfect lead-in to what Randolph had come to say.

"Trust me, this was not made by the devil, Uncle William. Rather, it was baked just for you by an angel," he said, his mouth sweet with the taste of victory. "My angel. My fiancée."

William stared at him, not moving a single muscle. Every inch of the old guy was fixated on what Randolph had just said.

Electricity charged through Rand's veins. This was, indeed, a treat.

"That's what this visit is about, I'm sure. So let's get to it, shall we?" William tried to push himself straighter against the bank of pillows. Rand reached to assist him, but his uncle shot a look so defensive it halted his move. He let his arm fall to his side.

Finally satisfied with his arrangement on the bed, William turned his steely gaze to Rand. "So, a fiancée? Max tells me you've not been forthcoming with the lady's identity. Is there a reason for the suspense, Randolph?"

"Just that I'm planning a surprise for when I give her the ring. And, I wouldn't want any, shall we say, interference with my plan. You understand, don't you, Uncle? A proposal is special."

"Well," William chuckled like an old witch. "I know *my* proposal is quite special. Odd, isn't it? That I propose that you be married in order to inherit my fortune and, presto, you've got a fiancée? Now *that's* special. Unbelievable, even."

"Trust me, Uncle William, she's real. The only

thing unbelievable is what a great baker she is."

"What's her name?"

He knew if he gave her name Uncle would have his bloodhounds on it before nightfall. But he had to give the old man something, a bit of information. Yet, somehow he just couldn't say it. *Daisy* just seemed to ring with commonality—a country-bumpkin kind of name.

Then it came to him like a gift. "Her name's Cameron."

"Cameron, huh? Cameron what?"

Randolph smiled. "I promise to give you a full introduction when the time comes. But for now, until she gets her ring, that's all I'll say."

William stared at Randolph, studying him like a bull in the ring. Rand was unfazed, a confident matador. Victory was within his grasp.

"Then let us not delay, son. I'll expect to meet your Cameron on Friday, as arranged through Max Willoughby. So, I suggest you not tarry, and commence with your *special* moment."

Although the smile was still on Randolph's face and his handshake with the old man a firm, confident one, Rand had started to sweat. His mind was already focused on his four o'clock meeting.

Chapter Eight

Daisy's hand still shook. Of all today's painful phone calls—the back and forth with the insurance company, the rental car ordeal—this last call had definitely been the worst. J. Randolph Press, Jr.'s voice echoed in her brain. Now her head ached.

She closed her eyes and breathed in deeply, forcing air into the constriction in her chest. She went into the kitchen to pour another cup of coffee. Adam—barefoot, hair a mess, and wearing boxers—stared into the open refrigerator like he was waiting for something to pop out at him.

"Hungry?" She slipped in under his extended arm to reach for the container of milk.

"I don't know," he said groggily. He shut the door, walked over to the kitchen table, and sat in a chair as if he was made of bricks.

"Have something." Daisy stirred the coffee she'd poured into her favorite daisy-decorated mug. "Want some coffee?"

"Nah."

Daisy joined him at the table, folded her arms onto the cool surface of the oak, and waited for him to begin. Adam continued to stare at the floor.

"Adam..." She kept her voice calm and steady, quelling the building desire to wring her handsome son's neck. "We need to discuss last night."

"What's to discuss? I fucked up."

"So true, and so eloquently put. The good news is that no one got hurt. Also, the fact that you were the designated driver is another good thing. Actually, it's what's kept me from wigging out on you."

The boy gave an anemic smile. Slowly he lifted his downturned head and looked at her. "Since when do you 'wig out,' Mom?"

She thought of the string of phone calls she'd had to make since she got up this morning. "Since today."

"Have you heard from Mr. Martino? How's the car?"

"That's my next phone call. In the meantime, I called the insurance company and they're going to pay half the cost of a rental car. So, that's something, at least."

"I'll give you my paychecks."

"Adam, I'd like to know how this happened in the first place. Did you know you were going to a party with no adult supervision? Did you know there would be alcohol? You lied to me about the movies. You said you and the guys were going to see the new fright flick."

"Mom..." Adam's voice was robust now, as though he had finally fully woken up. "I told you we were going to the movies because that's what I thought we were doing.

"When Paulie's sister's team qualified for the finals in their soccer tournament, they got the idea for a keg party."

"Who bought the keg?"

"I don't know. I walked in on it. I wasn't drinking, remember?" Adam's voice was too close to snotty for his own good.

"Okay, so you were the victim of an impromptu kegger." Now she sounded snotty herself. She sipped her coffee to chase it away. "So, what were you doing while your friends were drinking beer?"

"I was with Elizabeth."

"And Elizabeth would be?"

"A friend."

"What were you and your *friend,* Elizabeth, doing?"

"That's personal."

"Adam, I hope you're being smart. We've talked about this. You've got too bright a future ahead of you."

Adam groaned like a bear caught in a steel trap. "Look, Mom, I know this is going to cost you. I'm really sorry. I can give you my paychecks from the Y to help with the expense of the car and the rental. I mean, what else do you want from me? I'm sorry, okay?"

"I appreciate that, Adam. I'm not going to take your entire paycheck. We'll come up with a reasonable weekly amount. You don't seem to have much cash as it is. I hope you're saving some of what you make. You're going to need it for spending money when you get to Pratt."

The boy sighed, drawing the fingernail of his index finger along a groove in the oak tabletop. "I get it. No fun money."

"Yes, fun's on hold for a while."

Adam bolted up from his chair and went to the refrigerator again. He took the milk container into his hand, popped open the spout, and drank from it.

Daisy saw red. "Don't drink from the carton, Adam. That's disgusting."

He shoved it back on a shelf and shut the door. He turned to her. "Am I grounded or something? Is that what you're saying?"

"I'm saying for now you need to concentrate on school and work. It's necessary if you're going to keep your dream of Pratt alive."

He left the room and Daisy heard his bedroom door close with a heavy hand.

****

If she'd had a headache before, now Daisy's head felt as if it might crack like an egg dropped onto the floor. When her phone rang, she lifted the receiver with one thought. *Now what?*

"Hey girl."

"Hi Candy." Daisy felt herself smile against the mouthpiece, relieved and glad to hear her friend's voice.

"How's it going?"

"Okay, I guess. You know, compared to leprosy or the heartbreak of psoriasis."

Candy chuckled. "Bruno's got your car. He says the front axle is definitely bent and that's going to cost some dough. Too bad they couldn't total it so you could put the payout toward a new car."

"Yeah, but then I'd be back to a car payment. I can barely make my bills now. At least this one's paid off." Daisy blew out a breath. "But, hey, could be worse, right?"

"Well, your skin is scab-free, true."

Now Daisy laughed into the phone, the lighthearted moment feeling like an elixir. "Thanks again for rescuing us last night. And thank Bruno for all his help."

"No problem, honey. I'm just so glad everyone's okay."

"Well, I appreciate it."

"So, did you yell at Adam, but good?" Candy chuckled. "I hope you didn't, like, take away his birthday."

"Something like that."

"He's a good kid, Daisy girl."

"I know he is, Candy, but he's changing. He's moody and secretive. I don't like it."

"He's just lucky you're not an Italian mother. My mom would have broken a wooden spoon on my butt. I'm forty years old and she'd still be yelling at me to this day if I had wrecked her car when I was eighteen."

"I asked him what he was doing while his

friends were getting wasted and he said he was with some girl named Elizabeth." Daisy's voice was just above a whisper now. She craned her neck to peer down the hallway. Adam's door was still closed. "And, when I asked him what he and this girl were doing he said it was 'personal.'"

Candy laughed. "Well at least one Cameron is getting a little action. Do you need me to do anything for you? Make any calls, like maybe call that rich guy so you can take him up on his job offer?"

"Speaking of him…"

Daisy could hear Candy suck in her breath. Curiously she found herself enjoying a feeling of daring. "You did it!" Candy said. "Oh my God. You called him!"

"I did."

"Holy smokes. I'm impressed. Okay, so what's the scoop?"

"I'm meeting him at Bradigan's in the Colonial Arms at four today."

"You have to, I mean you absolutely have to, call me after you talk to him. What are you going to wear? Want to borrow something? I just got my little red dress out of the cleaners and it would look great with your blonde hair."

"No, no, no. No little red dresses. I'm not going on a date, Candy. This is a job interview. I thought I'd wear my suit. You know, the charcoal gray pinstripe."

"Boring."

Daisy sighed. As much as she loved her friend, they did not share fashion tastes. Where Daisy leaned toward the conservative, Candy leaned toward the fashion fast-lane. Though she'd never laid eyes on the dress in question, Daisy knew enough to decline the offer.

"Thank you anyway, Candy. I think I'll stick

with the business look."

"Well, it's Saturday and you're meeting a good-looking gazillionaire in the nicest hotel in town. At least wear a fun camisole with the suit."

"We'll see."

****

As Daisy stepped through the lobby doors she took in the newly refurbished Colonial Arms Hotel.

The décor was a far cry from its former patriotic theme. Now, instead of deep Americana red and Federal blue accents, the space had been transformed into modern elegance as if it had taken a ride in a time capsule. Everything was sleek and shiny new. The former tribute to the town's colonial heritage had been discarded like a used-up pack of matches. It irked her.

That only served to ignite the agitation this whole arrangement caused in her gut. If she had any sense left, she would high-tail it right back out along the marble-tiled floor, and go home.

Off to the right of the escalator the tall doors of Bradigan's loomed at her like a paned-glass and oak sentry. Daisy eyed the path back to the turnstile doors at the hotel's entry. She spied the doorman, under the exterior awning, who appeared to be giving someone directions.

Daisy needed direction, too. Stay or go? Her gut said to bolt, but her wallet said to stay.

Smoothing her hands over the thin wool fabric of her suit, she made her way toward the pub's doors. She reached a hand up and fingered the button on her jacket. Suddenly she wished she hadn't worn the ice blue camisole that peeked out from the lines of the lapels, but had gone with the silk blouse instead. She took a deep breath as she pulled open the door.

Bradigan's had escaped the modernizing renovations of the hotel's lobby. It was the same as Daisy remembered. Three bars, all hewn of thick ancient wood, sat in alcoves aligned along the back wall. The center bar, the largest of the three, had the most action today. Men and women in business attire were crowded at the counter talking animatedly, drinking ale. None of them was J. Randolph Press, Jr.

Daisy scanned the small dining room beyond the bar area. It was nearly empty at that hour with the exception of an older-looking couple sharing a meal. She turned back to the bar, letting her eyes travel along the row of stools. She wondered if the "gazillionaire" had changed his mind. That, she decided, would be a godsend. As the thought entered her head, J. Randolph Press, Jr. entered her line of vision.

"Have you been waiting long?" he asked. A smile played at his mouth. Dressed much more casually than she was, he wore trendy jeans, a gray V-neck sweater, and loafers.

Now that he was there in front of her, any and every doubt that had misted through her thoughts now pelted her like rain. If she had a kingdom, she'd have given it at that moment just to disappear. But, she didn't have a kingdom. Now, she didn't even have a car to drive to her imaginary kingdom.

She found her voice. "Not at all, I just arrived."

"Good." He extended his hand. "Thanks for coming."

Daisy shook his hand and was the first to pull free of the grasp. Touching him felt awkward and intimidating.

When she saw his green eyes find the wedge of light blue fabric of her stupid camisole, annoyance pushed its way into her veins and overtook her sense of intimidation. She was not about to let this man's presence affect her, and she'd be damned if she'd stand for being looked at like the daily special on the pub's menu.

"I don't want to take up too much of your time, Mr. Press."

"Oh, please. Stop with the 'Mr. Press.' Call me, Rand. Come on, let's have a seat." He touched her elbow and his hand acted like a rudder, guiding her to one of the side bars.

The bar, tucked in its alcove, was up two steps from the others and empty except for the bartender. Daisy felt as if she was watching a movie as she allowed the man to steer her to a stool.

"Michael." Rand reached over the wooden counter to shake the man's hand. The tender, a friendly-faced redhead with graying temples and thinning hairline, pumped Rand's arm like he was trying to draw water from a well.

"Good to see you, man."

"What's good today for my friend here, and me?" Rand asked.

"We've got two specials—O'Hara's Stout and on tap we've got Southern Tier's pumpkin ale," Michael turned his gaze toward Daisy. "I'd recommend the ale for you. It's smooth, and just right for a day like today."

"I think I'll just have a cup of coffee," Daisy said.

"Oh, no, that'll never do," Rand said. He gave a nod to the bartender.

Michael winked as he reached for an empty glass and held it up to the brass tap. He pulled the lever. "Here try some. Trust me, you'll enjoy this."

"I'd listen to the man. He'd never steer you wrong." Rand chuckled.

Rand's face was, without question, handsome—chiseled by nature's ablest sculptors for sure. But, there was something about him that Daisy didn't like, beyond the pomposity and loftiness he exuded. He was smooth, all right. Maybe what coursed through his veins was a river of pumpkin ale.

Michael handed off a sample amount of the

amber-colored liquid. Courteously, she took a tiny sip. It was indeed smooth and creamy. Its coolness chilled her throat as she swallowed, then a radiating warmth followed on its coattails and settled inside her. This was no ordinary beer.

"Well? What's the verdict?" Rand asked. Amusement lit his green eyes, turning them almost emerald.

"Delicious," Daisy offered. In spite of herself, she downed the rest of the sample. "But I'd still better stick to coffee."

"Humor Michael," Rand said in mock whisper. "He's quite serious about his brews." Then in his normal tone he added, "We'll each have some of that. I'm going to trust her reaction that it's good."

Daisy stiffened against J. Randolph Press, Jr.'s ignoring of her request. That sort of treatment brought her right back to the frustration of being on the wrong end of privilege. If she had any brains she'd leave right this minute.

Apparently her wallet wasn't the only thing that was empty. Her head was pretty damned empty now, too. She wrapped her fingers around the handle of the frosty mug Michael had placed in front of her and tapped it gingerly against the one Rand held up to her. *This guy better have a job that will make it worth tolerating his insufferable condescending attitude.* Daisy lifted the drink to her lips and took a sip.

****

Rand decided to make small talk until Daisy's mug was half-empty. It was obvious she wasn't a big drinker, which was a good thing. But she wasn't a teetotaler either. She was also willing to try new things. And, dressed up like this—out of that waitress getup—she looked good, very good.

She needed to relax though. She was rigid, her frame squared, jaw set.

He'd need to convince her to join him for something to eat in a little while, so that they could move the conversation to a more private table. The one close to the fireplace would be ideal. He looked toward the back wall. The table was still open, but it was getting closer to when early diners would start to arrive. *Come on, girl, drink up.*

"So," she said, "this job you have available…"

"Before we get to the business at hand, why don't you tell me about yourself?" Rand held his glass just short of his mouth, then took a deep pull. He figured the faster he drank maybe she'd try to keep pace.

"What would you like to know?" Her voice was cool, but not unfriendly.

He sensed she was a strong person, but hopefully did not come with a chip on her shoulder. That would suck. He knew that type—too much baggage, too little fun.

He liked her eyes. They flashed with confidence, intelligence.

He needed to ace this. There was no other option. "Let's see," he said with a tilt to his head. "How did you wind up here in this part of Jersey? Are you from the area?"

"Yes, this is my hometown."

"Ah, a townie. Lived here all your life?"

He watched her trace a fingernail along the frost outside her glass. "No. For a while I worked in New York. I've been back for two years now."

"Tell me about New York. What did you do there?"

"I worked for a large marketing research company."

Rand watched her as she fiddled with a button on her jacket. She crossed and uncrossed her long legs. Obviously she wasn't fond of divulging her information. The pumpkin ale was not melting her guardedness.

But Rand was a pro. He'd managed to wrap plenty of women around his pinky and Daisy Cameron would be no exception. He leaned in closer to her and put an elbow on the bar. "Enjoying the beer?"

The question seemed to throw her, which was of course just what he wanted it to do.

"Um, sure. Yes."

"Me, too." Rand said this in a way that made it sound like they had decided to be on the same team.

Daisy reverted her attention to her idle task, continuing to trace along the outside of her mug. The frosted sides now melted in rivulets that she caught with the pad of her index finger.

"You know," Rand said, "I could go for something to eat. Are you hungry?"

"No. No thank you. I, uh, I have an engagement to get to."

"Would you mind if I ordered something while we talk?" he asked.

She hesitated. Her mouth slanted in what looked like a moment of indecision. He watched her pretty eyes, almost seeing the wheels in her head turning, debating her answer. "Not at all."

Rand felt that satisfying little jab he always got when he'd won a hand. He turned to the bartender who stood at a discreet distance behind the bar. "Michael, we're going to get a table. Can I settle up with you now?"

"Nah," Michael said. "They'll add it on your tab. Enjoy."

"See you soon." Rand stood from his stool and grabbed both beers. They made their way into the dining room and took seats at the table by the fireplace. Within a moment a young waitress brought waters and two menus.

It didn't take him long to convince Daisy to

share a unique item from the appetizer menu, a cheese and fruit tray called the Blarney Platter.

"Okay, now with that business out of the way, let's get back to ours. You were saying that you worked in New York in a market research firm. Sounds interesting. What did you do there?"

She took a deep breath and let it expend slowly. "I was their focus study manager. I orchestrated the studies, managed the interviewers, supervised the moderators, things like that. Does any of this sound like something that would benefit your company?"

She gave a little laugh. "I don't even know what job opening we're talking about. You haven't said."

"We'll get to that," he said with what he knew was a reassuring curve to his lips. "Why did you leave New York?"

Daisy cocked her head, hesitated a moment, then spoke. "A number of reasons. The biggest being that my mother died."

"I'm sorry to hear that. My condolences. I've lost both my parents."

"How sad." Her voice resonated with empathetic warmth, a new soft lilt he liked. "How long?"

"They died in a car accident when I was twelve."

She reached up and fiddled with the button on her jacket again. Rand wondered if the button would eventually pop free.

"How tragic. I'm sorry."

"Long time ago. But, still hurts, you know?"

"Yes."

A server delivered the Blarney Platter which held a decoratively arrayed selection of cheeses, water wafers, grapes and enormous hot house berries. Rand ordered another round of pumpkin ale and was glad that Daisy didn't protest.

They sampled the offerings and Rand began again. "So, let me tell you about what I'm looking for."

Daisy held his gaze.

"I'm going to cut right to the chase, as it were. As unorthodox as this may sound, I have a very special need right now. That need is for you to pose as my fiancée convincingly enough that my dying eccentric uncle won't cut me out of his will."

The button from her jacket finally succumbed to her fingers' fret and Rand watched the disk fall and clack onto the tile floor.

Chapter Nine

Daisy watched as J. Randolph Press, Jr., wealthy snob that he was, scrambled to the floor to retrieve her errant button. If she weren't so stunned, she'd laugh at the scene—and laugh louder at the proposition he'd just offered. If Adam were here, he'd tell her she'd been "punked."

The most startling thing about Randolph Press's proposition was that the look on his face seemed sincere—as though this was not lunacy.

Whether it was the absurdity of the moment, the sight of him crouched on all fours like a well-dressed Labrador retriever, or perhaps it was the affects of nearly two mugs of pumpkin ale, but suddenly she decided this was hysterical. When Rand was back in his chair—perfectly coiffed hair now flopped over his forehead—Daisy eyed him incredulously and laughed like hell.

Rand joined her now in a chuckle of his own. He held the button out toward her. "I believe this belongs to you."

She ignored the gesture and watched him place it on the tabletop near her plate.

"I know how odd this sounds—"

"Odd?" Daisy asked. The moment's humor had dissipated like a burst soap bubble. Now she felt a froth of anger.

This guy had duped her, dangled a prospective job offer over her head like a carrot, all in an effort to humiliate her with some ridiculous scheme. "You're crazy."

"I know it sounds crazy. Please let me explain."

"Nothing you say could make it any less insane."

"My uncle has decided that I'm not living as stable an existence as he'd like, so he's concocted this preposterous stipulation in order for me to receive my rightful inheritance. I'm in a somewhat desperate situation."

She threw her napkin onto the table and pushed back her chair. "Well, I guess it just sucks to be you then."

Oddly, he grinned at her. His eyes flashed like the green lights at a racetrack giving the signal to accelerate. "That's what we have in common. We're both desperate. So, I'd amend that to say it *sucks to be us.*"

Daisy itched to slap the smile off his face. Instead she picked up the button he'd placed on the table and threw it at him. He expertly dodged. She'd be willing to bet that wasn't the first thing ever thrown in his aristocratic face.

"Sir, I'm not desperate. And I'm certainly not going to venture further into this cockamamie proposal." She reached for her clutch at the end of the table.

Rand put a hand out and touched her forearm, halting her move. Daisy gave him a narrowed glare that any normal person on the planet would have known was a demand that he let go of her. But, J. Randolph Press was not normal, apparently, and he didn't pull away.

"Please consider this," he said, his tone imploring. "Forgive my use of the word 'desperate.' I certainly wouldn't want to insult you in any way. What I meant by it was that I know you're a hard-working single mother looking to find the funds for your son to attend a very prestigious art school. If you take this on, I promise you your son will go to Pratt and it won't cost you one cent."

"Don't worry about my son and me." She kept

her voice low, forcing herself not to scream like she wanted to. She wrenched her arm away. "We don't need your money."

Eighteen years later and I'm saying the very same words again to a rich asshole that thinks his money can buy anything—even my cooperation. She bolted up from her chair.

"Please just think about this…"

"I'm leaving."

"One quarter of a million dollars," he said, enunciating each syllable clearly as he leaned forward. "Can you really walk away from the answer to your son's future?"

Daisy's heart stalled in her chest. The usually quick mathematics of her brain that routinely could calculate more complex equations than what Randolph proposed, could not process this offer. Yet the number, with all those zeroes, formed in her head like rings of smoke. Her mouth was suddenly dry. She lowered herself back onto the chair, reached for her dwindling ale, and took a swig.

Randolph sat back in his chair. She could see his chest rise and fall, heard the whoosh of air escape him. Momentarily numb, she just stared at him.

"Please help me. And let me help you."

"Out of morbid curiosity, what…" She wet her lips nervously. "What exactly are you asking of me? I mean, what specifically does this mean?"

As she said the words she couldn't believe they were coming from her own mouth. Was she actually considering this? Now she was feeling psychotic. Maybe J. Randolph Press' insanity was a contagious fungus.

She willed herself to flee the pub, but her feet would not budge.

"I will make this failsafe for you," he said. "I'll draw up a document that we'll both sign so that you will be protected.

"Essentially, what I need you to do is play the role of my fiancée. I'll get a ring for you to wear and then I'll introduce you to Uncle William. As I've stated, he's an old, ailing man and for whatever reason he's decided that his sole heir be married in order to inherit his estate."

"Won't he be suspicious of the fact that no wedding takes place? That we don't have any plans for that to happen?"

"It won't come to that. He's very ill. We just need this charade to appease his dying wish."

"But, it's a lie. And, it's not fulfilling a last request. It's fraud."

Randolph twisted his lips forming a deep crease on his face that gouged his laugh lines. "I know what you're saying. Believe me, I do. But, this is not just my uncle's money. It's my family's fortune, the Press legacy. I want to preserve that."

"When, uh, when would this act start?" She was incredulous that she was still involved in this conversation. The smoke rings in her head had clouded her logic, apparently toasting her brain.

"Friday."

"*This* Friday?"

This reminded her of fifth grade when her teacher had asked her to fill in as narrator for the class play. She'd had to go on stage and wing it in front of the entire student body of Mountain Peak Elementary School. She hadn't had time to practice then, and it appeared as though she wouldn't have that luxury now—if she were stupid enough to agree to any of this.

"Yes, does that work for you?"

Daisy racked her brain, searching her head for some rational thought. All she could see was the billowy numbers and zeroes floating within her grasp.

"I'd have to see the paperwork first," she said as

though this were a legitimate business transaction, and not an invitation to the funny farm.

Randolph smiled. "Let's meet back here tomorrow evening... say at seven? I'll have the paperwork ready to sign."

Daisy stalled, hoping for a cognitive thought.

Randolph added, "I've already thought of a couple of stipulations that I'll share with you. One being that I'd like to call you 'Cameron' rather than 'Daisy'."

"What? Why?"

He shrugged, tucked his chin toward his chest. "Pardon my saying so, but Cameron sounds more sophisticated. My uncle will not flinch at hearing it."

"Oh, but he'd *flinch* at Daisy?" Her anger surfaced again. He was just so damned pompous. "I'll have you know I like my name. My parents named me Daisy for a reason and I don't appreciate—"

"Hold on, hold on," he said in a soothing tone. "Please don't mistake my request. It's not me that would, say, question your colloquial name. It's Uncle William. Believe me. It's just an act, Daisy.

"During the charade you'll be Cameron Day. This way Uncle will never be able to investigate your identity. It's a harmless request."

Daisy detested everything about this. Yet she heard herself ask, "What else?"

"You'll have to nix the job."

"Excuse me?"

"You can't be seen waitressing. Uncle would know it's a fraud. Trust me on this, too."

"I cannot quit my job."

"I'm not asking you to quit. I know you're the Brookside Café's bookkeeper. That's okay, I suppose. We'll hope to keep that on the down low. But, you can't be slinging hash if we want this to work."

Warning flags pinched her brain. "Wait a

second. How do you know I'm their bookkeeper?"

Randolph laughed with what looked like pride shining in his eyes. "I went to the Brookside Café earlier today, to get a piece of that great mocha cake for my uncle. I asked for you."

She didn't know how to feel. Her mind was not functioning like it usually did. *But, then again,* the voice in her head scolded, *she wasn't herself, was she? Apparently she was Cameron Day.*

"Anything else, Mr. Press?" she said icily.

"You'd better start calling me Rand, if we're going to pose as engaged," he said with a sinister smirk. "Oh, and, one last requirement—our arrangement is to remain confidential. Just between the two of us."

Daisy nodded dully. "I wouldn't tell a soul that I'd even entertain something like this. But there's no way I could keep it from my son, of course. I'd have to tell him the truth."

"No one, Daisy. You must tell no one."

She stiffened. "You don't understand. I don't lie—as a rule. And, I especially don't lie to Adam. He doesn't lie to me, nor I him."

"I'm sorry, but in this instance you must not divulge our agreement. You don't know my uncle and his tactics. The wool isn't pulled over his eyes easily. If he were to discover the truth about our arrangement, it would be a disaster."

"Another thing is my best friend knows I'm here today to talk to you about a job opportunity. What am I supposed to tell her?"

Randolph thought a moment then smiled charmingly—as big fat liars are wont. "Tell her it was a ruse. Tell her I was so captivated by you at the diner that I made it up just to get you to meet me for a drink."

Daisy laughed, releasing the tension that had walled up in her chest making it ache. "I may not know your Uncle William, but you certainly don't know my friend. Candy isn't easy to fool."

"What's her name? Candy? Seriously? Is that a requirement of your working establishment? That you be named after a noun?"

"You're an ass, and *that's* a noun." She was aghast that she was still speaking to him. "Candy will not buy that you lured me here on the pretense of just meeting me."

"Why not?" Randolph said with restored brightness to his tone, his green eyes dancing with good cheer. "Look at yourself, woman. Who wouldn't believe that I fell head over heels at first sight?

Daisy pulled her eyes away, unable to hold the man's gaze. She was astounded at the way the sugary malarkey seemed to roll off his tongue. No wonder the man's menu selection had been a "Blarney Platter."

What came to Daisy's mind was how true the old adage that claims we are what we eat, for certainly when it came to blarney J. Randolph Press, Jr. was full of it. In spite of that, Daisy agreed to meet him the next evening to go over the paperwork.

Surely by then someone would save her from herself and strap her in a straight jacket.

Chapter Ten

Daisy found Adam watching television. The volume was louder than she liked, especially since whatever was on the screen involved piercing sirens and screeching sounds of a car chase.

Sitting with her son on the sofa were two of the four Martino's—Candy and daughter, Gina. Sharing a large bowl of popcorn everyone was riveted to the screen. No one heard Daisy come in.

"Hello!" she shouted.

Adam reached for the remote and tapped the volume button. The sound lowered to a whisper compared to what it had been. "Hey, Mom."

"Hi! Surprise!" Gina was a nine-year-old ball of energy with curly chestnut hair. "We're watching Kindergarten Cop."

"Hey, girl," Candy said. Anticipation was written all over her face. "Gina and I had to run to the store for bread. So, we thought we'd stop by and say hello."

"I see," Daisy said. She slung her purse onto the coffee table and kicked off her pumps.

On the way home she had rehearsed how she would begin a lie-fest with these people that she loved. She hadn't expected to face both Candy and Adam at the same time. She felt intimidated as though she were hooked up to wires and a machine was monitoring her—as if anything she'd say would be detected in a split second.

"How'd the interview go, Mom?"

"Yeah, how'd it go?" Candy's chocolate-colored eyes were bright and shiny.

Daisy cleared her throat and let the first lie tumble from her tongue. It tasted sour, like Brie left out too long. "It wasn't an interview after all," she said. She forced her tone to be lighthearted, but her heart did not feel light. It felt like lead.

"It wasn't?" Adam asked. "What was it then?"

"A ploy—apparently to get to know me."

Candy laughed loudly and clapped her hands, the bowl of popcorn on her lap pitching forward. Gina reached and steadied it and admonished her mother with a curt, "Mom!"

"Really?" Adam said. "The guy just wanted to hit on you? That sucks."

"Details, Daisy. Give us details," Candy said. She put the bowl of popcorn onto the coffee table and sat up straight, looking expectant.

Daisy shrugged, gave Candy a *not-now* look, and said "We have a date tomorrow night."

"You're kidding!"

"Seriously?" Adam said. He hit the remote again. The screen went black.

Daisy felt herself flush, her skin hot. She shrugged her shoulders, trying to appear nonchalant. "He seems very nice."

"Nice?" Adam said. "You're joking, right?"

"I'm not joking. I have a date tomorrow night." The words tasted like metal on her tongue. She had a mouthful of nails.

"Whoa," Candy said. Her mouth formed a circle like the doorway on a birdhouse. "Well, I guess if you didn't haul off and slug the guy for bullshitting you, then hell, you must have liked him."

Daisy forced a smile. "Something like that." She thought of the way she'd thrown her button at him. She was not a violent person, but she was known to be reactive. The man was lucky all she'd done was toss a tiny disk his way. Besides, she'd missed him by a mile and all she'd gotten out of it was a lost button.

"Well, well," Candy said. She checked her watch. "If this wasn't a school night and I didn't have to get this munchkin home I'd interrogate you."

That's what I'm afraid of, Daisy thought, *the interrogation.* She didn't know how she was going to pull this off with Candy...or Adam. Each of them was skilled at reading her, knowing her to be straight-forward.

If the *purse* wasn't the quarter-million-dollar answer to her dilemma, she'd sit down and tell the two of them what Rand had really proposed. They could then all share a good laugh. But, that was not what she would do. Instead she sat in the club chair angled away from the sofa and closed her eyes.

"Come on, Gina-Beana," Candy said. She gently tugged a tendril of her daughter's hair. "Time to get you home."

"But, Mommy, the movie's not over yet."

"Honey, you've seen this so many times you were lip-synching the script. Come on, get your jacket."

As Gina headed for the coat hooks by the front door, Candy whispered into Daisy's ear. "You've got a reprieve for now, Daisy-girl, but I'll be first in line at your office door in the morning to pick your brain."

The events of her meeting with Rand replayed little clips of their preposterous conversation in her head. Candy could try picking her brain all she'd like. Based on her entertainment of the outlandish scheme, Daisy figured her friend would find it slim pickings.

****

The first thing Rand would do in the morning was call his florist. Ordering flowers would get the rumor mill started. He knew all too well that the florist's clerk had an in with one of the assistants at

Press Industries, and speculation would begin about Rand's latest conquest. He knew the game and now he'd let it play in his favor.

Then, he'd need to get the ring. He would avoid Gallerstein's Jewelers, although the quality of their stones was superb and he had a long-standing relationship with their gemologist, Ethan. Rand knew Uncle could very well question Gallerstein about a ring purchase, and a hasty acquisition would send up a flag.

No, Rand would go into New York, buy a dazzling finger-ready engagement ring and present it to his intended. It struck him that he had no idea what size ring to buy. He decided to stop off at The Brookside Café in the morning before heading into the City to ask the lovely, newly-christened "Cameron" her ring size. It would be a good idea for her coworkers to see him show up, perhaps he would hand deliver the roses himself and create a bigger impact. It would be a win-win.

Chapter Eleven

Daisy wasn't in her little upstairs office at the café for longer than it took her to turn on the light before she had company. Candy appeared at the doorway to the cramped space, and next to her stood a wide-eyed Ima Ardellis.

"Okay, we want details," Candy said. She plopped herself down on a rickety folding chair near Daisy's desk.

"Can you give us the Reader's Digest version? I have soup on the stove. Not sure how much I trust Pete to make sure to stir it." Ima was a small, wiry woman with graying mid-toned brown hair that she wore to her collar bone, straight and plain. Today the sides were pulled back in tortoise shell combs.

"Candy said you met a millionaire with a job that wasn't really a job because he just wanted to meet you. Well that part is good because you're not leaving us. You're family now."

Daisy sat at the old pock-surfaced mahogany desk. The faded green blotter was littered with sticky notes of hastily jotted reminders—all things she needed to accomplish today, right after she lied her head off again.

She put her elbows onto the desktop and looked across to her comrades, preparing to lay the groundwork for her impending false existence. "Ima, don't worry. I'm not going anywhere.

"The story starts with J. Randolph Press coming in here on Saturday and having some dessert. Apparently, I, um, dazzled him so much that he concocted this whole thing about a job opening in his company just to spend time with me."

"And you didn't drown him?" Ima asked, apparently recalling the incident at the café when a customer grabbed Daisy's ass and she poured an entire glass of water over his head. "Well, that's impressive."

"I know, right?" Candy said. "It's not like our Daisy."

"He was, um, cute about it," Daisy said. She sounded lame to her own ears.

"Well, he's a sly devil. I'll give the guy that." Ima's lips turned up into a rosy-pink grin. "Well, good. At least he's not looking to steal you away from us. He's just a man with a mission."

Oh, he's got a mission, all right. Daisy dashed the thought, trying to ignore her inner voice—the reasonable one. "He's actually rather charming." Daisy said. Her smile felt like a rubber band that had been pulled beyond its comfort zone.

"Rather charming, huh?" Candy asked. She narrowed her eyes. "Just like that? This big-time pompous ass—your reference as I recall—traipses in and scams you into meeting him, and you—our very own Norma Rae—calls that 'charming'?" Candy let out a sarcastic-edged laugh. "I'd have thought *you* would've punched him in the nose."

Heat rushed to Daisy's cheeks. How she managed to maintain a playful tone amazed her. "I guess that's just how charming he is. I was enthralled."

"Enthralled, she says." Ima turned toward Candy. "The girl was *enthralled*. Not much can be added to that."

"Well, I've got three utility workers at the counter looking to place an order and they're *not* enthralled," a male voice said from the hallway outside the office. Pete stood wearing a white bib-front apron and a Mets cap squashed down over his curly gray hair. Silvery little springs poked out at the sides, like fringe, over his ears. "You three anywheres near done with your coffee klatch?"

"Okay, okay," Ima said. "We're coming. I hope you kept an eye on the beef barley."

"Your soup is fine."

Daisy heard Ima's typical, lighthearted admonishing as they descended the staircase. "Peter, how many times do I have to tell you that barley has a mind of its own? It expands.

"Yeah, yeah. I know. It's like *The Blob*."

When they were no longer within earshot, Candy paused at the office's doorway before heading down to wait on the guys from public service. "Duty calls. Hey, let's go out for margaritas tonight."

"Um, can't."

Candy's mouth opened then closed. She eyed Daisy with a side glance. "Can't?"

"I have a date, remember?"

Before Candy could comment, Pete was in the doorway again, breathless from what had to be a hurried climb up the flight of stairs. His eyes were bright with amusement. "Daisy, you better come downstairs, too," he said. "There's a man here to see you, and he's carrying an armload of red roses."

Daisy and Candy locked eyes. Daisy felt her insides twisting on themselves. Her muscles played a game of Tug of War. She wondered how she could possibly do his for any length of time. Her phony existence was only a few minutes old and already the lies were tying her in knots.

The three paraded single-file down the wooden stairs, led by Pete. Candy, ahead of Daisy, stopped short when she reached the last step, blocking Daisy's view of the interior of the café. She leaned forward and peered out like a thief looking for a getaway, then turned back to Daisy, her mouth a crooked smirk. "Pete wasn't kidding," she whispered.

"He's got an armload of roses, all right. There's got to be at least three dozen of those babies in a glass vase."

Daisy pinched her hands to her waist, massaging her fingers to loosen the muscles of her torso that wrenched like the woven bamboo of Chinese handcuffs. She wet her lips, a gesture that felt like a slick of fuel for her lying tongue. "Told you, Candy. Charming."

****

Rand did not miss the disparaging looks shot to him by the tool-belted guys, lined up on the swivel stools like trained seals. He was immune to their scrutiny, ignored the way they elbowed one another as he stood there waiting with his roses. If they knew what was at stake, they'd follow suit. Rand had no doubt about that.

The guy that said he'd go find her came back down the stairs followed by that other waitress from Saturday, what was her name? Oh yes, another noun—Candy. She poked her head from the stairwell, an apparent drop-out from the school of subtlety. He deliberately caught her skeptical eye and offered her one of his impish grins—a school boy with a shiny red apple for the teacher.

Cameron emerged. His brain registered the new name. Excitement lit inside him at the sight of her. She was his ticket, his solution, a flare in the darkness of what could have been a financial nightmare.

"Good morning." His voice was as smooth as silk.

"Good morning," Daisy said softly. She let her blue eyes dart briefly to Candy then quickly glanced back at him. He hoped he was the only one to notice that the smile on her lips—a pretty, full-sized grin—did not reach her eyes.

"These are for you," he said. He held the flowers

toward her.

"Goodness," she said. "How lovely."

As she reached for the vase Rand said, "They're heavy. Can I put them here on the counter?"

Daisy nodded, surveying the others in the room. Rand followed her gaze and noticed Candy whispering with that older woman, "Ima Waitress," he had seen on Sunday. Their eyes were on him.

"Happy anniversary," he said, loud enough for them to hear.

"Anniversary?" she asked. The word was punctuated by a nervous laugh.

"Yes," he said. He was glad she had taken the bait. "It's our three-day anniversary. We met three days ago. A dozen roses for each day."

"Well," she cleared her throat. "That's so, um, sweet of you. Thank you."

"I have some business in New York later this morning." Rand leaned in closer to her. Lowering his volume, he asked, "Would you have a moment to talk?"

Again she looked to her coworkers before responding to him. "Sure."

Rand ushered Daisy toward the café entrance and as they stood facing each other he reached for her hand. It was ice cold. He rubbed her ring finger with his thumb and whispered, "What size ring do you wear?"

She hesitated and he watched the pink tip of her tongue dart out from her mouth to moisten her lip. The gesture stirred something in him—a mere physical response, for sure. "I'm going to get the ring today and, unfortunately, I'll have to find something ready-made. You need to be sporting it by Friday."

"I still don't know how I'm going to do this," she whispered, her mouth frozen in place as if it was held fast by wires.

He gently touched around her ring finger. He

kept his eyes on her, enjoying the way her pupils dilated like black moons in the middle of a daytime sky. "I'd guess five or six. Am I right?"

He saw her swallow hard, her mouth pinching at the corners. "Five-and-a-half, I think. Yes, five-and-a-half."

"I look forward to our evening," Rand said. He was louder again, an actor playing to the café crowd. "Until then."

Rand lifted her hand to his lips and placed a delicate kiss on it, like a prince right out of a fairy tale. He thought he heard the two on-looking women gasp in unison. This was more fun than he'd thought it would be.

Chapter Twelve

Luckily Pete was debating animatedly with the utility workers on the topic of some sporting news, and was too involved to razz Daisy as she guessed he would. Thankfully, Ima's pot of soup with the incorrigible barley that needed monitoring only left her time to let out a cat-call whistle before heading back into the kitchen. That left Daisy virtually alone with Candy. That was bad.

"I know this *looks* like the Brookside Café and *smells* like the Brookside Café', but this is Disney World, isn't it?" Candy said. She shook her head.

"Oh come on, Candy." Daisy's tone contained as much nonchalance as she could muster. She plastered a smile and went over to the roses, preening them with admiring hands.

"Who *are* you?" Candy asked, coming close. Her glossy eyes were filled with question. "And how did we get to Fantasy Land?"

Daisy leaned in and took in a breath of the fragrant bouquet. The scent of three dozen roses was powerful, almost overwhelming. She stifled her urge to cough.

"Daisy, look at me."

She pretended to fuss with the arrangement, fiddling with a sprig of baby's breath. Daisy heard the café door open and the chatter of customers entering the room. She said a silent *thank you* to the strangers that saved her from Candy's scrutiny.

"Good morning," Candy called to the three older ladies taking a booth by the window. "Coffee?"

"Decaf," they said in unison, then chuckled

among themselves.

Candy put an arm around Daisy's shoulder, giving her a squeeze. "If you're really into this guy, then I'm as happy as a friend can be. But, I don't know...I'm just worried that's all."

"Don't worry about me, Candy. I'm fine. I'm *more* than fine," Daisy said. Her smile was full of saccharine.

When Candy moved toward the coffee station, Daisy seized the opportunity to go back up to the solitude of her tiny office. She welcomed the truth of numbers to displace all her own lies. She took the stairs two at a time.

****

Rand walked into the store at the corner of 47th and Fifth. He'd never been inside the place, but immediately had a hunch that this was a good choice. He liked the appearance of the woman at the front counter, a wise-looking matron with well-coiffed silver hair.

She looked up from a printout and peered at him over half-lens reading glasses. "Good morning," she said pleasantly in a rich alto. "How may I help you today?" She gathered her paperwork and slipped it behind the glass counter.

"I'd like to see engagement rings."

"Oh," she said, "My favorite kind of shopping. Such a happy time. Let's move down this way. We have some lovely, lovely stones."

Rand followed her along the glass casings, she on one side, and he on the other. Toward the back of the store, a case at least four feet long housed a selection of diamond rings with brilliance that could knock an eye out. He scanned the items poking up like flowers in a bed of sapphire velvet.

"Do you have something in mind? A style preference? Setting?"

"Well..." Rand said. Sounding charmingly

overwhelmed, he watched the woman's face turn to sympathetic putty. "I'm a bit confused, I'm afraid. I want something jaw-dropping, but not gaudy."

Rand knew that whichever ring he chose it would have to pass Uncle William's inspection. Even though the old guy was failing, he'd know a lesser quality stone with his naked eye. The ring had to be top quality, clear and colorless if this engagement were to appear believable.

"Do you see anything that interests you?" she asked. "Let's start that way."

He studied the rows of jewelry. He had no idea of Cameron's taste—the pseudonym was becoming quite natural for his mind. Did she like round solitaires? Marquis? Rand quickly realized that it didn't really matter, did it? This wasn't real.

He pointed to a nice-sized traditional-looking solitaire. The jeweler smiled as though he had chosen well and unlocked the case. She delicately removed the ring and placed it onto a display of velvet positioned directly under a facet-flattering beam of light. The diamond sparkled like nothing Rand had ever seen.

"That's breathtaking, isn't it?" she asked. "You have impeccable taste."

"It's a beauty, all right. Tell me about it."

"It's a six-prong two-carat solitaire, nearly flawless. Platinum band, obviously. You'll see by the grading specifications that this is a very unique ring."

"For a very unique woman," Rand said. He enjoyed the idea of so easily convincing this established gemologist that he was a dream customer in love. He hadn't even asked how much it cost. It didn't matter. After all, the ring was an insurance policy.

"I'm sure she'll love your choice. What is your lady's name?"

"Cameron."

She smiled appreciatively. "Lucky girl, Cameron."

"Can we have this sized? It's just what I've been looking for."

As she proceeded with Rand's transaction, she made small talk, chatting happily about the delights of love and surprises, and such. Rand smiled and nodded in all the appropriate places.

"Did you know, Mr. Press,"—she referred to his gold card information—"that the word diamond is derived from the ancient Greek word 'unbreakable'?"

"No," he said. "I didn't."

"And, diamonds are from the heart of the earth. Isn't it lovely to think that you will bestow such a treasure to your Cameron? May your hearts remain rooted deeply in each other and may your love be unbreakable."

Although Rand smiled appreciatively at her words, something inside him slithered in his gut, something sour—like spoiled milk had sneaked into his system. Suddenly, he wanted to bid this place adieu.

Driving back to Jersey, Rand was troubled by his thoughts despite efforts to distract himself with music on his MP3 player. The soothing sounds of Sarah Chan's violin came to life with a click of the button. He did not want this today. He tapped the button again. Even her more rousing Vivaldi would not do.

He wanted something loud and raucous, music that would bang around in his head, filling it to capacity and not allowing any thoughts to formulate. Rand selected Santana and cranked the volume until it nearly hurt his ears.

Even this did not chase away the visions that came to his mind—old images, memories he thought he had buried, burned, and obliterated when he was a boy. Damn that woman behind the counter and her blabbering about love and its fortitude.

In his mind's eye, he pictured his mother as she was just before the accident. She was young and beautiful with sleek, dark, shiny hair—like his own. She'd had the same green eyes he saw now in his rearview mirror. Lori Doran Press, thirty-seven years old, just about three years younger than Rand was now.

The day she and his father, John Sr., left for Florida came into Rand's mind. An oncoming billboard of October first 1982 pictured his father driving his car, appropriate for the scene.

It had been his mother's idea, Rand remembered. When Lori bubbled with that enthusiasm of hers, well, it had been impossible for his father to resist. She had convinced her husband that going to the impoverished towns of Lee County, Florida, to assist in an eight-day project for Habitat for Humanity was all she wanted for her birthday. She didn't crave more jewelry, or trips to Tuscany.

According to the patriarch of the Press clan, Grandfather Randolph, Lori Doran had done the extraordinary—and to him, the unthinkable. She had recruited a Press man to abandon his familial conventions for a life of philanthropic pursuit.

Rand's parents were the family's black sheep. He didn't realize this until they were long gone and he himself had become a young man.

He saw now the image of their Olds Cutlass Cruiser, a silver bullet of a station wagon, as it eased down their long brick driveway. Rand had waved his arm until it ached. The next time he saw them his parents were in side-by-side caskets. He cranked the Santana song to its loudest.

Rand turned onto the familiar ramp that led him off the highway, hoping that the string of memories was not following. He waited for the crazy guitar riffs to fill his head, to banish all other thought. What he heard were the echoes of his boyhood loss, drowning his senses with the muffled sounds of his own sobs.

He could not shake the image of himself, a boy attired in a new black suit he hadn't even remembered shopping for. He could nearly taste the fabric now, wooly and rough against his lips, as the broken boy in his head held an arm over his face—too ashamed to let anyone see him cry.

Rand remembered his grandfather and Uncle William scoffing at the wake, whispering to each other with pinched disapproving mouths as they sat in the stiff-backed chairs receiving the flood of mourners.

It had been Florence, Uncle William's housekeeper, who had comforted Rand. He remembered now the scent of lilacs of her perfume as she embraced him against her strong torso. She ran fingers through his hair and hummed a melody that he didn't recognize.

Damn it all! As Rand pulled onto his street, he remembered what had sparked this ugly reminiscence—the ring—that saleswoman and her insufferable sentimental drivel about diamonds. It was her words that had conjured it all.

Now the key image popped into his head. His mother's folded hands as they lay atop her upper body, waxy fingers laced around her white, leather-bound prayer book. She wore her wedding set, a plain band nestled against the matching engagement ring, a simple diamond solitaire. She was buried with it.

Rand guided the Jag into his garage, turned off the ignition, and hit the button for the electric door which hummed as it closed away the daylight outside.

He was left alone in the dark and sat for a

moment in the silence, letting his mind settle. Santana had let him down today. His music had not done its job. Suddenly the name of the song came to his mind with the abruptness of a slap—*Soul Sacrifice.*

Chapter Thirteen

Daisy stared at herself in her full-length bedroom mirror. On an ordinary day, she would say she looked pretty good, neat maybe, tailored in her tan dress slacks, a coffee-colored boat-necked sweater and a long, dangly multi-strand chain necklace. But, now what came to mind was that she was dressed for a masquerade. Her attire might as well have been a bunny suit, a costume hiding the person inside. She was not Daisy Cameron now. She was Cameron Day.

Adam sat at the dining room table, books splayed on the surface. The wrought iron chandelier suspended above him was lit to its fullest brightness. The remnants of his dinner, his favorite take-out Chinese, were still there amidst his school work.

"How was the Kung Pao?" his mother asked as she headed to retrieve her purse from the hall closet.

"Really good this time. You look nice, Mom."

"Thank you." She turned and saw that his face and his tone were absent of the sullen mood that had clung to him since the accident. He was his usual relaxed, genial self. This boy simply melted her heart, making her remember why she was allowing herself a temporary detour from sanity.

The open book in front of him was his Art History text, turned to a chapter headed "Pioneers in Abstraction." To Adam, this was not work, it was passion. Knowing that, she marveled once again at his talent. And now, thanks to J. Randolph Press, she would make sure he would realize his full potential at a top-rated school.

Daisy took her purse and a light jacket from the closet, closing the door. "I'm sure I won't be late, but, I don't think I'll be home in time to watch Law & Order tonight. You can fill me in on the episode."

"So, tell me again about this guy?" Adam said. He crunched on a fried noodle from the open waxed-paper bag sitting on the table. "What's his name again?"

"Randolph."

Adam made a face. "Who name's their kid Randolph? I'll bet when he was in school the kids enjoyed throwing spitballs at him all day."

"I think it's an old family name or something. He's got this lineage that goes way back."

"Well, I know you haven't dated anybody since we moved here. Take your time, okay Mom? I mean, what do we know about this guy?"

"I know he's, uh, very nice. He seems so, anyway." Daisy stopped herself from elaborating too much on the appeal of J. Randolph Press. It felt false in her mouth, like chewing on lint. She knew better than to babble. Adam would suspect something was up. She had to be herself, even if she was now a new creature named Cameron.

"Just take it slow, Mom. Isn't that what you're always saying to me?"

"Yes," she said warmly. She touched her hair again and fingered an earring. "So, I look okay, right?"

"You're a hottie."

Daisy laughed. "And you're not at all biased."

"Hey, ask my friends. They'd agree with me."

She halted that conversation. "Have a good night, Adam. Don't forget to clean up."

"I know, I know. Have fun," he said. He reached for a cellophane-wrapped fortune cookie and tossed it at her. "Read the fortune before you go. It'll give you good luck."

The cookie landed in the crook of her arm. She put her purse and jacket over the back of a chair. Pulling open the wrapper, she cracked the cookie between her thumb and forefinger. She withdrew the little white paper and silently read the words.

"Well?" Adam said. "What's it say?"

Daisy felt a dull ache settle inside her chest. She looked up at her son's expectant face and offered a smile she did not feel. Without referring back to the slip of paper she recited the words, *"Mountains can move. But not your character."*

Adam looked disappointed. "What's that mean?"

She felt the hint of a tear sting her eye—Daisy Cameron's eye. "It means that no matter what, hold onto who you are."

"In bed."

"I beg your pardon?" she asked.

"That's what you're supposed to say after you read a fortune. Read it out loud and end it with *in bed*. You know, like you will be lucky *in bed*. You will have great success *in bed*."

Adam started to laugh, presumably from the way Daisy held her mouth agape. "Come on, Mom, chill. It's funny. And make sure you don't take that seriously."

Daisy threw the paper at him, which didn't sail far, but fluttered to the tabletop right in front of her. "Who taught you that? Elizabeth?"

Adam groaned.

"Just making sure you follow your own advice. Okay now, good night, and finish your homework. Your mother's had enough *education* for one night."

****

Daisy spotted Rand at the same table by the fireplace they'd shared the afternoon before. He was already sipping a drink, the ice in the clear liquid reflecting sparks of light from the flames coming from the nearby hearth.

It was more than the way the man looked in his dark sports jacket, more than the way the light played against the angles of his face that made Daisy's heart thump in her chest. It was the circumstance she had gotten herself into. The words from the fortune cookie traveled through her mind like a ticker tape. How on earth could she remain true to her character when she had sold herself to this high bidder?

As she approached she ignored the way he looked at her, eying her with amusement. His mouth was pursed in what looked like an effort to not laugh. "Hello." She forced a smile when suddenly she felt like bopping him.

"The fair Cameron Day," he drawled. "You look lovely."

She swallowed hard and sat down in the wooden chair even harder. She had a feeling everything she did from now on would be just that—hard. Certainly none of this would be easy—torturous maybe, but not easy.

"That name's going to take some getting used to," she said. "And I still don't know how I'm going to lay that one on my son or my friends."

"You'll think of something," Rand said. That amusement still danced around in his eyes. "I'm convinced you're a resourceful one."

"Thank you, but frankly I'm concerned about how I'm going to explain my engagement to a veritable stranger."

"And, it's Wednesday. You have to be wearing a ring by Friday night when we visit my Uncle William," Rand said. He motioned for the waitress who immediately came over to their table, her face aglow with willingness to please. "The lady would like a drink, please."

For once, Daisy thought, J. Randolph Press, Jr. spoke the truth. She indeed wanted a drink—a big one. "I'll have a glass of merlot, please."

The waitress nodded, jotted something on her pad, and turned to leave. Rand touched a hand to her arm, halting her movement. "Bring us a bottle, Amanda, the Duckhorn Three Palms. Two glasses."

"Right away," she said. She hurried to retrieve his request.

"Now, what were we saying?" he asked. "Oh yes...our limited timetable. My thoughts are that we'll have to be utterly inseparable between now and Friday, to give the people in your immediate surroundings the picture that you're in an impetuous frenzy of a whirlwind romance."

Thankfully, Amanda brought the wine promptly, pouring a sample for Rand. He swished it around the bowl of his glass, sipped, and then nodded approval. She poured them generous portions and Daisy immediately took a taste. She was not a wine connoisseur by any stretch of the imagination, but she knew good, and this wine was very good. Its velvety smoothness bathed her throat. "That's going to be rough. I have a job and a high school kid at home. What do you call inseparable?"

"I think you should be absent from your normal routine for a few days. You know, show up late for work maybe, come in very late in the evenings. Make sure people notice the difference in your behavior."

"Oh, don't worry about that. People are already noticing." She sipped again.

"That's a good thing, Cameron, my dear. Let's order."

The ever-eager Amanda took their orders of the highly recommended salmon special, and soon brought them their salads. The vinaigrette dressing arrived in a small glass sauce boat with ladle.

"Ladies first," he said. Rand motioned to the bowl.

Her hand shook as she drizzled the dark

pungent dressing onto her greens. When she offered it to Rand, their fingers touched in the exchange.

Without thinking, Daisy met Rand's eyes. The green in them tonight was riveting, bright pools of beryl in the firelight. She released her hand abruptly. The hasty move tipped the bowl and the ladle clacked against its rim. If it were not for Rand's quick grasp of the sauce boat their table would have been bathed in balsamic vinaigrette.

Daisy turned her attention to her salad, kept her gaze down into her plate, breathed steadily, and willed the blood that had rushed to her face to beat it. She stabbed at the lettuce as though to punish it, realizing of course that the romaine had not betrayed her.

****

By the end of the meal and the consumption of good wine, Rand had made a self-confession that could prove interesting or, to be more accurate, detrimental to the plan. The truth was evident. He liked her. This woman who had agreed to it all—the name change, the stipulation of his agreement that she not tell a soul—had signed the detailed statement he had presented between courses without much hesitation.

There was something about her. It wasn't all about her looks, either. He'd been with plenty of beautiful women. In fact, he had not been without the company of some such glamorous eye candy for any stretch of time.

Rand observed her as she sipped her wine, staring into the flames of the fire as though in deep thought. He got a good view of her profile, the arch of her brow, the shadow of lashes cast onto her face. He watched her mouth greet the rim of her wine glass, the stem pinched delicately between long, elegant fingers. She had a new manicure, the polish a translucent pearly pink.

Her lips parted, providing entry for the last of the burgundy liquid and he watched it disappear into her mouth. Rand stirred—a sensation that felt wrong—the kind of thing that in another time would have spurred a suggestion to take their charade to a physical level. *But no, not Cameron Day.* She was no man's dalliance. Rand had gathered that much.

There was something clearly genuine about her. He could feel that, even through the mud of their pretense. He would never cross the line—to do so would be the end of his plan. He felt that, knew it at gut level.

He must never entertain the idea again. He needed to stay on his game. Rand would not touch her other than for deliberate public displays of affection meant to fool anyone that needed fooling.

Rand motioned Amanda over to their table and ordered a cup of dark coffee. Cameron decided on a decaf cappuccino. They each agreed to no dessert, but lingered over their coffees. The hot, rich coffee, no milk, two sugars, tasted good. The caffeine was just what his blood needed. Adrenalin spiked through him, the moment of lapsed judgment now gone.

"Dinner was nice. Thank you," she said. She pressed the white ceramic mug between both her hands. She blew lightly over the surface of the foam, wiggling it in her effort. "I guess I should be heading home. It's late."

Rand looked at the large wood-framed clock on the wall above the mantelpiece. "It is late, but there's more we need to discuss."

Daisy put the cup down and folded her hands in her lap. "We've each signed the agreement. You're going to make me a copy. I think we're set for now, don't you?"

"On that end, yes. But, my uncle is going to grill me and, honestly, he'll grill you more. You're going to have to prove you and I know each other enough to be engaged. You need details, crib notes. And, I need them from you."

"Well, that could take all night, Rand. Where do we start?"

"The basics. Where did you grow up, what about your parents, what did they do for a living? How about school? Where did you go to college? Your son—all I know is that his name is Adam, he's a senior in high school, and he has enough artistic talent to convince a woman like you to join forces with me in this crazy scheme."

Daisy let out a long, slow breath and lowered her gaze to her hands. When she looked back up at him Rand saw doubt in her baby blues, a hint of overwhelm. "It's a lot, I know. But, let's just start with these things. Tell me about Adam."

"He's a great kid," she began, her tone warm like their proximity to the fire. "So talented."

"When did you first know he had artistic ability?"

Cameron chuckled, her eyes lighting up, cloudless skies now. "When he was in kindergarten. I went to his Back-To-School Night and saw all the kids' art projects on display. They were asked to make something with colored leaves they found on the playground. Adam's was three dimensional. He made a house."

"Wow. How'd he do that? I mean, what held it up right?"

"Twigs," she said.

"By the way, where is Adam's father?"

He saw the clouds come back into her eyes. "He's not part of Adam's life. Never was. I wasn't married when I became pregnant. I was a sophomore in college. Adam's father was my boyfriend. He...let's just say, he didn't have a baby on his radar."

"Well, where is he?"

"Who knows, and who cares?"

"He's never contacted you in all this time? Never helped you financially?"

"No, and no." She said. Her words were like spat poison.

"What does Adam know about his father?"

He saw her chest rise with the intake of a deep breath, then fall as she exhaled. "The truth. Remember? Truth is our credo, which now I've blown to smithereens."

"For a good cause. For him."

Cameron nodded. "My father was the manager of security in a big office complex in Florham Park. He was several years older than my mother. He was a smoker. He died ten years ago—throat cancer.

"My mother died two years ago. I was still working in the City. She was living with us in Hoboken, keeping an eye on Adam for me. When she died suddenly—one wicked stroke—I left New York and moved back here."

"Sisters? Brothers?"

Daisy shook her head.

"So, no extraneous relatives I need to know about?"

She shrugged. "I have an aunt and uncle on my father's side. They have two kids. But they live down in Florida. I never see them."

"What about your job in New York? You just up and quit?"

She closed her eyes briefly, then wet her lips as he'd seen her do before. If this was a poker game he'd guess she had a bum hand.

"When my mom died it became too difficult to go back and forth into the city *and* be a parent to Adam. So, I resigned and came back to Jersey. Jobs were scarce and I was grateful to get the job at the café." She shrugged one shoulder. "I wanted a stable home life for Adam."

"You're a good mother."

"I hope so."

"Okay, my turn. I'm an only child. My dad was J. Randolph Press, Sr. He married his college sweetheart, Lori Doran. After I was born, mom concentrated on parenting and community involvement. Dad was involved with Press Industries. As you know, they were killed in a car crash on their way home from Florida when I was twelve. My Uncle William took me in and raised me. I guess that covers it."

"How about previous relationships? Have you been engaged before?"

Rand chuckled. "I guess that depends on who you ask. Since you're asking me, I'll say emphatically no, I have never formally proposed to anyone. However, there's a woman or two who might dispute that."

"Like Jada Jefferies?"

Rand laughed aloud this time. "My darling Cameron, you've done your homework I see. No. Jada and I were never engaged. Granted it was a messy break-up, but we were never headed toward the aisle."

"Anything else I should know?" she asked.

"My birthday is January first. I was a New Year's baby. That's the deadline my Uncle William has newly imposed. I must be married and settled into domestic bliss by my fortieth birthday. Happy birthday to me."

"Let's clarify that one. I mean, our pretending to be engaged is one thing. Faking a wedding and a marriage, well that would be impossible."

"It won't come to that," he said.

A chill ran through him in spite of the warmth of the fire. His guardian was dying. And even though the old guy had really pissed him off with this nonsense, Rand was already feeling loss. This surprised him initially—when the feeling sneaked into his senses. But, after all, Uncle William was the last of the Presses. After he was gone Rand would have no family. No one. He would truly be alone.

"Well..." Daisy startled him from his reverie. Her tone was soft, a near whisper, as though she could tell he'd been mulling his list of losses and didn't want to intrude. She offered a tiny grin, a polite curve of her lips. "I guess that's all then."

"One more thing," he said.

"Shoot."

"When's your birthday?"

Rand watched her glance down at her coffee cup. The remnants of her cappuccino now clung to the sides of the mug looking like suds left in a washing machine. When she lifted her head Daisy's eyes held a hint of something he hadn't yet seen since they'd met. Playfulness flashed in them, and she seemed almost sly as she let her eyes lower to half mast. The effect was sexy and it unnerved him.

Her mouth turned into a smirk. "September twenty-fifth," she said. Before Rand had the chance to react or respond, she added, "Which would be Friday. Happy birthday *to me*."

Chapter Fourteen

Daisy dragged herself to work the next morning. When she had gotten home late last night she had tiptoed to her room, robotically shed her outfit and yanked on her pajamas. Although she'd felt like a zombie, she had been too wired to actually sleep. Now, standing at the coffee station in the café, Daisy yawned.

"Late night, pumpkin?" Candy asked, hand to one hip.

Daisy offered a rueful smile. "Kind of."

Candy shook her head. "Staying out late on a school night. Shame on you. What kind of example is that for my favorite teenager?"

"Ha, ha."

"So, are you in like, or in love, or in flux?"

"I'm 'in' something, that's for sure," Daisy said.

"Let's invite your gazillionaire to your surprise party!" Candy said excitedly. "We can all get to know him."

"Whoa, wait. What surprise party?" Panic stepped into her gut and started to cha-cha.

"Oh come on, Daisy. You know I throw you a surprise party for your birthday every year."

"Every year? I've only known you for two."

"Okay so this will be your second. It's a tradition now."

"No...no. Uh-uh. Please, no party. Honestly, Candy, I appreciate the offer, really, but I'm just not up for it."

"Too late," her friend said happily. She turned on her heel and walked away. "It's all planned. Tell

Prince Charming...Friday, my house, seven o'clock."

"Candy, I can't. I have plans with Rand on Friday." Now panic had invited fear to tango through her insides. Bad enough she had to face this Uncle William character on her birthday. She couldn't continue the hoax with her son and friends all in the same day. She touched a hand to her midsection and gave it a gentle rub. She willed her nerves to sit this one out.

Candy sauntered back, her face contorted into an exaggerated pout. "Your son and I have made plans for you. You were ours first, Daisy. You'd better tell Mr. Press he has to share."

"Candy, look..." Daisy felt a stab, hating the new frontier of juggling lies. "I'm meeting his uncle on Friday. He's a very sick, old man, and it's, uh, very important that I meet him."

Candy's shoulders slumped. "What time are you meeting the uncle?"

"I'm not sure."

"Can you meet him and then come to your party?" Candy's voice was a pathetic whine now, the kind for which she usually admonished her fourth-grade daughter.

Daisy's heart swelled in her chest. "We'll work it out." She took the reins in this piece of the deception without thought to Rand's reaction.

****

By Friday Daisy was exhausted. She had been out again with Rand last night, this time receiving her copy of their signed agreement. It still blew her mind to see the numbers on the page—a two and a five, followed by all those zeroes.

Adam would get his chance at Pratt and surely forgive her once he learned she had been part of this scam that had paid for it. When she got home she tucked the paper into an old shoebox on the top shelf of her closet.

Rand had been amenable to the news of the impromptu birthday party at Candy's house.

"Guess we'll lower the boom of our intended nuptials all in one fell swoop. We'll tell Uncle William first, spend a little time convincing him of our sheer and utter happiness, then take the stage over to your friend's house."

Her head still pounded with Rand's cool ability to roll with the lies. He seemed totally unfazed by what they were doing—it was a walk in the park, nothing out of the ordinary. Well, for Daisy this was more than extraordinary. This was, in her estimation, the worst thing she'd ever done.

When she got to the Brookside Cafe she found that Rand had sent her more flowers—this time, white roses. Daisy's first thought was *Dear God, bridal roses!* The man really was amazing. After this stint, Daisy thought he should get himself a theatrical agent.

When Daisy entered the luncheonette, Ima cast her a genial smile. "You're turning my luncheonette into a florist's shop."

"Or a funeral parlor," Pete added, and then laughed. "Old man McGreggor was in here a little while ago getting his coffee and asked who died."

Daisy felt a pang stab at her. *Who died, indeed? Daisy Cameron, apparently.* She pretended to be amused by Pete's comment, then made like she was delighted by the obscene number of blooms crowding the counter. "Aren't they gorgeous?" she cooed.

"Happy Birthday, by the way, Daisy," Ima said. "We can't wait to meet your man tonight at Candy and Bruno's. What an exciting birthday party this will be!"

Oh, yes, she thought. *Maybe we'll play Pin the Tail on the Donkey.* She already knew there would be an ass in attendance. Her name was Cameron Day.

****

He found himself whistling. Rand hadn't whistled since he was a carefree kid, skipping along the easy street of his existence. Somehow he felt like that kid now.

His plan was in the bag. He felt it, knew it, at gut level. Cameron was totally on board, had signed on the dotted line. Nothing could interfere now.

He dressed in his favorite suit—the charcoal Versace—new white shirt, the Vitaliano Pancaldi silk tie with the matching pocket square. Rand eyed himself in the full-length antique cheval mirror, an heirloom that had belonged to his father. He looked like a million bucks. Actually, now that he was about to fulfill Uncle's demand, he would be worth more than that—much more. He started to whistle again.

Making sure he had the ring tucked into his inside pocket, Rand left to pick up his date. What a night—first Uncle, then her brood. Rand felt a keen anticipation similar to placing his chips on the table. This was the kind of wager that couldn't go wrong, could only reap reward.

Rand pulled into Cameron's condominium complex, struck again by the luck of its location. She lived in Moore Arbor, a rather prestigious community in Hanover Heights. Her unit was among those classified as "affordable." He could tell by the placement within the development's layout and by the less ornamental, more conservative facade of her building. It didn't matter. She lived in Moore Arbor.

If Uncle learned of her residence, he'd be fooled into believing she had one of the big, fancy townhomes with all the bells and whistles. It would be a natural assumption. Rand made note of the number on one of those buildings, just in case the question was ever posed.

Her front door was dressed with a grapevine

wreath, the mat on the floor offering "welcome" in black letters surrounded by a design of ivy. He rang the bell.

****

The sound of the doorbell pierced Daisy's ears, jarring her like an electric current. It was show time. She gave herself one last glance in the hall mirror. She had gone with the simple black sheath, a strand of pearls at the jewel neckline, single pearl stud earrings. She was as ready as she'd ever be. She opened the door.

"Happy birthday!" Rand smiled impishly over a bouquet of roses. *More roses!* Why did she feel as if she'd been bombarded by thorns? "You look lovely."

Daisy ushered him in, accepted the flowers into her hand with a polite "thank you," and was startled when he planted a light, soft kiss onto her cheek. Blood flooded her face.

"Let's save that for when there's an audience, shall we?"

Rand eyed the room. "Your son's not home?"

"No. He's already gone to Candy and Bruno's to help get ready for my *surprise* party."

He followed her into the kitchen while she pulled a vase from a cabinet and put it in the sink under the open faucet. She unwrapped the cellophane from the blooms and carefully snipped the ends of each stem with scissors. She arranged them one-by-one into the ceramic receptacle. The entire time she felt Rand's eyes on her. "I'm getting good at this," she said. She did not look at him, but offered a little laugh. "How many does this make?"

"Who's counting?" He leaned against the counter as she cleaned up from her task, wiping her hands on a dishtowel.

"I'd offer you something to drink, but I'm thinking it wouldn't be a good idea to show up to visit your Uncle William smelling like alcohol," she said.

Rand tilted his head and gave a little nod as though mulling her rationale. "Might be a good idea. But, Cameron, shouldn't we have something to toast your birthday privately? Provide the perfect moment for me to give you your present?"

"Present?" She hated the way he made her feel as if she was a school girl caught cheating by the teacher.

"Your ring, my dear. We can't have you meet Uncle without a diamond on your hand. So..." He paused, and then rubbed his hands together like a hungry man about to dig into a hamburger deluxe. "What do you have, Cameron, my love?"

She opened her refrigerator and pulled out a half-empty bottle of chardonnay by its neck. Her grip was vice-like on the cool glass. "I have some white wine. That's about it."

"White wine's fine," he said.

She handed him the bottle. She withdrew two glasses from a shelf, placed them on the stone counter, and watched Rand pour two generous splashes of the golden liquid.

"Just a little," she cautioned. There was no way she was going to allow herself any effects from wine tonight. Her nerves would have expressed appreciation if she downed the portion in one gulp.

Rand grabbed both glasses, strode from the kitchen opening to Daisy's living room, and headed toward the sofa. He sat down placing the wine onto the coffee table and looked up at her with a clownish grin. Unabashedly, he patted the seat cushion beside him.

Daisy detested the way he seemed to make himself at home, as though he belonged here. Rand was bold, presumptuous, and everything that made her bristle. Right now the last thing she wanted to do was pretend to be in love with him, let alone react to his summon that she sit beside him.

But she did. She had to. She parked herself on the sofa and watched with queasiness as Rand reached into his jacket pocket. He withdrew the little black velvet box and extended it her way. He dramatically lifted its lid in slow motion. What blinked out at her nearly stopped her heart.

It was a magnificent ring. It was so pretty, so like what she would have chosen had this been real—or if she'd died and gone to jewelry heaven. The phoniness of what they were doing made her sick, especially with it being celebrated with such an outstanding ring.

"Nice, isn't it?" His tone was almost taunting. Apparently he was amused by the moment.

"It's..." She sounded like a frog, her voice a sorry croak. She took a breath and started over. "It's gorgeous."

"You like it?" he asked. "It's important that you like it."

She didn't see why it was important that she approve of the bauble. After all, this was but a smoke screen. "Who wouldn't like it, Rand? Seriously, it's spectacular."

"I just want to make sure you'll feel comfortable wearing it. You know, be at ease sporting it around your family and friends."

Daisy looked him in the eye. He had more faith in her than she had in herself—faith in her ability to be a fraud. There was no compliment in that, for sure, but Daisy decided that coming from someone like J. Randolph Press, Jr. it had to be some sick form of praise. Like a robber admiring another thief's heist.

"Let's see how it looks," he said. He lifted it from the case. Rand reached for her left hand and slid the ring onto her finger. It was a perfect fit. Daisy looked down at it and felt as though she was having an out-of-body experience. Her hand seemed a prosthesis, and not her own flesh and blood.

"I guess I should say something, shouldn't I?" Rand said. He looked up at the ceiling as though a script were written there. "How's this: My darling Cameron, will you make me the happiest man in the world and be my wife? Will you marry me?"

He was Laurence Olivier practicing his soliloquy. Daisy snatched her hand from his grasp and Rand let out a hearty chuckle.

"This isn't funny."

He laughed some more. "Oh, lighten up, sweetheart. It's all part of the game."

Yes, Daisy thought, *and the game has just begun.* "And, I'm not your sweetheart."

"Oh yes you are," he said. Playfully he reached for her hand again, held it up in front of her face. "See?"

Daisy pulled free of his grasp and reached for her glass. She put the rim to her lips, but Rand quickly grasped her wrist and commanded, "Wait! We need to toast."

"No we don't," she said. She downed the fruity wine in one swallow.

Chapter Fifteen

During the excruciatingly long, achingly slow ride to their destination Daisy kept her hand on the door handle as she sat stiffly in the passenger seat of Rand's Jaguar. Her fingers itched to turn the metal lever. Realistically, she supposed jumping was not an option.

William Press lived in Jacob Hill, a small, elite town tucked into the hillside ten miles outside downtown Morristown. They drove through the maze of winding streets bordered by vast lawns whose mature shrubbery worked to keep the privacy of those that lived in the sprawling estates. The only thing Daisy knew about the area was that the locals referred to it as "The Hill." *Yes...Snob Hill, for sure.*

The driveway of the Press property was marked by two stately, large stone pillars topped by brass lanterns that lit their way up the macadam. The palatial, stone-front residence came into view as they crested the incline of the land. Rand parked his car in the surround outside the grand double-door entrance.

Rand turned to her as they sat in the parked vehicle. "Ready?"

She took in a deep breath. "I guess so."

"Come on. Piece of cake."

"Right."

He leaned in and kissed her on the lips, startling her beyond comprehension. He held her firm when she tried to push him away. When he did release her from his clutches she found herself gasping for air, her chest heaving. "What are you doing?" she rasped.

"Just being cautious. There're surveillance cameras all over this place. In case anyone's watching—and trust me, someone probably is—I want them to see two young lovers."

She pushed her hand at his chest that still invaded what Daisy considered her personal space. "Warn me next time, will you? For God's sake. No surprises."

"Yes, darling." His smiling lips were insufferable—although they had tasted good—and she hated him for it.

The arched-top double-front doors were massive. The door chimes sounded like church bells. In a moment a woman appeared in the doorway. By the description Rand had given her Daisy knew it was Florence. Rand had said Flo, as he called her, was a good woman. She cared about him, and this engagement would be a tough sell to the smart housekeeper that had helped raise him after his parents' death.

"Hello," she said. Her tone was deep, balmy. Her eyes were gray welcoming pools. "Please come in."

They stepped into a vast foyer, empty except for the oval mahogany pedestal table on which was displayed an intricately painted vase filled with fresh flowers. Daisy did her best to keep her eyes from wandering the expansive space, not staring too long at the imposing stairway that swept upward to the second floor.

She fixed her eyes onto Florence, smiled, and extended her hand. "Hello, you must be Florence. Rand has told me so much about you. I'm Cameron." The word tasted plastic.

"Yes," the woman said. She took Daisy's hand into hers and covered it with her other hand, their handshake two-on-one. "It is a pleasure to meet you, Cameron. Rand was right, you are lovely."

Rand took the opportunity to wrap an arm around Daisy's shoulders and tuck her close to his side. "Isn't she? I'm one lucky man."

Daisy thought she saw an exchange between Rand and Florence. *A question perhaps, from her eyes to his?* Whatever it had been was gone in a flash.

"William's waiting," she said kindly. She turned and crooked her arm through Daisy's guiding her toward the white marble staircase. "Randolph's uncle has been most anxious to meet you, my dear. Most anxious."

Daisy smiled at Florence appreciatively, although what popped in her head was, *I'll bet!* They ascended the stairs linked together, arm in arm like comrades. Rand followed closely behind.

Daisy listened as the two exchanged small talk about the weather and the latest repair to something that had gone on the fritz in the old house. There was a pleasant, familiar air between Rand and Florence, like kinship, family even. Florence laughed softly at some quip that he uttered and Daisy turned to see that Rand's face was bright with satisfaction.

At the top of the stairs Florence released Daisy's arm and walked ahead down a burgundy-carpeted corridor. Rand reached for Daisy's hand. When she turned to him with question he gave her an exaggerated gesture that said this was an essential part of the game—as necessary, apparently as that random kiss that he'd sprung on her in the car. She had refused to allow herself to react physically to it then, and she'd be damned if she'd let the memory of it come to her senses now.

She looked down at their mingled fingers and felt the pressure of a squeeze which charged her skin, reminding her that the hand was alive and not a prosthesis for sure. No, hers was a real live appendage, one that stubbornly ignored her will of it to play dead. Why did her hand feel warm and safe in his? Daisy thought sourly that what dangled from her wrist may as well have been Benedict Arnold's hand.

****

So far, so good—excellent, actually. Randolph squeezed the hand he held, hoping Cameron knew he was silently telling her she had done a good job with Florence. She had.

After so many years of conducting himself with the woman, Rand knew the nuances of her behavior. The double-grasp handshake was an indication of sincerity. Florence was not what Rand called a "gusher." She didn't overtly bestow affection. She was reserved in her mannerisms and in her judgment of others.

He had witnessed plenty of occasions over the years when Flo had sent a workman or a gardener packing if she determined they had misrepresented themselves in some way. She had been loyal to her care of Rand as an orphaned youngster and a faithful attendant to Uncle William. Their relationships now, over time and experience, were a familial evolution.

The door to Uncle William's bedroom suite was ajar, and Rand could see the mellow glow of light within its depths. *Oh, the old guy was ready for this, all right.*

Rand felt a zing of anticipation poke at his insides. He squeezed Cameron's hand again, noticing how nicely hers fit in his, as though they were meant to clasp together like partners. Confidence surged through his veins as Florence rapped her knuckles lightly onto the door and then pushed it gently open.

Uncle William was sitting up in his bed, perpendicular to the dark expanse of the headboard. In his tan and black checkered robe, his hair was combed neatly over his crown. He did not look like a dying man—old and frail perhaps, but his skin tone was no longer the ghastly gray Rand had seen the other day. Nor were his eyes sunken dull disks in his craggy face. William's eyes shone like wily beacons tonight.

Rand could not help but feel amused at how Uncle's eleventh-hour will change had given the old guy a reason to live. And thus, in Rand's rules of the game, William Press deserved the deception he was about to receive. "Uncle, you're looking well this evening," Rand said cheerfully.

He and Cameron crossed the room where guest chairs had been arranged bedside at a conversational angle. Tea was served on an antique Chippendale piecrust table along with a tray of Flo's shortbread.

"Bring that Cameron of yours closer, Randolph, let an old man get a better look at her," William croaked, with a theatrical sweep of his arm, an infirmed Napoleon dictating from his sickbed.

Rand could feel Cameron's hand stiffen in his grasp. He squeezed in response and turned to meet her gaze. Her cerulean eyes shone with fear, but Rand was not worried that Uncle would spot it as a sign of their sham. He knew the ego he was dealing with.

William, if he detected Cameron's trepidation, would chalk it up as a reaction to his own awe-inspiring presence. Rand was sure Uncle would find that pleasantly endearing.

Rand saw the line-up of pill bottles positioned behind a white ceramic water pitcher on the nightstand at William's bedside. He was sure it had been a deliberately discreet placement. Yet, it served as a stark reminder to Rand that there was a clock in the room, and it was ticking.

"Uncle, may I present the soon-to-be Mrs. J. Randolph Press, Jr. Meet Miss Cameron Day." They stood at the side of his uncle's bed. Rand leaned and placed a delicate kiss at her temple. Her hair smelled sweet and clean, like honeysuckle after rain.

Daisy reached across the bedclothes and offered her hand to the aged patriarch. Uncle lifted his spotted, gnarled hand to accept her smooth ivory one into his. He smiled at her, his chapped-in-the-corners lips cracked with the effort.

"Well, well," he said in his gravelly tone. He chuckled as he shook her hand. Rand watched the loose fabric of his robe's sleeve sway like a flag on a skinny pole. "No cataracts could hide such beauty, my dear. I see why Randolph *chose* you."

Rand bristled at his uncle's emphasis on the word. Although delivered with a lilt of pleasantry and cleverly piggybacked with his opening endearment, he knew that for the man to say Randolph *chose* Cameron implied doubt of their union.

Instinctively Rand let his arm circle Cameron's narrow waist. He felt a brief stiffening of her body before she relaxed against him.

"Destiny *chose us*, Uncle. Cameron and I knew it almost immediately. Didn't we, darling?"

Daisy looked at him with incredulous eyes. He was putting her on the spot, he knew, but she had to chime in now. Uncle needed to see the personality behind the face, had to know she was substantive and not just a pretty package of fluff. Rand did his best to flash her a look of encouragement.

"Yes," she said. She let the smile return to her lips. "Although, I have to admit, that at first I thought Rand might be a pompous ass."

William Press laughed out loud and then let go of her hand to slap at his own chest. His gaiety turned into a series of phlegmy coughs. He cleared and cleared his throat, and then resumed a low chuckle. "Randolph, pour me some water, would you, so I don't keel over and die right here and now."

Rand attended to pouring water from the pitcher into a crystal glass and handed it to William. "That would serve you right, Uncle, for laughing at my beloved's joke," Rand said. His joyful tone lacked admonishment.

"I'm sorry for making you cough, sir," she offered.

"Oh, nonsense, honey. Everybody could use a good laugh now and then and when the joke's on our Randolph here—well, it's delightful."

"How about we have some tea?" Florence said from the corner of the room. Rand had nearly forgotten she was there. He needed to keep in mind there were two judges in this courtroom.

"Randolph, I made shortbread." Florence's face beamed.

She loved him. Rand knew this was the closest thing to a mother he had now. He appreciated her, although their relationship was pale in comparison to the one he had shared with the effervescent Lori Doran Press.

It struck him as odd now that it had only been over the last couple of days that thoughts of his mother had entered his mind—ever since buying the ring.

"The ring!" he said aloud. "Cameron, show Uncle...and Flo, you too. Come see the ring that persuaded this magnificent woman to agree to marry a pompous ass."

William reached for his reading glasses when Daisy extended the ring toward him. He scrutinized the stone at close range.

Randolph stifled the urge to offer to rake the stone over the surface of a mirror and demonstrate its ability to scratch it. Florence leaned in but not nearly as blatantly as William, so near it now that he could have given it a kiss.

"It's breathtaking," Florence said. She looked to Rand. "Congratulations, again."

"It's a stunner, all right," William said. He tugged the spectacles from his face, tossing them to his nightstand. "And, yes, yes...by all means, congratulations." Then he turned full-faced to Rand, smiling enough to make his dry skin nearly bleed, exposing his teeth—yellow like ancient ivory. "You're one lucky man. May I ask how this wonderful occasion came to be? Now of all times."

The question was a snide one. Randolph knew it and he was sure Florence was well aware of its connotation. "Today, dear uncle, is Cameron's birthday. What better time to celebrate our having found each other?"

Rand's blood surged with warm pleasure at the old buzzard's clamped mouth. He and his accomplice had passed the initial inspection.

"Darling, come, have a seat and taste this unbelievable shortbread Florence has made for us. It's irresistible," Rand said.

Cameron sat erect in one of the spoon-back Victorian armchairs. She looked too prim, Rand thought. She needed to relax in front of the scrutinizing eyes taking in her every move, drinking in her presence.

Rand reached for the shortbread and held the silver tray before her. She pulled a small square napkin from the table and delicately placed a triangular-shaped cookie onto it. She kept her eyes on Rand as he bit into one, savored it audibly, and made an exceptionally big deal about the home-baked confection.

He was a director giving his actress a pointer on how to play the moment. He wanted her to bite into the damned cookie and call it the best she'd ever tasted. He was pleased when she lifted the cookie to her mouth and bit the pointy edge off of it. Rand waited for her to react before he spoke. He wanted the first words to come from her.

"Florence, this is incredible," Cameron said, right on cue. "Just delicious."

"Flo, you've outdone yourself," Rand added.

"Thank you. Please enjoy," she said, obviously gratified. "It's an old recipe from my mother, and her mother before her. Scottish, you know."

"Well, it's the best I've ever tasted," Cameron added sweetly.

"Perhaps you could give Cameron the recipe sometime, Flo. I'm marrying quite a baker," Rand said, his voice loaded with pride. He turned to William. "Uncle, this is the little lady that's responsible for that chocolate mocha cake you enjoyed the other day."

"Well, now," Uncle William said, "Cameron, dear, you'll have to bake a cake for me sometime soon. I love the sight of a woman in the kitchen. I may even venture downstairs to watch the show if these old legs will cooperate. Let's make a date."

Rand smiled a broad grin, a winner's smile and looked to Daisy. She was staring at him with horror on her face so comprehensible that even a dying man would be able to read it.

Chapter Sixteen

Daisy's heart whirled in her chest like a top. The rest of their visit—more like an audience with the Pope—zoomed on fast forward. Although she went through the motions of sipping tea, dabbing at her mouth with the starchy antique linen, and commenting or nodding sweetly at pauses in chit-chat—all she could think of was getting back in the car so she could sock Rand in the nose.

First he had blindsided her with that wicked kiss. And now, for some reason she couldn't fathom, he had decided she was Betty Crocker. His uncle was soon expecting to see a baking exhibition, as though she were a trained monkey.

Thankfully having the excuse of Daisy's imminent birthday party, they bade Uncle William good night. Daisy soon found herself descending the long marble staircase alongside Rand. Luckily, Florence was ahead of them and did not see her swat at Rand when he attempted to pull her hand into his grasp. She wasn't going to touch him unless she absolutely had to.

Florence waved to them from the open front door as Rand slowly drove around the paved circle. When they were far enough down the driveway, when Daisy felt sure that no spy cameras would catch her, she turned to him and whacked her knuckles onto his solid shoulder muscle.

"I can't do this. I don't know what made me think I could, but I can't."

"Whoa," Rand said. He turned quickly and gave her a look, his brow knit into a crease. He focused back on the roadway. "You did a great job in there. What are you talking about?"

"You're a good liar, I'll give you that, but I'm no match for you. I can't keep up with what spills off your tongue."

"You played it fine," he said in a condescending, soothing tone one would give a petulant child.

"Well, you don't *play* fair. What the hell was that about, telling your uncle that I'm this great baker? Are you nuts? You want a pot roast? Great. You want spaghetti and meatballs? You got it. But, I can't bake for the life of me. If you saw what I do to box-mix brownies, you wouldn't be smirking right now. You'd be crying."

"Now who's the good liar?" His smirk was gone. His mouth was in an angry twist. Apparently, the man was not fond of being told a thing or two. *Tough.* Daisy folded her arms over her chest and looked forward. "What are you talking about?" she asked through a tight clench.

"You told me yourself, when I was in the diner, that you baked that cake. Are you denying it now?"

"What? I did not. You speak lies and you hear them, too, apparently."

"When I asked you if it was fresh you said you had made the damned cake that morning."

She thought back to the moment and felt irritation rise in her like mercury in a thermometer. "What I said was 'Ima made the cake'. Ima, you know, my boss? She's the baker. Not me. I would never claim to make a cake unless it was in an apology for attempting to do so. You're hearing things."

Rand was silent, but Daisy could see his jaw tighten. She watched his Adam's apple rise and fall with a deep swallow. "Ima baked it," he said. "Ima Waitress. Shit, you said 'Ima'?"

"I'm a waitress?" she asked. Indignation caused

her voice to quake. "Did you say 'Ima Waitress'?"

"Oh for God's sake, Cameron. Who names their kid Ima?"

"You're a mean, small man. And, I quit."

"You can't quit while we're winning. Don't be ridiculous."

"Thanks to your big erroneous announcement, your uncle's gearing up for a bake-off that I can't perform. It's over before we even start. Let's face it. This isn't going to work."

"Hold on, hold on. Calm down. First of all, I apologize for mocking your boss's name. I'm sorry, okay?

"And, we'll find a way to avoid your having to bake for Uncle. He's an old man...maybe he's forgotten it already."

"And Florence? You think it'll slip her mind, too?"

"Maybe," he said. "Or maybe not. But, there's no reason to throw in the towel, for crying out loud. It was one little slip-up. You're making too much out of it."

"I'm not good at this...and I hate it."

"You'll get better," he said. He turned to her, his green eyes sly. "What's your friend's address? It's time for the second show of the night, birthday girl."

****

On the little cul-de-sac in the Knolls section of Hanover, all the lights were on in Candy and Bruno's Cape-Cod-style house. Daisy felt a renewed appreciation for the blue-collar neighborhood as she and Rand approached Candy's driveway. Knolls had roots, it had heart.

Back in the fifties most of the men in town, Daisy's grandfather included, worked for the Liskie Paper Company that had flourished along the river. It used to be that she knew everyone—the Michas brothers who owned the local food store where Daisy held her first job as cashier, the grouchy man who smelled like cigars behind the counter at the Sweet Shop.

Candy's white house, with painted maroon shutters and matching front door, was right smack dab in the middle of a neighborhood of similar families—with kids in grade school and mini-vans parked in their driveways.

Tonight, Candy's driveway had several cars aligned in a tight row and Daisy recognized each vehicle. As Rand squeezed his little coupe behind Ima and Pete's Malibu she felt her insides turn over on themselves. The people in her world—her people, her son—were in that house waiting for her, anxious to meet her new man.

She looked up at Rand as he opened her car door, trying to view him as Candy would, as Adam would. What would they see? Would they see him as an ideal match for her or would they see through the opacity of their charade? Daisy wanted to run. Instead she placed her hand into Rand's extended one, and he assisted her from the vehicle like the gallant knight that he was—*Sir Malarkey*.

Candy opened the door with a ceremonious swing. "Surprise!" Her two children—little Bruno, with his gel-slick hair and his father's broad grin, and Gina, ponytailed and in a trendy hot pink and black leggings ensemble—hovered beside their mother, their eyes filled with expectation. Behind them Daisy saw her son staring at her curiously.

Her stomach pitched, rendering her queasy. *Dear God, I must be insane.*

"Happy birthday!" Bruno and Gina chorused.

Gina jumped up and down, stepping on her brother's foot. He yowled, "Watch out, moron!"

Her jumping ceased. "Mommy..." Gina whined.

"Oh kids, please, stop already. Come on in you two," Candy said jovially, her kids squabble of no effect. "You're Randolph." She ushered them through the doorway. "Hi, I'm Candy."

"Rand, please," he said. He extended his hand, which Candy took immediately, wrist bent like a southern belle.

"Pleased to meet you," she gushed.

"Good to meet you, Candy."

They made their rounds in greeting the others. Candy's husband Bruno, a burly-looking man full of fun, grabbed Rand in a bear hug and gave him a good squeeze. "There he is!" he boomed. "Been hearing plenty about you, buddy. Let me get you something to drink. Want a beer?"

"Uh, sure. Whatever you have."

While Bruno went to the kitchen, Daisy and Rand made their way deeper into the dining room, its table set with a festive multi-colored balloon-dotted vinyl party cloth. Bowls of chips with dip, Candy's famous Chex mix, hotdogs wrapped in dough, and other snack foods had been set out. Daisy was immediately ashamed at the flush of embarrassment that struck her as she watched for Rand's reaction to the table fare.

He fooled her. Instead of condescension in his eye, she saw something that resembled appreciation. *He was good,* she reminded herself.

She watched him reach over to a napkin-lined basket and pull out a bright orange cheesy coil and bite into it. "Cheese Doodles!" he said. "God, how long has it been since I've had one of these?"

Her muscles relaxed. She didn't know if he was just playacting and masking his appall of the food, but it didn't matter. Daisy saw that he had garnered smiles of approval from most of the other guests in the room. However, the jury was still out on Adam.

She couldn't tell if that look of consternation in his baby blues was concern, doubt, or perhaps—hopefully—just curiosity about this man with an arm around his mother. Adam came to Daisy for a hug, forcing Rand to disengage his hold on her.

"Happy birthday, Mom." He smelled of cigarettes. She remembered that he reeked of tobacco the night of the accident, but she had chalked that up to it having been from one of his friends. *Is he smoking? Since when?*

When they broke from the embrace, Rand extended his hand and revealed a big, toothy smile. And yet, his eyes were narrow and the crease was back in his brow. The big handsome bullshit artist wasn't fooling Daisy with that genial façade.

She gave Adam a quick once-over, trying to take in what Rand was seeing with his snob-green eyes. It was true that her son had an unusual appearance. Sometimes she forgot that he dressed Gothic and had that penchant for heavy silver rings adorned with things like serpents and wolf heads.

Other times, like now, someone else's startle at his look would remind her that Adam could be considered by some to be an eyesore. She felt her shoulders press straighter, her frame became taut. Silently she dared this pompous phony to say something snide.

In that instant she didn't care about the money or how it could be Adam's ticket to the future he deserved. All that mattered was that this momma bear didn't like the way this oaf was scrutinizing her cub.

****

Rand took the kid's hand, feeling the coolness of the hunks of metal that decorated his fingers. "Hello, Adam. I'm Rand." He said this as pleasantly as he could although in his mind he was screaming. *Shit, who's this kid's father? Gene Simmons?* An image of Uncle William being introduced to this son of Kiss appeared appallingly in his head.

He needed to make sure this kid didn't get near

his uncle, whatsoever. Surely, it would be a dead giveaway that this was no real love match. Old Will knew his nephew enough to ascertain he'd never sincerely entertain a life-long liaison with a woman whose kid looked like a vampire.

Rand didn't miss the sharp light that cast from Cameron's eyes. She'd caught his immediate reaction, subtle as he felt it had been. Nonetheless, his partner in crime bristled and he needed to keep her happy. Okay, maybe not happy, but at least willing to stay in the game.

"So," Rand said with much enthusiasm, "you're the great artist I'm hearing about all the time. I'm glad to finally meet you, Adam."

He didn't need to look at Cameron to know her feathers had settled back down. He heard her breath soften, mollified. The kid's eyes were just like his mother's, pretty, girlish. His lashes were brushy and full like hers, too. Rand peered at them again. *Jeez, this Rocky Horror Show has to be wearing mascara.*

"Thanks." Adam's tone was warmer, his look less leery. "I don't know how *great* I am, but I sure love it."

"What's your specialty? Oil, watercolor?"

"I'm a sketch artist, drawings."

"Ah, and do you use ink or pencil?"

"Pencil...yes, sometimes. I like charcoal also. I work with pastels, too. I like color, but I mostly focus on the definition of the lines on the paper, you know?"

Rand was impressed with the kid's ease in talking about his artwork, very forthcoming with what Cameron described as his passion. Although he looked like a freak, he spoke well enough and engaged in eye contact, albeit eyes that were intimately acquainted with Maybelline.

The big guy came back with the beer, finally. "Thanks, man," Rand said. He took the brown bottle from Bruno's hand.

"Hey, you need a glass?" Bruno asked. He held a beer of his own in his other paw.

"No thanks, this is fine," Rand said. He lifted the Michelob to his lips and took a deep swig. It felt good going down, cold and crisp. He saw that Cameron was handed a glass of red wine.

He tapped the neck of his beer bottle to Bruno's. "That's good. Thanks." Then he tapped the rim of Cameron's glass. "Happy birthday, darling."

Rand saw her immediate reaction, as though he had thrown ice water into her face. She did an impressive job of trying to conceal her shock. Her smile looked almost genuine.

His endearment did not go unnoticed by her son, either. Adam's mouth had fallen as though his jaw had lost its hinge.

Bruno couldn't let it go without comment. "Candy, get over here," he boomed. "These two are calling each other 'darling' already." Then he made some kind of whoop noise that brought the rest of the room to attention. "You work fast, buddy, I'll tell you that."

Candy sidled up to her husband with a beer in her hand, also. She looked expectantly from Cameron, to Rand, then focused on Bruno. "What are you yelling about now?" she asked, her voice was light and playful, but Rand noticed her eyes darting to Cameron with consternation.

"Well, *darling*," Bruno said. He emphasized the term as though speaking to someone just learning the language. "I'm thinking Cupid's found a target."

Everyone chuckled at Bruno's theatrics— everyone but Adam and Candy. That worried Rand. But it was time to forge ahead and let the chips fall.

He put his beverage down onto the absurdly draped dining table. Then he turned to Cameron and placed his arm delicately around her waist, pulling

127

her close. She was a two-by-four.

"I guess now would be a good time for us to make our announcement," Rand said. He saw Cameron's fingers tremble on the stem of her wine glass. He needed to get this over with, sever the tension in this wooden woman tucked into the crook of his arm. "Shall we?"

Cameron smiled brightly in spite of her body's rigidity. "Yes," she breathed.

"Ladies and gentlemen," Rand said in his most-grand voice, "I am delighted to announce that this wonderful, beautiful, charming woman has agreed to be my wife."

The roomful of guests sucked in their breaths in unison providing nearly enough movement in the air around them to pull the walls in. The little old diner owners, standing on the opposite side of the table, were huddled next to each other. About the same height and breadth as each other, they reminded Rand of a couple of Hummels. The wife—Ima, as he'd sadly come to know—clapped her hands together, clearly pleased. *One down, many more to go.*

"What?" Candy's mouth was a lopsided gash, her voice a rasp.

"Come, darling, show everyone your ring," he urged. He scanned the rapt onlookers. "It is her birthday, and yet, when she accepted my proposal, I was the one given a gift."

Ima gave a loud, "Ah!" Her hands were still clasped in front of her. Her husband put an arm around her shoulders and gave her an affectionate squeeze. His face, amazingly unlined for a man of his years, was alight with joy. *Two-for-two.*

Rand glanced to the silent, stoic Adam, a wax figure in front of a house of horrors. He offered the boy his best sincere grin, the one that never failed. *Come on, kid, loosen up. Give me a break.*

He turned back to Cameron who slowly levitated her left hand. She looked as though she might be ill, and Rand needed to nip her obvious fear of the other's reactions. He put his hand beneath hers, giving it a brace as she held it up for inspection and eliminating the chance for someone to see her quiver.

"Holy mackerel," Bruno said. He eyeballed the rock. "Get a look at that, would you."

Candy inspected the ring, intermittently looking up at Cameron's face. But, Cameron's gaze was focused on Adam, who still stood motionless.

"Well," she said. She laughed nervously, "Adam, honey, what do you think?"

"I...uh...I'm speechless, Mom." The kid's voice was but a haunted acoustic. "I mean"—he continued with a shrug of one shoulder—"yeah, wow." The "wow" had as much exuberance as a dead fish.

"We know it's sudden," Rand interjected, providing the necessary liveliness for the moment. "But, we're not kids and, well, when you know, you just *know*." He turned to Cameron, willing her to add to the remark.

"Yes," she piped in. "Believe me, I was shocked when Rand proposed, but it's, um, I know this is, ah, the right thing."

"I can't believe it." Candy was still hunkered over Cameron's hand, as though bowing before royalty. "I just can't."

"Can I be your flower girl?" Candy's little girl asked. She was a cute kid, with the best sense of timing in the room. Everyone laughed at the question. If Rand were inclined toward children, he'd have hugged the little rug rat.

"Don't look at me to carry any stupid pillow or anything," the son added. He placed his hands on his hips. "I saw Anthony do that at Aunt Teresa's wedding and he looked like a total dork."

129

Again there was a round of chuckling. The comment even produced a laugh from the scrutinizing Candy. Rand saw that Adam's mouth had closed and pitched into a crooked smirk. Little Bruno's protest was miraculously amusing even to him.

"Whoa, you two, who said you'll be invited," Bruno said.

"We've got plenty of time to think about things like that," Cameron said. She gave Candy a look. "Rand and I aren't planning to rush into the wedding."

"Oh?" Candy asked.

Rand tightened his arm around Cameron, leaned in and kissed the soft spot at her temple. He turned to Candy. "Right now our plan is to simply enjoy the engagement and celebrate our having found each other."

That seemed to satisfy their doubtful hostess. She put her arms around first Cameron, and then Rand, offering congratulations. One by one, the others in the room did the same—Bruno, the kids, Ima and Pete, the other two waitresses; the old one and the fat one, whatever their names were—but not Adam, not yet. Rand went to him, his left hand extended.

"Adam, I hope to make your mother the happiest woman on the planet."

The kid accepted his handshake, but Rand was aware of the anemic pressure Adam supplied to the effort. "I hope so, too."

Cameron was at Rand's side now. She pulled her son into her embrace and his arms wound around her like cords. His eyes were closed as he embraced his mother. When he opened them, the blue spotlights were fixed on Rand like bare bulbs in an interrogation room.

Chapter Seventeen

Daisy had made it through the muck of their spectacle without throwing up. At this stage of the game, she'd call that a great success.

When Rand had made his grand gesture, whet, of course, by his calling her *darling,* Daisy saw the look of utter shock on her son's face. Adam had gone from a vibrant, interactive human to a cement-pallored stone alien.

In hindsight, she wished she had told Adam separately. It wasn't fair to spring it on him like that, with an audience.

Candy would be a problem, but Daisy knew that going in. When her friend pulled her into that hug she used the gesture to deliver a message in a low, curt whisper, "Come into the kitchen, pronto!"

Daisy would face that soon enough. For the moment she was concerned about Adam.

When everyone had officially seen the ring and offered their good wishes, they dissipated to the living room and onto the deck to either smoke cigarettes or just enjoy the cool night air.

Thankfully, Rand had taken Bruno up on his suggestion to go outside and see his latest handiwork—a wooden shed with a gabled roof and dormers that matched the line of their house.

That left Daisy alone with her son. He downed the rest of the soda in his cup. Holding it with one hand, he tapped it with the fingers of his other. The hollow sound was the only noise between them.

"Adam..." Daisy took a step toward him.

"Mom, it's okay."

131

"No, it's not 'okay.' I can see that. I should have told you privately. I'm sorry, honey. We'll all get used to this. Believe me. It's all new to me, too." She laughed a little, hoping to lighten the air between them.

"Are you sure about this? I mean, God, you just met the guy, didn't you? What'd he do, say 'hi, my name is Rudolph, will you marry me?'"

She laughed—not because it was funny, but because it was pathetically close to the truth. "Not exactly. And, his name's Randolph. Rudolph was the reindeer."

"Right," he said flatly. "The one with the shiny nose. Looks as if this guy's got a shiny everything."

"Adam…"

"How much do you know about him? It's so fast, Mom."

"I know, but we're not rushing down the aisle any time soon. We're going to, you know…enjoy this time, as Rand said."

"I don't know if I like him."

"Why not?" Daisy felt her heart stutter in her chest. She pleaded with him silently. *Please don't do this, Adam. Don't delve so deeply that you see the rotten, stinking truth.* She couldn't bear the thought.

Adam shrugged. "I don't know, Mom. It's just a feeling, I guess. He's, I don't know, too smooth, maybe. Too sure of himself."

"I understand. I made the same misjudgment. Get to know him, Adam. That's all I ask."

Finally Adam offered a feeble grin. Stepping forward, he touched his forehead to his mother's. This move between them had originated when Adam turned thirteen and had sprouted up to stand at nearly Daisy's height. It was their sign that their heads were in sync, and their relationship was solid, no matter what.

Adam spoke first. In a gentle whisper laced with

132

the uncertainty that Daisy had heard plenty of times over the years, he asked, "Do you really want this, Mom?"

"Yes," she whispered back. Her heart ached with regret.

She did her best to focus on the end result, the day she would get her financial due for this unsavory ordeal. At that time she would tell one more lie about how she and Rand had decided they weren't destined to be together after all. She and Mr. Press would go their separate ways. *And I'll never tell another damned lie again, so help me.*

He lifted his head and gazed into her eyes. "I guess I just worry about you," he said.

"That makes two of us," Candy said. Daisy startled at her friend's sudden appearance in the room. "Adam, honey, want to give Bruno a hand in bringing the burgers outside? The grill's ready."

He gave one last glance at his mother, and then nodded. "Sure."

"You, *darling,* can help me toss the salad," Candy said. She ushered Daisy down the short hallway to the kitchen.

Adam had disappeared through the back screen door. Daisy did her best to act as though flipping the salad utensils to sufficiently distribute the vinaigrette over the romaine was her only thought.

"Okay, stop." Candy reached to halt Daisy's frenzied manipulations. "Talk to me."

Daisy released her hold on the long-handled spoons and forced a grin. "I'm in love."

"You're in love?" Candy said. Her hands flew to her hips and her head cocked. "Okay, when's the punch line?"

"Candy, really, there's no punch line."

"So, bam! You're engaged?"

Daisy laughed as realistically as she could muster. "We just fell really hard."

"Well, when you fell, it must have been right on your head, because your screw's loose."

"I know it's a shock, Candy. I'm pretty shocked myself. Now, I...uh...I know what they mean by *whirlwind*. I feel as if I'm caught up in one big happy whirlwind."

If she didn't shut up, Daisy knew she'd make herself vomit. She figured that might just cast some doubt on her story. She closed her mouth and gave Candy a tight, brief hug. "Trust me on this."

"I'm trying."

"Thank you."

"But, you have to promise me you won't change."

"What are you talking about? Don't be silly."

"He's loaded—and if you recall, you thought he was obnoxious when you first met him. I just don't want you being bamboozled by this guy's charm and the lure of his lifestyle."

"You know me better than that, girlfriend."

"Even when you're Mrs. J. Randolph Press, Jr.?"

Daisy felt the words stab her like a blade. Keeping up this falsehood was a festering wound. One truth she knew was that she would *never* become Mrs. Press, so her comrade would not have to worry about the moniker changing her into someone she was not.

"Candy, I promise. I will always be me."

"You'll always be my Daisy?"

"Yes."

****

Rand strolled over to Adam who was staring out into space over the railing of Candy and Bruno's redwood deck. Adam's shoulders were hunched. His lean, entirely black-clad torso resembled an upright snake.

Rand's tightly clenched mouth ached. He wiggled the lower part of his jaw to loosen it. "So, Adam..." Letting out a breath, he was ready to wing it, confident that he'd figure out the right approach as they went along.

Adam straightened, looking Rand in the eye. He said nothing. His countenance was blank, but the flash of distrust in the boy's baby blues was unmistakable.

"I know this comes as a shock," Rand offered.

Still nothing from the kid. Rand would not be dissuaded. "Believe me, your mom and I are both a little stunned ourselves. I'll tell you we...uh...sure didn't see this coming."

Adam nodded, his mouth curved down in a frown. His eye contact was unwavering. Clearly this heavy-metal artist had a stubborn streak—like his mother. It almost made Rand smile, the heady sense of conquering an affront piqued him like a hot craps table.

"I'm an art fan. I'd like to hear more about your interests, Adam. Who's your favorite artist?"

Adam's eyes darted to their surroundings as though searching for his mother's whereabouts. When he turned his attention back to Rand, he shrugged, hesitating as though carrying the conversation any further went against his religion. "I've got a few"—another shrug—"I guess that depends on what you're talking about."

Rand calculated his response, searching for what would garner a greater number of words out of the kid's mouth. He decided to wait him out. He punctuated the pause with a façade of keen interest—one he knew just how to paint on his own face.

"I like different artists for different things," Adam said.

"Interesting," Rand said with just the right nod. "I just know when I like what I see, being a non-artist, you know."

Adam merely nodded. Rand's comment caused

him to clam up again.

"So, give me a *for instance*." Rand said. "For example, tell me something that appeals to you specifically about a certain artist. It's intriguing to hear commentary from someone involved in the study."

He had him now. Rand knew it. It was a direct request that required an answer. Adam either had to comment or appear rude. If Rand knew anything, he'd bet the house that Cameron raised him better than that.

"DaVinci's Last Supper."

"Really?" Rand was unable to keep the surprise out of his voice.

Adam's mouth curved into a half-smile, his eyes alight, perhaps with appreciation for the ancient master painter. "Yes, he brilliantly captured the precise moment when Jesus knew he would be betrayed." And, then the boy resumed his narrowed stare.

Well, Rand thought. *This painted pony is going to give me a run for my money, I see. All the more interesting.* He smiled at the kid, keeping his gaze steady, yet wide and appreciative, innocent of the jibe in that comment.

"I'm a fan of Van Gogh. Do you like his work?" Rand asked. He took a swig of his beer, washing down the sudden urge to spill the fact that he wouldn't give a rat's ass what this beanpole thought of Van Gogh, or Picasso, or his opinion on betrayal.

"Yes. A big fan, actually."

"Great. I'm interested in why you're a big fan. I mean because I just know I appreciate his paintings, but I couldn't tell you why."

"What works of his appeal to you?" Adam's question made Rand feel as though he was now being tested. Silly boy didn't know the measure of a successful man's preparation.

"*The Red Vineyard,*" Rand said. The title rolled from his tongue as though it were an all-time favorite. "I also like the *Public Park* and the *Café Terrace at Night.*"

Adam nodded his appreciation. "They're all images of the same city."

"Yes, Arles, in the south of France," Rand said. Accessing that little tidbit he'd stored in his brain gave him a zing of pleasure, giving him to enjoy Adam's look of defeat even more.

"How about you, Adam? Tell me about Van Gogh's appeal to you."

"It's the soul of his art. The techniques may have changed in modern times, but the soul of art remains the same. I'm in awe of his use of shadow and light."

"It's really nice to hear an artist's opinion. Fascinating, really."

"Well, I also respect the works of Arshile Gorky. Do you know him?" Adam asked.

The kid had him there. Rand had never heard the name, so there was no use pretending otherwise. He knew that Adam would love nothing more than to catch Rand in some bullshit response. So, in this instance, he spoke the truth. "No, can't say I have, Adam. Tell me about him, or her."

"Gorky painted what is known as abstract expressionism. In my opinion, he was a master with pencil and charcoal."

"I'll have to investigate his work sometime." Rand knew he would do no such thing.

"My favorite of his," Adam offered unasked. "*The Artist and His Mother.* A captured moment of unwavering loyalty."

Rand's stomach twisted like a dishrag. *Okay, Oedipus, you can have your mother just as soon as she fulfills her obligation to me.*

Rand smiled to disguise that he was about to

spew his Cheese Doodles. "My Cameron's a lucky lady."

The boy's face contorted into an angry grimace. After uttering a hasty "Excuse me," he bolted across the deck and pulled open the door to the kitchen.

****

Adam burst into the room, making the hinges on the screen door cry in pain. "Mom!"

Daisy and Candy stared at the boy in the doorway. He let the door slap closed behind him and folded his arms over his chest.

"You mind telling me why this guy's calling you *Cameron?* When did you change your name?"

Two sets of eyes were glued on her. Her tongue was tied. She had forgotten she needed to come up with a plausible reason for why Rand called her by her last name.

The truth was the last thing she could use. *Oh, it's nothing, just that Rand's rich uncle might question why his money-hungry nephew would even contemplate getting engaged to a country mouse by the name of Daisy.* Yeah that would work. She swallowed hard, trying to come up with an excuse.

"You're Cameron now? Since when? And, better yet, why?" Candy asked. Her mouth was agape.

"Mom? What's that all about?"

Daisy managed somehow to pop a giggle out of her throat, as if a peach pit had been blocking her windpipe. "It's cute, don't you think? He, Rand, well, he thinks I look like Cameron Diaz, and when he found out my last name was Cameron—"

"So, when you look like someone else you have to change your name to be that person?" Candy asked. "Okay, I think he looks like Rob Lowe. Should I start calling him 'Lowe'?"

"It's low all right," Adam added. "Didn't you tell him the reason you were named Daisy?"

"Sure I did, but..." Of course this was a lie. The

fact that it came so easily was what bothered her. No, she had not explained the details of her naming, but now she worried that one of these two inquisitors would quiz him on it. She felt sick again. She was not getting any better at this.

"I mean, I think I mentioned it to him, but, to tell you the truth, I don't see the harm in his calling me by my last name. It's an endearment like any other, really. What's the big deal?"

Adam and Candy exchanged a look. "It's just that..." Adam stopped.

"It's just what, honey?"

"Forget it. It's nothing." He turned to the door and exited to the deck where the smell of burgers sizzling over open flames would entice anyone. At least they'd entice anyone who wasn't feeling too nauseous to eat.

"So much for not changing, huh?" Candy said dejectedly. She grabbed a basket full of buns and a tray of American cheese slices and took them to her husband at the grill.

While the guests waited their turn for their hamburgers or hotdogs, Cameron stole away to the restroom and stared at herself in the mirror over the sink. The stark light from the fluorescent bulb overhead gave her skin an ugly bluish hue. She looked dead. Daisy snapped off the light and stood alone in the darkness.

Chapter Eighteen

In the narrow hallway outside Candy's bathroom, Daisy stumbled into Rand.

"We have to talk."

"Yeah, we do," she said. In the darkness of the little tiled space she had decided to do her best to undo this nightmare, confess to the crowd, apologize and hope that they would forgive her—considering it was her birthday and everything.

"Listen, it's going well enough, honestly." His tone was irritatingly soothing.

"You think so?" she asked, her voice laced with bitter sarcasm. "What was your first clue? When my son and best friend wigged out about your stupid need to call me Cameron? Couldn't you wait until I had the chance to tell them first?"

"I'm sorry. It just slipped out. I saw the way Adam looked when I said it, but he didn't wait around long enough for me to try to give him a reason. I figured it was better if I didn't follow him in after you. I knew better than to join the crowd."

"How chivalrous of you. Drop a bomb and wait for it to explode. Nice."

"I don't believe that describes the situation. Think about it, would you?" he said, his voice dangerously elevated.

"Can you please keep it down?" Her eyes scanned the hallway to make sure they were still alone. "Unless you want to expose it this way— which at this stage, I'm not sure would be such a bad idea."

"Cameron—"

"Stop it." She spat. "Just...Just don't." She heard the sob in her voice and tried to swallow the urge to cry.

Rand put his hands on her shoulders, his touch softer this time than any before. "Please listen. Okay?" he asked calmly, bending his head down to look into her eyes.

Daisy couldn't respond for fear of encouraging the threatening tears.

"Come on," Rand said, still gentle. "We'll make it right with them about the name. Adam and I were making some good progress before I blurted your name out."

"What kind of progress?"

"We were having a really nice conversation about art and famous works. He really knows what he's talking about. And, I'm glad for him, and for you, that he's going to be able to study his passion in the school of his choice."

"You're patronizing me. I hate this. *Everything* about this," she whispered. "I just do."

"We'll talk to Adam together about the name thing. How's that? We'll come up with something to appease him."

"Well, I think I better explain something to you about my name. The first thing Adam asked me was if I'd told you why I'm named Daisy. I said yes, then got worried that he would question you about it. Since you don't know anything, it would catch you off guard and—"

"Can you fill me in right now, and then we'll go find your son and cool his jets?"

She held his gaze, wondered why on earth she would trust the manufactured sincerity in his emerald eyes. But for some crazy reason, at that moment, she did. "Okay."

"Talk to me," he smiled.

Daisy took a deep breath, let it expel audibly,

and tried to unscramble her brain. "All right, Reader's Digest version. I was born two months early, and back then a three-pound baby was in major danger. For the first week I didn't make a sound, didn't open my eyes. It was very touch and go. Then one early morning my father, a writer who loved poetry, was talking to me. I opened my eyes and, according to the lore, I looked right at him, my eyes as blue as they are now. He named me Daisy, from a line in the Canterbury Tales. Chaucer referred to a daisy as the *eye of day.*"

****

Rand could only stare at her. Looking into those crystalline blue eyes, he tried to picture her as a tiny, frail baby. He wondered what a three-pound baby looked like.

How scary had it been for her parents to peer down at their miniscule infant and wonder if she would ever open her eyes? She honored her first name and yet she had agreed to allow his notion to ditch it during their scheme. As much as it apparently meant to her, her love for and belief in her son mattered more.

For the first time in a long time, guilt wound around Rand's heart, and knotted like a rope. In a flash, anger boiled in him. This was no time for sentiment, no time to be taken in by old stories about sappy families, or to feel anything besides determination for his cause. He needed to pull his eyes away from the blue ones in front of him, and keep his eye on the prize.

"Lovely sentiment," he said. "I'm sorry it upsets you to be called Cameron. But look at it this way, it's temporary. You'll be back to Daisy again soon."

Rand forced himself not to think about what would have to occur before she could resume her real name. It was one thing to want the fortune he was entitled to, it was another to all but wish for his uncle's demise. He was angrier at himself now. He wanted another beer.

"Okay?" he asked with forced gentleness to his voice. "We good now?"

She didn't answer him, but he could see by her expression that she had calmed down. He touched his hand to the small of her back. "Come on, birthday girl, let's get you a burger. I want to find myself another beer."

They stepped out onto the deck, lit now by the string of plastic Chinese lanterns suspended above them on the edge of the canvas awning. Although the lights themselves were a dime store variety, their affect was nice enough. Everyone looked as though they were aglow.

Rand retrieved two balloon-patterned paper plates that matched the plastic cover on the dining room table. Balancing a hamburger on each one, the weight taxing for the flimsy plate, he brought one to Cameron.

As they stood at the railing eating, Adam strode over to them with purposeful steps. Rand braced himself for the confrontation.

"Did you get a burger, Adam?" he asked. The boy's eyes were on his mother. Rand glanced at her and was impressed to see that she was attempting to appear at ease.

"They're good, huh, sweetheart?" He regretted the question as soon as he saw that she had taken just one bite of hers. As if his words were a command, she lifted the bun to her mouth and took a small nibble.

"Delicious," she said as though she meant it. "Adam, honey, could you get me a can of soda? Anything diet."

"Sure, Mom," he said. "But, first I want to say something." He turned his attention to Rand, then fixed his gaze back on his mother. "I want to apologize for the way I've been acting. I think I've upset you, and I'm sorry.

"I guess I'm just not used to any of this yet. The news is, you know, like out of nowhere."

"Honey, I know. I'm sorry, too. I'm sorry that I didn't get the chance to tell you myself first." She shot Rand a look.

"That's my fault, darling. Adam, I was just so excited about our news that I announced it ahead of your mother telling you."

"I understand," he said. He offered a feeble smile. "Or, at least I'm going to try."

"And, about your mother's name…" Rand said. He slipped an arm around Daisy's shoulders. They were cool in the evening air despite the gas deck heater positioned nearby, burning orange under its wide stainless dome.

"I know, I know…" Adam said. He lifted his hands up as though in surrender. "I was out of line. He looked at his mother. "If you like being called Cameron, then I'll respect that."

"Thank you, Adam," Daisy said.

Rand could hear the quiver in her voice. "I am very touched by the story of how your mom got the name Daisy. Don't be mistaken. I think it's lovely that she was regarded as such a gift to her parents. Truly. I can't recall now how I first came to call her Cameron, but it's how I've come to think of her. She seemed to like it and it's sort of like our code for *I love you.*"

He closed his mouth to cease spilling any more utter, blatant bullshit. The hamburger in his stomach careened like a pinball. Thankfully, it appeared as though Adam was satisfied. Yet, something else occurred to him.

Curiously the fact was that the tenderness involved in her naming had affected him. It brought to mind the name his own mother used to call him.

Bruno had put on some country music, no surprise to Rand. However, the songs were better than he thought they'd be—not that of a twangy, cry-baby cowboy lamenting the death of his hound dog. Simple ballads with appealing sounds of steel-pedal guitars, many included violin. Rand was particularly partial to strings.

"This music…"

"I know. You hate it, I'm sure," Cameron said.

"No." Rand laughed. "Trust me, I'm a bit surprised about that myself. I've never been a fan of this kind of stuff. I mean *at all.*"

"That would have been my guess."

"But, well, who is this now? Do you know?"

"Sugarland. It's a duo. The song is called 'Settlin'."

"They're good," Rand said. He listened closer to the lyrics. "Do you like them?"

"Very much, actually. This song in particular."

Rand didn't miss the flash in her eyes, something he'd guess was as close to playful as she would allow in their situation. The singer's lyrics vowed to never, under any circumstances, settle for something that wasn't all she deserved.

Rand looked at the woman next to him, some long-ago young couple's *eye of day*, and felt a stab of longing he did not understand—or want.

"Ima-Waitress" and her Hummel husband joined them, followed by the other two waitresses. The old one, Rand learned, was Bridget. She had a raucous laugh that bubbled from her lips whenever something struck her funny, which was often. The other one, Millie, although rotund, had a cherubic face that Rand found pleasant. He did his best to stay engaged in their conversation.

Adam had returned with a dripping, cold can of Sprite and joined the circle of conversation. It wasn't long before the host and hostess of the evening had joined them. They all, being familiar, were in tune with the pulse of the conversation.

Periodically Rand stole a glimpse of his cohort, alive now with her speech and demeanor. She was in her element. She laughed with genuine heartiness, a nice sound to his ears. He watched her fingers cradle the soda can, watched her lips cover the opening as she sipped. He stirred.

Maybe it was the two beers, or maybe the dichotomy of the September air and the warmth from the heater that bathed them. Whatever it was, Rand did not fight it. He made the decision to just enjoy the moment and allow himself to relax and be a part of the celebration.

And that was when Bruno decided to incessantly tap the side of his beer bottle with the metal edge of his grilling tool. The sound rang into the night with a message clear to everyone, including Rand. Soon, any person holding something that could make a noise did so even if it was merely to clap their hands.

Rand turned to Cameron whose eyes had grown wide with dread. He needed to dash that look before someone recognized it.

"Oh, come on, buddy. Kiss her," Bruno taunted. The crowd responded with a loud cheer.

Rand put his beer down on the top of the railing and took the soda can from Cameron's mannequin grasp. He slipped his arms around her waist and pulled her close, feeling her resistance. He leaned close, his mouth just above hers and whispered. "No choice."

Her lips parted as though to remark. He silenced her by covering her mouth with his own. He heard the onlookers' cheers, yet there was nothing alive to his senses but the feel of her—the scent of her skin, the soda-sipping coolness of her lips, and the warmth he sensed was beyond them.

Cameron's mouth softened under his. Her lips

were lush and welcoming. His tongue dabbed inside to the warmth that beckoned him, and her mouth responded with open accommodation. Finally, a hand on his shoulder brought him back to the reality of the moment, and he became aware of laughter.

"Holy smokes, you two. You trying to set the place on fire?" Bruno cajoled.

"Oh, leave them alone," Pete spoke up. "I could go for a kiss like that."

"Be quiet, you!" Ima's voice was light and joking. "You're all talk. That kind of kiss would send you to the cardiologist."

"Come on everybody, let's have cake! It's all set up in the dining room," Candy called over the din.

"You, too, lovebirds," someone else said as they all filed slowly in through the back door.

They were alone, Cameron and Rand, each unable to speak or meet the other's gaze.

Chapter Nineteen

Daisy took a step away. Rand reached for her hand. "Cameron," he said softly.

"Please don't," she said. She pulled her hand away as though he were a live flame. "We need to go inside."

"I—"

"They're waiting." She hurried toward the kitchen.

Daisy hadn't realized her hand was shaking until she reached for the handle of the screen door. She tried to pull enough air into her lungs to unleash the clench of her chest.

She licked her lips and regretted it. She could still taste him, salty, yet sweet. Daisy closed her eyes, silently praying her common sense was inside the house because for sure it was nowhere on the deck outside.

Candy was at the counter pouring coffee into a thermal carafe. She turned to the sound of the door's squeak as Daisy came in. "My, my…" Her mouth had a smirky twist.

Daisy didn't know how to play the moment. She was unable to come up with a comeback as she normally would—not surprising as there was nothing normal about her now. She had lost her mind.

"Can I, um, can I help you with anything?" Daisy's voice was meek. She cleared her throat, trying to find her usual tone. "Want me to bring in the milk and sugar?"

She watched Candy screw the carafe's lid into

place. Her friend then turned in Daisy's direction. Her mouth was a broad goofy grin. "Well, girl, let me just say this..." Candy said in her sultry voice. "If I didn't understand how you could wind up engaged in such record time, I sure as hell do now."

"What does that mean?"

"That kiss convinced me. You two are nuts about each other. I stand corrected, sweet pea. You go for it, girl. I'm with you," Candy said. She threw her arms around Daisy who hugged back robotically. She was too stupefied to challenge the conversation, or even pretend to confirm it.

Inside the dining room the guests were gathered around the table. A homemade chocolate-iced cake sat in its center, pastel candles poked in the frosting, lit and waiting for her. The light fixture hovering from the ceiling had been dimmed low.

"Make a wish!" someone implored.

Daisy closed her eyes and blew, her mind chanting a sole wish. She wished for the speedy return of her brain functioning.

When she righted her stance and opened her eyes, she spotted Rand across the table, his countenance blurred by the skinny ribbons of smoke that undulated into the air from the doused wicks. He looked surreal and ghost-like. He was a hologram—that could kiss like nobody she had ever known.

"What'd you wish for?" Excitement sparked Gina's voice.

"She can't tell, dork," Little Bruno said. "Or it won't come true."

Daisy smiled at the little girl but inside she felt doom closing in on her. *Oh, it better come true,* she thought. *She'd make sure it did.*

Candy doled out slices of cake, receiving praise from Ima, the resident baker in the bunch. Daisy was reminded of the baking dilemma instilled on her by Rand's ranting brag to his uncle.

They might still have to deal with that if the uncle brought it up again. That would be nothing short of a fiasco. Right now she had a bigger problem than being forced to follow a cake recipe.

She looked up again to eye Rand and was surprised to see that he was no longer in the room. She surveyed the entrances to the kitchen and the living room. He was in neither place.

If he'd split now, left her here holding the bag, so to speak, she'd kill him. The mean feeling came as a relief. Daisy welcomed the negativity when it came to thoughts of Rand.

A hand on her shoulder startled her back to the moment. It was Adam, holding a Styrofoam cup in his hand. "I got you coffee," he announced.

Daisy smiled at her son. The impish look on his face was so endearing it made her heart pump. "Thank you, honey."

"One sugar, right?"

"Yes," she said. She lifted the cup to her mouth, blew over the surface of the liquid to cool it, and took a sip. "Mmm. Good."

"Um, I think he might be okay. I mean, he likes art. And he likes you, right?"

Daisy offered an encouraging nod, admired her son's effort to try to accept the crazy situation foisted upon him. She hadn't known that Rand liked art.

Perhaps that was another lie, though. He was an expert liar. She must never forget that.

"Thanks for putting up with this, Adam. I promise I'll never make another big decision without warning you. Deal?"

"Deal."

Rand was back, now standing beside the two of them. "Hi, there," he said genially.

"Hi, there," Daisy said.

"Good cake," he said. "This is the third time I've

had cake since I met your mother, Adam. I'm going to have to go on a diet."

"You like cake?" Adam asked.

"Love it."

"Hope you don't expect my mom to ever make you one. She can't bake at all. I mean *at all*." Adam laughed.

Rand and Cameron exchanged a look, conspirators sharing the only thing they had in common, their need to carry out their falsity.

After the "thank yous" and "good nights," the majority of the guests had left. Candy's two children had reluctantly gone up to bed. Adam and Bruno were outside tidying up the deck while Daisy assisted Candy with putting the rooms back in order.

Daisy was surprised to see Rand pitch in with the effort by taking the job of emptying the cooler of the beer and soda cans. He even dried each off with a towel and found room for them in the refrigerator. It was surreal to witness him working so dutifully on a task that seemed too menial for a Press.

Helping Candy with the dishes, Daisy dried platters that were too big to put into the dishwasher. Soon Bruno and Adam joined them in the room. "I'm going to run Adam home," Bruno announced.

"That's not necessary, Bruno. We can take him home," Daisy said. She looked toward Rand.

"Sure," he responded. "Let Adam come with us."

"No, no, no," Candy said. She waved a dismissive hand. "Bruno's running out for more milk anyway. The kids will want cereal in the morning and we're out."

"I can't keep it in the house," Bruno said. He shook his head. "Wish I had stock in cows."

"But, still, we're going right there," Rand said.

"You two lovebirds can be alone tonight. You just got engaged!" Candy said.

Daisy felt a stab of concern. She hadn't stopped to think that people might find it normal these days for an engaged couple to cohabitate. She had to dash that idea and fast. "But, I'm going home tonight."

"So, enjoy the ride together," Candy said. She winked. "You know, take the long way home."

Daisy wasn't sure if she liked Candy being on "Team Rand." She had thawed toward him, acting chummier ever since witnessing their kiss.

The kiss! Daisy chanted a reminder, *It's fake, it's fake, it's fake.* She prayed that would be the antidote to the image that popped into her mind.

****

On the way home, Daisy felt uncomfortable in the quiet. Rand seemed deep in thought. In spite of herself, she rehashed the evening in her mind. If she were to be honest—something she used to be all the time—the truth was that Rand had been a pretty good sport.

He'd made a real effort to be nice to Adam, had been congenial to the others, and helpful to Candy and Bruno. She was sure that her friends found it believable enough that she would fall in love with such a man. They had fooled Rand's uncle and his long-time caretaker, Florence. And now they had done the same with her people.

"We might have a problem," Rand broke into her thoughts.

"What?"

"Florence called."

"She did? When?"

"While we were having cake."

"Oh," Daisy said. *So that was why he had gone missing for a while.* "What, uh, what's the problem?"

"Uncle has asked her to arrange a small engagement party for us."

Daisy groaned. Another event to get through—she couldn't take it. "Can't you just say no? That

152

we'd rather not?"

"You don't know my uncle. He's not doing this for anything other than to watch us in action. He's going to be looking for flaws in our story to find evidence of us trying to pull one over on him."

She took a deep breath and let it out audibly. "Then I guess we have to do it."

"Yes, but that's not what I'm worried about."

"What then?"

"He wants your family and friends to attend."

"Well, all it would be, really, is Adam, Candy's family, and maybe Pete and Ima. Are you worried it would be too big a crowd?"

"Not at all. It's just..."

It started to dawn on her that he was worried about his uncle meeting the people in her life. That really pissed her off. "What, Rand? What then?"

She saw his chest rise and fall. "I like Adam. I really do. He's a nice, well spoken, intelligent kid..."

"But?" Daisy seethed.

"Come on, Cameron. His look is outlandish to say it mildly. My uncle would be aghast at the sight of him. Let alone Florence."

"You're a pompous pig."

"Cameron—"

"Do not call me *that* when you don't need to. Thanks by the way—you've taught me to despise my own last name."

"For crying out loud, you're being irrational."

"What?" If she hadn't wanted to get home in one piece, she'd have hauled off and slugged him right then and there—without care to the fact that he was driving a car. "You don't know anything about my son. How dare you infer that he's anything aside from a good, noble person—regardless of how he dresses or wears his hair."

Rand pulled into a guest space in the parking lot of her apartment complex. He shifted the transmission into park and turned to her. "Please listen to me. I'm not saying anything disparaging about Adam. It's my uncle's reaction that I'm concerned about."

"I hate this whole thing," she said bitterly. "I hate it! Do you understand?"

He reached for her and she yanked free. "Don't. I detest you, too."

"You're getting much better at this, aren't you?"

"I beg your pardon?"

"The lying—it's starting to roll freely from your tongue."

"I am not lying."

"Yes you are."

"Oh, believe me. I do detest you."

"No you don't." His voice was a tease.

Taken aback by his arrogance she stared at him, wide-eyed and speechless.

"I hate your guts. How's that?"

Rand leaned in dangerously close to her. She could see his eyes alive with amusement in his dimly lit car's interior. She held her breath.

"You may hate my guts, madam, but you're rather fond of my lips."

Daisy bolted from the car and slammed the door. She could hear his laughter as she stormed to her front entrance. Fumbling with her key, she cursed it for not cooperating. Finally her door opened. She locked it behind her, turning the deadbolt with a flourish.

Chapter Twenty

Daisy couldn't let it go another day. It was time to lower the boom to Ima and Pete that she would no longer be available to waitress on Saturdays.

Pete leaned against the doorway to Daisy's little office. "I saw this one coming." He turned his gaze to Ima. "What'd I tell you?"

"He bet me you'd nix Saturdays." Ima said.

"I'm psychic, what can I tell you?"

"Hush, Peter. If you're so psychic, then you already know I need you to get started on making room on the pantry shelves. The delivery guy will be here later this morning."

"Okay, okay, I know the *brush off* when I hear it." Pete turned to leave, but then turned to look back at the two women. "Just to warn you, Daisy. I smell a lecture."

Daisy laughed, cringing inside. She couldn't take another *talking to*. But, she supposed she deserved one. After all, she was leaving these folks in the lurch for Saturdays.

With Pete gone, Ima sat down in the chair positioned in front of Daisy's desk. The way she fiddled with the pins holding her bun in place told Daisy that whatever Ima was about to say was not easy for her. Daisy held her breath.

"Honey, you know we love you around here. Pete and I, well, you know how we feel about you. Don't you, Daisy?"

Yes, she knew how much this cute, caring couple cared about her. Her throat constricted and there was an ache behind her nose—the kind she got whenever she tried not to cry. She appreciated the way they all but adopted her when she arrived back in town without a job, a home, or a direction.

Suddenly, she felt like the worst of betrayers, an ungrateful bailer. "Look, Ima, really, if you need me to stay on Saturdays until you find someone, I can do that much." Rand would just have to live with her decision.

"No, no, no. Millie is interested in picking up some hours. And, if she can't do it every Saturday, I'm sure I can get Bridget to come in."

Daisy still felt awful. It was as though all she'd been doing these days was letting people down, herself included. "Ima, I'm sorry. It's just that, well, you know, with Rand and everything..."

"That's what I wanted to talk to you about, Daisy."

"Okay," Daisy said. She glanced down at her hands folded on her desk top. Her knuckles were white. The sharp edge of the ring's prong jabbed at her flesh.

"You and your young man seem like a nice match. You make a beautiful couple."

"Thank you," Daisy said. Her eyes were still on her white knuckles.

"But, I'm sensing something, sweetie. You're hesitant. I've come to know you pretty well since you showed up that morning two years ago." Ima chuckled.

"I remember the day as if it was yesterday. You were looking all business-and-purpose, wearing that buttoned-up suit and high heels. Pete thought you were the IRS. Remember that?"

Daisy had to smile. "Yes, I do. I was scared to death."

"I could tell. You never blinked your eyes while you made your pitch to Pete and me. I thought 'look at this lovely young woman scared like a rabbit. Too afraid to even blink.'"

Daisy lifted her head slowly, meeting Ima's gaze. She knew where this was going. She waited, knowing she couldn't stop her mentor from saying it.

"That's how you looked last night. You look like that now—a rabbit again. And I want to know why."

Daisy was at a loss for words. She was out of excuses today, absent of any more false reassurances. It was true that she was scared, and the fear of her actions grew stronger every day. She took a deep breath and deliberately blinked her eyes for effect. "I'm fine, Ima. What you're seeing, I guess, is just new-engagement jitters."

Ima shook her head as though she weren't having any of what Daisy dished out. "Jitters don't look like that." She pointed to Daisy's face. "That's panic."

Suddenly Daisy wanted to confess to Ima. She let the words form in her head, allowed herself to imagine how Ima would receive the news. Would she laugh? Yell? Kick her out?

It didn't matter, though, because Daisy was going to hold her tongue. "Ima, really, the only panic you see on this face is my anxiety to get the bills and payroll done by the end of the week. I better get cracking so I'll have time to, you know, take a breath or blink my eyes, maybe."

Ima pursed her lips and gave Daisy a sideways glance. "I'll leave you to your work, Daisy. But, I'm going to be watching you. Pete's not the only psychic around here."

Ima disappeared down the staircase that Pete had descended a few minutes earlier. In her solitude, Daisy tried to concentrate on her Excel spreadsheet. The numbers made no sense to her today. Inadvertently she erased the formulas from some of the columns and had to re-insert them, a tedious task. The ringing phone startled her out of her forced attention to the details.

"Brookside Café," she said. "Daisy Cameron."

"Okay, that's got to change."

Her jaw clenched against the receiver at her mouth. It was Rand.

"I beg your pardon?" Her voice was curt.

"You can't answer the phone like that. What if my uncle has one of his investigators researching you? One of them could have called you already. Did you get any unusual phone calls this morning?"

"Just this one."

Rand chuckled into her ear. "Still mad at me, my love?"

"Stop it," she said bitterly. She shot her gaze to the doorway to her office to make sure no one had sneaked up on her. She lowered her tone. "Why are you calling me?"

"Florence called. She wants to begin making plans for this engagement dinner Uncle has bid her to arrange." He let out a sigh. "It's unavoidable."

"Has she come up with a date?"

"Well, considering the matter of Uncle's health, Flo would like to have it very soon. She asked if we were available next Saturday evening."

"I can be," Daisy said dully.

"And, how about the rest of your crew?"

"The rest of my crew? I thought my family and friends weren't acceptable to you?" Her voice had elevated again, her tone sounded like a growl even to her own ears.

Rand hesitated before responding. "Cameron, I apologize if I insulted you and your people last evening. It's just that I have legitimate concerns about your group meeting my group—concerns about the appearance of the authenticity of our engagement. You don't know my uncle very well."

"Nor do I want to," she said. She felt a thud in her chest, regretting her words.

There was no reason to transfer her self-loathing onto the shoulders of a dying old man. "Next Saturday's fine, I'm sure. Hopefully, my pawn pieces will be available and we can only hope that they'll meet the standards of your inspection."

"Cameron, I'm sorry."

"What time on Saturday?"

"I'm not sure, but it will be for dinner. My guess is the invites will say seven, seven-thirty."

"Invites?"

"Oh, yes," Rand chuckled. "With the time constraints, I'm sure Florence will arrange for a courier to hand deliver formal invitations to everyone."

Daisy's insides wound on themselves like twine on a spool. She realized her eyes hurt and felt dry. During the entire conversation she had forgotten to blink.

"Do you think your Adam would agree to dress a bit more formally for the occasion? Perhaps lose some of the hardware?"

"Yes," she conceded. "I think he'll be amenable to looking more dressed up for the party."

"Thank you. See how nice it is when we're not working against each other?"

"Anything I go along with is simply to comply with our agreement. And, don't forget it."

He chuckled into the phone again. "Point taken. However, I've held you against me and I think we'd both agree it works."

"I have work to do."

"What time shall I pick you up later?"

"Later?"

"Yes, darling. We're so mad about each other we can't stand to spend an evening apart."

"Try me."

"Seven it is," Rand said. He laughed. "We'll do dinner at my club."

159

****

By early afternoon, Daisy's back ached. She stood from her desk and stretched herself like a cat rising from a nap—only she hadn't been napping. Daisy's number-crunching had allowed only debits and credits into her thoughts. Now, with her arms up over her head, eyes closed, she reached to loosen the knotting muscles in her neck and upper back.

"I thought you could use this about now," Candy said.

Daisy opened her eyes with a start, and then smiled at her friend holding a large ice-filled glass of lemonade. "Jeez, Candy. You should wear a bell."

"I'm glad I opted for this rather than iced tea. Looks as if you've had enough caffeine."

Daisy ignored the reference to jitteriness and gratefully accepted the chilled glass, taking a big sip of the tangy refreshment.

"Good, huh? Ima just made it."

"Yep. Good stuff."

"How's it going?" Candy asked, plopping herself into the chair. "My feet are howling already."

Daisy sat at her desk, folded her arms on the surface in front of her, and waited. She knew better than to believe this was simply a drink delivery. Candy was here on a mission. She raised her eyebrows and looked at her friend.

"Ima says you're off the waitress schedule."

Daisy nodded, her mouth automatically turning into a rueful smile. So this was it. She waited for Candy to say the rest of what was on her mind.

"To recap, let's see...first, you're Cameron, and now you're too good to wait tables. Have I got that right?"

"No, Candy. You haven't. Give me a break, okay?"

"I swear, Daisy or Cameron or whoever you are, if I didn't see the way you and your gazillionaire act

160

together I'd bet you had lost your ever-loving mind. I'm still wondering if you're off your rocker. I'm hoping this wacko behavior is because you're gonzo in love."

Daisy laughed out loud, at the absurdity of her friend's words and erroneous observation. The kiss Candy and everyone else had witnessed suddenly flashed through Daisy's head. The reaction of her senses was alive again. She was getting so good at lying that even her nerve endings were falling for it now.

"Don't get carried away, Candy, please. Rand and I are two adults with good heads on our shoulders. We're not teenagers that don't know what they're doing."

"Well maybe you better tell that to your hormones. It looks as if they forgot to read the calendar."

"Okay, I'll speak with them. Right now I've got to get back to work."

Daisy leaned forward and locked her gaze with Candy's. "Listen, I'm not waitressing on Saturdays because I have too much to do right now. That's all.

It's not that I think I'm too good to wait tables. I know you've got to be plenty smart to do the job. Hell, remember how long it took me to learn the menu items? You kept quizzing me until I got it down."

"I remember," Candy said, smiling. "And, I'm sorry if I sounded, you know, harsh."

"No offense taken. I realize how out-of-the-blue this all is."

"What kind of things are you so busy with these days? Wedding plans already?"

"Gracious no, not yet. But, Rand's uncle is planning a small engagement party for us. It's next Saturday evening...but I'm not sure what time yet. Of course, you and Bruno are invited."

"Whoo-hoo!" Candy clapped her hands and jiggled in her seat. "Now this'll be something. This shindig is going to be at the Press mansion?"

"Apparently. They're still working on the details."

"Oh, baby, I've got appointments to make. Hair, nails, toes. Finally, another occasion for that red dress of mine. I'll have to get Bruno's suit out of mothballs!"

Daisy swallowed hard. Dear God, this little soirée might just kill her.

Chapter Twenty-One

Before Rand arrived for their dinner date at his club, Daisy knocked on Adam's closed bedroom door. She found it somewhat annoying that he had taken to closing her out this way. Unless he was sleeping or getting dressed, Adam's door was always open.

"Come in," he called.

Adam sat cross-legged on his bed, a textbook open in front of him, and his binder on his lap. She let her eyes scan the walls in his room, lined with Adam's artwork. The one above his headboard was the charcoal drawing he had made of his grandmother's hand, Daisy's mom. Pinched between her textured, lined fingers she held one perfect daisy.

"Lots of work?" she asked, sitting gently at the corner of the bed, easing down onto the mattress so as not to disturb his arrangement. Above his dresser, where typically a mirror would go she saw a sketch of a young woman depicted from behind, looking out over a vine-covered wall. She was reminded again of his talent, and of her mission.

"Not too much," Adam shrugged. "What's up?"

"Rand should be here in a little while and I just wanted to touch base with you. I made chicken noodle casserole. It's in the oven now. Make sure you take it out in half an hour."

Adam nodded. "Okay. Thanks."

"Adam, honey, Rand's Uncle William is hosting a small dinner party next Saturday night. It's kind of an engagement party, but really it's just a chance for Rand's close family and friends to meet mine."

163

"Okay."

"Should we go shopping for you? Do you, uh, have a sports jacket that fits you?"

"Sports jacket?" Adam said, as though she'd asked him to wear a dress. "Seriously? A jacket?"

She felt her chest constrict. Her nerves were on edge and it felt as if she was attempting to navigate a tightrope, one tentative inch at a time. How was she going to bring up his jewelry, his "hardware" as Rand had so delicately put it?

"It's no big deal, Adam. After all, you're going to need some nice clothes eventually. You know, for when you exhibit your work."

"Mom, first of all, it'll be a long time before that happens, and secondly, I'm really not the suit type."

"Not a suit, Adam. A sports jacket and slacks. Khakis are fine, I'm sure."

"Do you hear yourself, Mom? You sound like you're trying to meet a dress code or something. Want me to cut my hair off, too? Get a crew cut? Is that what this is about? You think this guy's family is going to freak when they see how I look? Is that it?"

Adam pushed the binder from his lap, and flipped his textbook closed. Daisy inched closer to him. "That's not it at all."

"It's not. Okay, what then?"

"It's just that this is kind of a more formal event, that's all. Come on. Don't read more into this than it is. Just for this occasion I'd like you to dress up."

She watched Adam's chest expand and contract as he took a deep breath and let it out in a dejected sounding whoosh. "This is all too much too soon."

"I agree, it's a lot. I'm still reeling from it all, too. Believe me."

He met her gaze and shook his head. "A jacket?"

She knew by his tone that he had acquiesced. She loved this kid. "Do you know how handsome you'll look in a jacket?" She offered him a small grin. Her heart was swollen with affection.

"I'm drawing the line at a tie. No tie."

"Okay. No tie," she said. Suddenly she wondered how Adam would take the truth when he eventually learned it. The fear that crept into her bloodstream, she realized now, was that there might be no undoing this wrong even after she 'fessed up. Perhaps there would be no waking up from the nightmare she had created by signing that agreement.

The doorbell rang and Daisy felt a jolt as though the buzzer were connected to her brain. She stood, ready to leave. "Thank you, Adam. Don't forget to turn off the oven after the casserole is done."

She went to answer the door and Adam had the good manners to come out from his room to greet their guest. The two men shook hands and Daisy marveled at how easily Rand went through the motions. Anyone would think he was genuinely happy to see her son. While they chatted, Daisy retrieved her purse and jacket. When she returned, the two of them were chuckling softly.

"Chicken noodle casserole?" Rand asked with staged indignation.

Daisy looked to Adam who shrugged at her in return. "It's one of his favorites."

"Darling, you've got to promise to make it again soon. I absolutely love chicken noodle casserole."

She smiled in response, wondering if he were mocking the dish or if he was that good at faking it. Either way she could not picture the man dining on a chicken meal made with egg noodles and cream of mushroom soup.

"Sure," she played along. "Next time."

They said good night to Adam and were soon headed toward the River Edge Golf and Country Club in nearby Bernard's Village.

The scenic ride through Hanover Heights with the houses and postage stamp-sized lawns reminded Daisy of a well-played monopoly game. Closer to Bernard's Village the lawns grew as did the houses on them.

They turned into the gated entrance to the club. The long paved roadway was bordered by well-manicured shrubbery and abundantly mulched beds of flowering plants, their late blooms still vibrant and welcoming.

The building itself sprawled wide with wings that branched out like arms from the tall two-story pillared center of the facility entrance.

Inside the wainscoted anteroom, a coat-check clerk greeted Rand by name. He, in turn, introduced Daisy to the young woman as his fiancée, Cameron.

"Hello, Cameron," she chirped. "I'm Angela. Everyone's buzzing about you two. I'm sure all eyes will be on you in there." She motioned toward the dining room down the wide corridor.

Daisy's heart fell to the bottom of her stomach with a thud. She forced a smile. "Good to meet you, Angela."

"Enjoy your dinner!"

Their table was nestled near the tall windows that overlooked the golf course. Throughout their courses, club members stopped by the table to greet them—like royalty. Royal frauds, maybe. Through the Waldorf salad, shrimp cocktail, crab stuffed tilapia, and a half bottle of chardonnay, Daisy did her best to play her part. She smiled and offered her hand, made as if she was amused at jokes she barely heard, and said "thank you" to more "congratulations" than she could count. Thankfully, Rand responded with an unquestioned vagueness to anyone's inquiry about the date of their "big day."

The dining room was nearly empty by the time Rand and Daisy had coffee. The bartender sent over after-dinner cordials and Daisy, against her better judgment, sipped the dark, rich amaretto, enjoying its soothing warmth.

"I think that might be the last of them," Rand said. He tapped his glass lightly against hers. "You did a great job tonight, by the way. You're a natural."

"I don't consider that a compliment."

"Hey, come on," Rand's voice was mellow, soft. "Lighten up. We managed to convince all these people that have known me forever that I've decided at long last to take the plunge. I owe that to your believability. You're smart and sophisticated and"— he shrugged with a tuck to his chin, a gesture Daisy and her shot of amaretto found appealing—"perfect."

Her face flushed and she put down her tiny glass. There was nothing more than a hint of the dark liquid lingering at the bottom. She sipped from her water glass, hoping to flush away the appeal of Rand's mouth with the half smile that almost looked sincere.

Daisy watched his profile as he looked outside the window to the illuminated pond fountain. His was a classically handsome face. She could not deny that truth. She downed more lemon water.

He was the first to break the blanketing silence. "Did you enjoy the tilapia?"

"Yes," she said too eagerly, relief for the refocus of her thoughts. "We're big seafood fans, Adam and I. He likes to fish."

"I used to fish," Rand said. He appeared surprised by his statement. "A long time ago."

"How long?"

Rand chuckled softly. "When my dad was still alive." He looked at her long. "A lifetime ago."

"Good memories?"

"Yes. My parents were rather, how should I say it? Earthy." Rand said. He laughed. "Don't look so

167

shocked, darling."

Calling her by that endearment shot through her like an arrow. She would never get used to it, not coming from his lips. "I'm sorry. But, I can't picture you in rubber waders carrying a big net."

"I know," he said. He sounded jovial now. His look was absent the hint of emotion she saw flash through them a moment ago. "But, that was what it was like.

"My father was nothing like his brother, William. He and Mom were like hippies. My mother made macramé plant holders for our house and did pottery."

"Really?" Daisy was astonished and couldn't hide it thanks to her last beverage. "You're joking."

"Seriously. Oh, you should have seen Florence when she'd walk into our living room and see these beaded ropey things holding up my mother's ferns and the spider plants dangling in front of the windows." Now he laughed out loud. "They looked great with the damask draperies."

Daisy laughed, too. She liked the easy curve of Rand's mouth, the gleam in his eyes when he told the story. His countenance, his tone, his eyes—all of it beamed with truth. Daisy sipped more water. His lies were easier to deal with tonight. She continued to listen as he elaborated on another tale.

"One Christmas my mother used one of her glazed vases as the centerpiece of the holiday dinner table. Uncle William had turned his nose up to it. When he opened his gift, wasn't he surprised to see my mother had made one just like it for him? Uncle was appalled."

"That had to have been awkward," Daisy said, unable to hold back a smile.

"He twisted around like a top when he opened the box, trying to act gracious. We all knew he hated the thing."

"Must have been quite the scene."

"The best part?" Rand gazed beyond her as though seeing a movie screen in the distance that projected his memories. "My parents and I—after Uncle went home with his homemade clay vase— well, we sat in our big fancy kitchen eating ice cream out of these odd-shaped bowls my mother made, and we laughed like hell."

Daisy did her best to dash the endearing image that popped into her mind. "Do you have any of her work?"

Rand sobered, his smile fell. "Just a couple of things. Everything was, well, *disposed of* after they died."

Daisy felt her heart clench as though a fist was squeezing it. She wanted to say something. She felt the urge to reach over and cover his hand with hers, but she did not. Instead she asked where the restrooms were located.

In the ladies lounge, Daisy ran a cool damp towel over her brow. She implored herself to get a grip. She liked it better when J. Randolph Press was his typical pompous-ass self. It was easier.

But right now she could only picture him as a young boy sitting around a kitchen table late at night eating ice cream with his parents. Life had changed dramatically for him. That was for sure. Who would he have been if the tragic accident hadn't happened? What kind of man?

Daisy reapplied her lipstick, pressing her lips together to spread the color over them. She kissed the paper towel in her hand and tossed it into the trash. There was no sense in asking questions that had no answer.

Rand had taken care of the check and retrieved her jacket from the coat check. He stood waiting in the vestibule area of the club when she emerged from the ladies room.

"We're all set, darling," he said. Daisy noticed that Angela was still in place although her rack was now empty save for the row of wire hangers.

Daisy slipped her arms into her jacket that Rand held up for her. They bid goodbye to the lingering staff members. The valet retrieved Rand's Jaguar, and in no time they were belted in and retreating from their evening.

Daisy felt mostly relief, although her head throbbed mildly from the mix of liquors. She knew better than to combine a sugary after-dinner cordial with a couple of glasses of wine. Tomorrow morning would definitely include a dull headache.

"We haven't had the chance to discuss the engagement party. Florence is on the details like a mad woman. She's asked me, twice already, for your guest list so that she can have the invitations hand delivered."

Daisy let out a long sigh. "I hope I've got it in me to pull that off, Rand."

"It'll go well, you'll see. Just be yourself."

"Myself? And who might that be? Cameron? Well, I don't know how to be Cameron Day. Considering I never even met her until last week."

Rand reached over and covered her hand with his. His fingers were warm in spite of the chill in the air. She looked at him with wide eyes and gently pulled her hand away from his. "I'm worried about it and not just for myself. My friends and coworkers are good, honest, kind people. If anything were to make them feel unworthy or unaccepted by your uncle's scrutiny I'd be mortified. They don't deserve that. They were not part of our bargain, Rand, nor was Adam."

Rand watched the road, dimly lit by wrought iron street lamps, his car expertly hugging the curves of the countryside. He did not take his eyes from his task, but she watched the curve of his mouth force the skin of his cheek to define a crevice.

"We have no choice at this point but to hope for the best, Cameron. I mean, let's just hope that the evening goes well enough to satisfy everyone."

"My biggest worry is Adam. He doesn't deserve to be duped this way. He's so smart, I'm worried that he's going to figure out this is all a hoax. He'll be crushed, Rand. I'm serious.

"If I had the chance to go back to when you first proposed this preposterous idea I would have told you to find someone else for the job. But now, I have no choice but to see it through, if I'm to have any chance whatsoever of resuming my life as it was. It's making my head spin."

What was really making her head spin was the combination of drinks in her system. She felt the swerves of the road as he negotiated them. Each one sent her equilibrium into orbit. Closing her eyes didn't help, but rather enhanced the feeling of whipping around in a carnival ride.

"You okay?" He asked, stealing a glance at her.

"I think I drank too much, or at least I shouldn't have had the amaretto. It might have put me over the top."

"Uh-oh. You're not going to get sick are you?"

"Not unless you talk about it some more."

"Okay, then let's change the subject. Tell me more about Adam's father."

"The sperm donor? Nothing to tell."

Daisy rested her head back on the leather seat. The headrest hit her in an uncomfortable place nearly jabbing her neck. It occurred to her that Rand's last dalliance was probably shorter than she and the seat settings had been arranged for her.

God only knew how many women had sat in that very seat. Daisy's head continued to spin. Now, the whirling was enhanced with pictures as though someone had put on a movie at high speed. The images blurred together in her mind but she knew what they were.

She saw David Babbage staring at her in disbelief when she told him she was pregnant. His big brown eyes had been absent of the empathy she thought she'd be seeing in them. He sat opposite her at a small dining table in the student cafeteria at Farleigh Dickinson University.

His mouth had turned up into a false grin, a harsh curve of lips. She remembered her own shock and the way her stomach tumbled with dread. Her stomach tumbled now.

"Well, it's despicable that he'd let you assume the whole financial burden of a child."

Daisy snorted. Her hand flew up to cover her mouth too late to stifle the sound. "His parents tried to pay me off to disappear."

She kept her eyes on the road ahead of them willing the car to stay steady. Any turn, even a slight one, gave her a twinge. Another image snapped on in her fuzzy brain. Mr. and Mrs. Babbage's eyes were on her like prey, all but boring through her. She saw the check in David's father's hand, waving it at her like a teasing tongue. "Take me," it said. "Take this and leave us alone." She felt the bitterness in her throat and the urge to wretch squeezed her stomach like a vice.

Thankfully, the car stopped and she saw they were in her complex's parking lot. She bolted from the car and stood taking deep breaths of the night air. Slowly her stomach settled. She saw that Rand was there holding a bottle of water in front of her face.

"Take a sip," he said.

She accepted the bottle and took a tentative taste. It went down easily and stayed put. She drank again, suddenly thirsty.

"Okay now?" He touched her back gently.

She looked at him. His eyes were kind, his voice sweet. *Stop it. Please be awful. It's better when you're rotten.*

"Listen, I shouldn't have brought up the ordeal with Adam's father. I think that may have added to your upset. I, uh, I apologize."

"Ha," Daisy laughed. "Are you kidding? It's as though you wrote the guy's script. I read all that stuff about you on page six. I know about the women you've had to pay off."

"Cameron, I..."

He stepped closer and when she looked up into his eyes she saw compassion. How did he manage such realistic expressions? If he ever lost his fortune, he could always pursue the stage.

Daisy closed her eyes, blocking out the vision of his face. She opened them when she felt a fingertip on her chin.

"For what it's worth, Cameron, I think he was a fool."

"He was a fraud. I detest fakes," she said softly, a near whisper. "I'm not a fake."

"That's true. For the record, you're the most genuine woman I've talked to in nearly twenty-eight years."

In spite of the fact that she couldn't breathe, Daisy could still do the math. The man referred to the time when he still had his mother. Suddenly, she was clearheaded enough to do what she had always done before in her life. She bid Rand a good night and walked away.

Chapter Twenty-Two

Rand sat on his balcony facing the line of buildings that was the cityscape. Many of them were still dotted with golden light emitting from their windows. It appeared that he was not the only one awake at this late hour.

He repositioned himself on the cold, wrought iron chair. Chilled to the bone, he couldn't help but wonder if the culprit was not the chair, but rather the effect that Cameron had had on him tonight.

Rand let out a long sigh. He was mad at himself. Why had this little waitress managed to conjure memories in him? He didn't like it, didn't like thinking backward. There was no sense in it, no purpose.

What mattered most was the future. And that future would be just as he needed it to be, due to this unlikely alliance with this pretty woman. Succumbing to any feelings Cameron triggered was counterproductive. He knew it down to his very core.

So then why, in spite of the breezy evening air that rushed at him, could he still smell her? He closed his eyes, and gluttonously pulled a deep breath of the night into his lungs. Cameron's scent, a distinct combination of floral and musk, filled his senses by sheer memory.

He envisioned her eyes, filled with emotion as she told him about her ordeal with the *sperm donor,* as she'd referred to Adam's father. She was a proud woman that stood for something, and yet, her vulnerability had been apparent tonight. Maybe it was caused by the amaretto chaser, but whatever, she had shown him that side of herself.

That was the danger that lurked now in Rand's brain, that picture in his head of Cameron's pretty mouth and the way she pulled her lips into themselves when she paused in her revelations. Her honesty unnerved him and he needed to brace against the total effect of her.

He had to concentrate on what he needed to achieve with this partnership. He had to put it into the forefront of his head that Cameron was not in his league. In the darkness that surrounded him, he realized that the truth was that he was the one that fell short of Cameron's league.

****

The next day Daisy received a call from Florence. She had been expecting a return call from one of the café's vendors, so when she heard the older woman's familiar warm resonance, her hand gripped the receiver tightly. She closed her eyes.

"Florence, hello." She wondered if her cheeriness sounded believable.

Daisy had been wrong last night. She did not wake with a headache from the amaretto. What did greet her in the morning's light was a feeling of dread.

She relived the conversation she had shared with Rand. It didn't help to admonish herself for lowering her defenses, yet now it felt like lead in her belly.

"I apologize for disturbing you at your place of business, dear," Florence said. "It's just that I'm hoping to have the invitations printed later today and I do need your guest list."

"Yes," Daisy said. She rustled through the pages of a steno pad she kept near her phone. Guilt swirled within her as she had hastily jotted down the names and addresses of her immediate friends earlier this morning. "I have it here. I was planning to email it to you this morning."

"Lovely." Florence spoke with exuberance, as though this party was something Daisy wanted, too. "As soon as you can, dear. I hate to pressure you but, as you know, time is precious."

Daisy knew the woman referred to Uncle William's precarious health, but also remembered that the idea of this blasted party was his. According to Rand, its whole purpose was to expose some clue that their engagement was a sham.

"I'll get it to you immediately."

"Thank you. Shall I consult with you on the menu or would you like it to be a surprise?"

The last thing Daisy wanted to do was select food items for this dinner party. She wanted to think about it as little as possible. "Surprise us," she said.

"I shall, then." The older woman's tone was happy and clearly up for the challenge.

"I look forward to it," Daisy lied.

"One more thing, Cameron."

"Yes?"

"William would like for you to join him for lunch. Are you free today?"

"I, uh, I don't normally take a lunch hour, Florence," Daisy said. Her lungs locked.

"Might you, just this once? William is anxious for you two to get better acquainted. And, as I said, there isn't much time to plan these things."

Daisy knew a corner when she had been painted into one. "How's one o'clock?"

"Lovely!"

****

When she placed the receiver back into its cradle, Daisy stared down at it as if it was a rabid animal that had just bitten her in the butt.

She looked down at her outfit, casual black jeans and a sweater that had seen better days. There was no way she could show up at the Press estate looking this way. She needed time to get home, change, and do something with her unruly hair that she had shoved up into a clip.

She also needed to run her midday departure by Pete and Ima. They would most likely not be happy considering the billing was due.

"I won't be too long, Ima. I've got to get back and work on the accounts due."

"Go on then." Ima shooed Daisy out of the kitchen where she and Pete were chopping vegetables at a butcher block counter. She turned to her husband. "Tell her it's fine, Peter."

Pete gave his knife a wave in the air. "You better get going if you want to make yourself gorgeous first. Have you seen that hair of yours today?" He went back to his slicing and dicing.

"Don't tease her, Peter," Ima scolded.

"Who's teasing? I'm jealous. I just wish I *had* hair."

"Okay, you two. I'll see you when I get back." Daisy exited the café but not without first noticing the questioning look on Candy's face.

When she got back to her condo, Daisy hurried through the hallway, fished a more presentable outfit from her closet, laid it on her bed, and dashed off to the bathroom to jump into the shower.

As soon as she opened the bathroom's door, the steam hit her in the face like an assault. This was not nearly as stunning as the foggy sight of two wet, cringing bodies wrapped in her matching green velour bath towels.

The steam dissipated through the open doorway, moving fast as if it knew a storm was about to erupt. Daisy focused on the image of her wide-eyed son and the petite teenage girl whose long, dripping hair was plastered to her head. A nose ring was pinched into one of her nostrils.

"Mom!"

"Get dressed," she said through clenched teeth. She turned to Adam's wet, semi-naked friend who now had pulled the extra long bath sheet up so high it covered her mouth. "You, too."

Daisy slammed the door behind her, strode to her room and kicked that door closed too. Her hands shook. She sat on the bed not caring what her backside would do to the freshly pressed trousers she had placed there.

Adam and his...his...what...? Who was this girl? Daisy had the intimate knowledge that she had a Texas-shaped birth mark on her shoulder, but didn't even know her name. She stifled the urge to scream.

Her cell phone rang and she jumped at the sound. She dashed to retrieve the purse that she'd left on the kitchen counter. She tiptoed, like a cat burglar in her own house, past Adam's closed bedroom door. "Hello?" She said sotto voce. She made her way back to her room.

"Cameron. Hello. I just got off the phone with Florence. She tells me you and Uncle have a lunch date today."

"Rand," she said, her brain still scrambled. She plopped onto the bed. "I was going to call you after I got ready, but I might have to cancel."

"Not a good idea, darling."

"I just don't think I can go."

"You sound upset. Are you that nervous about this?"

"No. Yes. I mean, yes, but..."

"Okay, first of all. I'm glad that you were going to call me. We need to keep each other abreast of anything that has to do with Uncle because, obviously, that affects our plan. Don't be too concerned, but keep on your guard. This is going to be more than tea sandwiches, Cameron. I'm sure you know that. But, please don't cancel. Uncle will be suspicious."

She let out a deep breath. "Rand, it's not that. I have, um, a situation I need to deal with." She heard a door open down the hallway, heard whispering. "It's, uh, regarding Adam."

"Is he all right?"

"Oh, he's as fine as any eighteen-year-old boy would be when his mother comes home unexpectedly in the middle of the day and finds him enjoying a shower with a female friend."

The sound of Rand's laughter infuriated her. It figured that someone with his reputation would find this predicament amusing. There was nothing funny about this—not to her, anyway.

Not only was this a violation of Adam's grounding. He obviously was skipping a part of his school day, and he had been...well, at the very least, enjoying a shower for two. Everything about it angered her, including the continued chuckling on the other end of her line.

"Cameron, he's a red-blooded young man. You can't condemn him for that."

"That's not the point. He's supposed to be in school. Adam has never, I mean *never*, skipped school. He's the kid that goes to class even when he's sick."

She tugged the clip from her hair and shoved her fingers into the curly mass. "I can't deal with this, and then get ready and go make nice with your uncle. I can't."

"Aren't you making too much of the situation? He didn't murder somebody. He took a shower. He's hygienically correct."

"Only someone like you would see this as funny, or even admirable.

"He's also been grounded because of the car accident. I'm still paying for a rental car. My insurance agent says my premiums will be jacked up."

Daisy heard her voice rising higher as if helium had found its way into her voice box. "And, I think he might be smoking, too. I keep smelling smoke on his clothes—that is when he's not locking himself in his room."

"Tobacco?"

"What?"

"Do you think he's smoking tobacco?"

"God, I don't know. What I do know is that Adam's very different. This behavior is unlike him. He's acting out, and I think it's because of this stupid arrangement we made."

"You might want to lower your voice, darling, so he doesn't hear you refer to our undying devotion as a 'stupid arrangement.'"

"You are absolutely no help, not that I thought you would be."

"If the kid's grounded and he's skipping class to frolic with his girlfriend, then, sure he's in trouble. But, don't make it out to be more than it is, Cameron. He's growing up. He's going off to college in a few months, remember? I don't know what you did in college, but..."

"Spare me your reminiscing, Rand. I get what you're trying to say. But, I'm just, I don't know, *rattled* by the blatant disrespect."

"Tell him that," Rand said. "You've told me how mature and level-headed Adam is. Well, talk to him like you would any other adult that's disrespected you."

Daisy sat silent for a long moment. Rand's advice was unexpectedly sound. She found herself chuckling into the phone now.

"What's funny?" he asked.

"I'm taking advice on how to deal with my son's promiscuity from the biggest playboy on the eastern seaboard. That, sir, is not funny. That's hilarious."

"Okay, darling, keep laughing. Handle the

young man, and then go dazzle our benefactor. I'll call you later to see how you made out."

She groaned into the phone. "Fine. 'Bye."

****

Adam and the girl—dressed now in ratty jeans and a black tee-shirt with a ghoulish-looking face emblazoned on it—sat on the couch next to each other, so close their thighs were pressed together. Adam's arm was slung over the back cushions. The girl, small compared to his stature, appeared to be trying to disappear. Her hair was still damp and hanging around her head like twigs.

"Mom, I—"

"Wait," Daisy said. She sat on the ottoman opposite the sofa. She wanted to be close enough to them so they wouldn't miss a single syllable that she uttered. She still wasn't sure what would be coming out of her mouth. "You don't get to talk first."

Adam clamped his mouth shut. Daisy noticed the girl tuck herself closer into his side, her head nearly in his armpit.

"Who are you?" Daisy directed her.

"Elizabeth."

Daisy looked at Adam. Bits of the conversation they had the morning after the car accident now wafted through her head. "How did you get here, Elizabeth?"

"We walked." Her voice was low. She sounded like a much younger girl, one who'd be attired in smocked dresses with puffy sleeves rather than the faded, ripped getup she wore.

"From school?"

"Yes, Mom," Adam spoke up. "We decided to skip lunch and come here."

"To bathe?"

Elizabeth's mouth turned into a smirk. Daisy shot her a menacing look that dashed it right from her lips.

181

"I'm going to drive both of you back to school. It's not one o'clock, yet. So, there's plenty of the afternoon schedule left."

"Okay," Elizabeth said. She moved as though about to bolt from the sofa.

"But, when we get there, all three of us are going to the office."

"What?" the two freshly-cleaned teenagers said in unison.

"Whatever penalty the school doles out for skipping class is what you owe them. And..." she turned to focus on Adam. "You and I will discuss what price your actions will cost you when I get home from work. In the meantime, I need to get ready for an appointment. Stay put."

Daisy turned to head to her room, then stopped. She looked back at the two, sitting like recently washed statues on the couch. "Did you have any lunch, by the way?"

"No."

"While I'm getting ready, go make a sandwich."

"Thank you, Mrs. Cameron," Elizabeth offered meekly.

Daisy gave her a narrow-eyed look, which she then fixed on Adam. She turned and walked to her room, closing the door behind her.

****

The teenagers sat silently in the backseat of the rental car. Elizabeth was still nibbling on a piece of her peanut butter and jelly sandwich.

After parking the car, they strode to the office and approached the secretary who merely stared up at them with a look of *now what* on her tired-looking face. Daisy turned to Adam. "The floor is yours," she said. She waved her hand. "You can do your own talking."

Adam explained to the woman, a Mrs. Strellack, that he and Elizabeth had left campus for lunch without permission, and now they were late for their sixth period classes. She reached for her pad of passes and began to write in the spaces. Without looking up, she asked, "Are you both in the same class?"

"No," they chorused.

Mrs. Strellack blew air from her mouth and pulled a second pass from her pad. "Okay, we'll start with you." She pointed her pen at Elizabeth. "Elizabeth Lucent, right?"

Daisy felt her mouth pull into a smirk. It seemed as though the shower girl was a familiar face at the Vice Principal's office.

"Mrs. Strellack," Daisy interrupted. "Is Mr. Bruder going to speak with them? I mean, they're not just going to be given passes to class are they?"

The two kids looked at her as though she'd thrown them under a bus. This satisfied the hell out of Daisy. The secretary looked perplexed. "I assumed because you escorted them, Mrs. Cameron, that you were providing an excuse for their lateness."

"Not at all. I'm just delivering them to you."

"Have a seat, then." The words were now a sing-song, and a far cry from the drone of her previous speech.

Adam and Elizabeth moved like zombies and plunked themselves onto two bright blue plastic chairs.

"Will Mr. Bruder need to speak with me, also?" Daisy asked. "I'm already late to an appointment."

"Just briefly," she said. Mr. Bruder appeared from his office. "Then he'll handle the little darlings."

The secretary explained the situation and introduced him to Daisy. He shook her hand.

"Thank you for waiting," he said. He asked Mrs. Strelleck to keep an eye on his *guests* and escorted Daisy into his office, where they could speak more freely.

"Mrs. Cameron, is there anything you need to add to this story? Anything the school can assist with?"

"This is so unlike Adam. Has he ever even been to your office?"

Mr. Bruder offered a little smile. "Not for anything remarkable, I assure you. I'll assign them detentions. Have you alerted the girl's mother?"

"No."

"We'll take care of that. And, thank you for bringing them back to school. Could be early senioritis. What are Adam's plans after graduation? Is he going to college?"

"Yes," she was quick to respond. "Of course. He's a brilliant artist, but I'm sure you're aware of that."

"No, I didn't know. What kind of art does he enjoy?"

"Sketching mostly."

He looked deep in thought. "Mrs. Cameron, let me ask you something," he said finally. "Has Adam demonstrated any new behaviors lately? Ones that might send up a red flag?"

She felt herself stiffen. "Nothing out of the realm of typical teen behavior, I guess," she said. "What do you mean?"

"How long has his appearance been so, um, radical?"

"He's artistic. That's how he expresses himself."

"It can indicate a need for, um, concern," he said.

She clenched her jaw, held his gaze. "Artistic," she said. Her emphatic tone was absent of the agitation that threatened in her throat.

"Our school has been plagued recently by graffiti," he continued.

"And?" A flush climbed across her cheeks.

The man shrugged his droopy shoulders. "It's

rather impressive work, the graffiti. I'd say it was, *artistic*."

"Sir, I assure you Adam is not responsible. And, I disagree with your inference that the way he looks might indicate a problem. It would certainly not implicate him in defacing property."

"We're on the same team, Mrs. Cameron," he said in a tone that she assumed was meant to sound reassuring. To her ear, it seemed condescending.

"Mr. Bruder, I support whatever penalty the school has for skipping class. I'm still deciding what price I'll have him pay for breaking our rules. This is new for us. But trust me, I'll come up with something."

He nodded. "Good."

"But, please understand, I also support my son. And, I will not have you stereotype him. That's prejudice, Mr. Bruder. Have a good day."

****

Driving to the Press estate, Daisy had a mixture of emotions—a swirling of what transpired with the kids, with Mr. Bruder, and her conversation with Rand. How odd was it that his words to her had given her some sort of empowerment to deal with what she had viewed as a hand-trembling crisis?

As she watched the roadway ahead of her, the scene still impressed her with its grandeur. She felt her nerves twitching with anticipation, but she felt more equipped to handle this uncle of Rand's.

Florence seemed ready for her, dressed today in a smart skirt and blouse, with pearls at her neck. "Cameron, dear," she said. Her quick embrace surprised Daisy.

"I'm sorry for being late. I had an unavoidable situation to deal with."

"Oh, please," Florence waved her hand. "I understand. Thank you for calling ahead, however. William is just delighted you were able to join him today."

"It was so nice to be invited," Daisy said. The words felt like cardboard in her mouth. She had to keep in mind Rand's warning that this was more than a social visit. This was an elderly piranha trying to close in on his victim.

She took a deep breath and forced a grin, taking a step toward the staircase. She was at least pretty sure she wouldn't find the old guy wrapped in a bath towel.

"William's waiting for you in the breakfast room."

"Oh, I just assumed…"

"He's feeling chipper enough today to come downstairs. William hasn't dined outside his room in weeks, so this is a real treat for him."

"How nice."

The breakfast room's rear wall was a bank of floor-to-ceiling windows that faced the back lawn. William sat with his back to the view, a bed pillow stuffed behind him. He was not in pajamas, but rather wore a pale blue sweater vest and white shirt. He looked healthier today. Maybe it was the brightness of the room or the color of his vest, but he looked amazingly well and vital—an alert piranha.

The glass-topped table was set for two. Daisy was surprised that Florence would not be joining them as she seemed more like part of the family, rather than an employee.

"There she is!" he bellowed in a gravelly tone. "Don't you look lovely today, Cameron."

"Thank you, sir," she said. Intimidation poured over her as if an egg had been cracked on her head.

"'Sir' will never do. That's too stuffy. Surely you can call me Uncle William, can't you? After all, soon you and my nephew will be man and wife and we will then technically be relatives, won't we?"

"Yes, sir," she said. She winced. "I mean…sure.

That's true."

"Iced Tea, Cameron? Hot tea?" Florence asked.

"Hot tea, please." The last thing she needed was something to help chill her bones.

"A girl after my own heart," William said. He lifted his teacup and slowly guided it to his mouth. His hand shook with a Parkinson-like tremor and the cup clattered when he replaced it on its saucer.

Florence had disappeared, leaving the two of them alone in the room. The high ceiling and glass wall made everything echo. Even the way William cleared his throat reverberated with a sound like a car stuck in snow. Daisy felt her fingers coiling around the linen napkin in her lap.

"So, how are you on this fine day?" he asked, his mouth a broad, moist smile, his eyes focused on her.

"I'm wonderful, and I can see you are feeling well." She refused to call him Uncle William, so she decided not to call him anything.

"This is one of my better days. When a man has a beautiful woman meeting him for lunch it can be an elixir. So, thank you for joining me, my dear."

"I'm happy to."

Florence, accompanied by a younger female helper, served their lunch. The chicken soup with chunky vegetables and noodles was another of Florence's homemade concoctions, according to William.

Daisy watched Florence ceremoniously tuck a starchy napkin into the collar of William's shirt where it hung down in front of him like a large bib. "Really, woman, must you do this?" he grumbled.

Daisy could tell he was not seriously angry. Not by the way he smiled up at Florence, and the way her eyes danced with affection. Daisy felt as though theirs was a partnership that went beyond obvious appearances.

While she and William ladled soup into

themselves and nibbled on fresh rolls, he quizzed her about her relationship with Rand—how they met, their engagement, inquisitions she surmised were meant to trip her up in some way. Luckily, she knew their concocted story by heart. To her own ears she even sounded believable when she told him it was a case of love at first sight.

"Cameron, I thought you told me that at first you thought Randolph was, how did you put it? Yes, a *pompous ass.*" He chuckled, then coughed, the sound muffled by the napkin he pressed to his mouth.

Daisy felt her breath catch in her throat. William might be an old man on—as they say—his last leg, but his memory was better than hers. She had forgotten about her earlier quip.

"Well, sure, that goes without saying," Daisy said. "I mean, you can imagine. He comes into my place of business and I watch him eye the place with that regal disdain of his."

William guffawed, then coughed some more. "Priceless."

"Oh, he was priceless, all right," she continued, feeling relief at having made the man laugh.

"Yes." He sobered, and then patted in place the napkin that hung around his neck. "But, nothing's really priceless, wouldn't you say, Cameron? I mean, everything does have its price."

William's eyes danced as he held her gaze. The double meaning of his words pelted her like sand in a windstorm. He was mocking her. "Not necessarily, sir."

"There goes that word again, Cameron. Please, humor an old man. Call me Uncle."

In her life Daisy had been asked to say uncle before. There were the times in grade school when a playmate would hold her down and wouldn't stop tickling her until she said the word. William's request felt akin to one of those childish bids for control. She hated it then and hated it now. She smiled at the old man, but did not use the moniker he implored.

The kitchen helper removed their lunch plates, and Florence brought in dessert. She set a place for herself at the table. Apparently, it was acceptable for the woman to join them for this part of their meal. Daisy felt her mouth pinch. These highfalutin rules were insufferable.

An appealing slice of pie with cookie crumbs topping its fluffy white cream sat before her. Florence refilled everyone's teacups.

"Florence," William said with smarmy appreciation. "You made another one of your delights for us today."

"It looks delicious. What kind is it?" Daisy asked.

"Coconut cream. Another of William's favorites." Florence looked at the elder with pride beaming from her dove-toned eyes. "Fresh coconut," she added.

William precariously lifted his dessert fork and sunk the tines into the confection. He lifted a puff of cream to his lips and gobbled it. "Whipped to perfection," he said.

An old fairy tale popped into Daisy's mind, the one where the snotty little princess needed all those mattresses with a green pea tucked under the stack in order to determine her royal status. This, she decided, was a king without a kingdom, but he sure had a royal subject in this caretaker. Daisy wondered if Florence had climbed a palm tree herself and hacked down a fresh coconut for His Highness.

She sighed, and then gently touched the end of her fork into the pie. A morsel melted in a sweet softness in her mouth. "It's wonderful, Florence."

"Thank you, Cameron. I do love to bake, but you understand that, don't you, my dear, being a baker yourself?"

Daisy let her fork fall from her fingers and it hit the china plate with a loud "ping." Thankfully, she hadn't put a blemish on what had to be heirloom dishes. She feared what was coming next.

"Oh yes!" William said. He picked up the cue instantly. "Another baker in our midst. Don't forget, Cameron, you promised you would make the mocha cake again for me. I'd like to watch you while you work, if I may."

Daisy didn't remember promising any such thing. But, she knew there would be no debating it. The old guy wanted her to perform something for which she was ill-equipped. Daisy closed her eyes and willed away the image of fire trucks circling the estate when her attempt at mocha cake went seriously awry.

No. She would not acquiesce to this ancient barracuda. She merely smiled at him, so sick of the feel of a false grin stretching across her face she thought she might spew her lunch.

"Let's make a definite date," William said. He smiled over the rim of his teacup.

"I, uh, don't have my calendar with me, but I can let you know at a later time," she said. She feared her words may have sounded desperate, because they were.

The cagey codger's rheumy eyes swam with delight. He was reading her unease, she knew it. She straightened in her chair. *And I thought just having to endure the engagement dinner would be a challenge. Now he expects me to pull a miracle out of an oven.*

Florence cleared the table, brushing it clear of any crumbs. She delicately removed the napkin from William's shirt front—doing so, Daisy noticed, with the gentle manner of a mother doting over her precious child.

He beamed up at her, then turned his gaze to Daisy. His eyes still bore the light of trickery, a disarming image of liveliness wrapped in the wrinkles of age and ill health.

"Cameron, my dear, this has been a wonderful visit. Thank you for making time in your busy day to join me."

"My pleasure," she said. Her jaw clenched against the blatant lie.

"By the way, my dear, I do so appreciate your name. Cameron." He mulled the word, savored it like a candy on his tongue. "Is there any history to the name? Or, did your parents take one look at you and decide you were Cameron?"

The fist of self-reproof punched her insides. Yes, she wanted to say, my name has great personal meaning. But, she was not Daisy in this man's presence. She was Cameron Day and she felt like a big nobody.

"Not really," she managed.

"Well, it's a lovely name for a lovely woman."

"Thank you."

"I hope you don't mind, dear Cameron, but I've taken the liberty to get you a small gift, a token really, of appreciation for your joining me today for this visit."

"That wasn't necessary," Daisy said. Instantly she felt a twinge of sympathy for him. *Is this what he was used to? Buying the attention of others? Is this what he had done with Rand all these years?* She swallowed the sour taste that burned in her throat.

As if on cue, Florence appeared at his side. She placed a small box, wrapped in floral paper, topped with a crisp fabric bow, on the table. Florence offered Daisy one of her smiles and discreetly left the two of them alone.

Daisy's stomach wrenched with caution's twist. To protest the gesture any further would be an insult to the man, yet accepting a gift merely for joining him for lunch was bizarre.

He pushed the package in her direction using one bent arthritic finger. Daisy could not stand the way the effort appeared as taxing to his strength as if he were pushing a ship's anchor. She partially rose from her chair and reached across the square tabletop as a form of rescue for what she had suddenly felt was a lonely old man.

"Open it, will you, my dear? The best part of giving a present is witnessing the recipient's reaction."

"Of course," she said. A rush of errant affection surprised her. "This is so nice."

A shaky hand fiddled with the bow. A mix of confusion and warm emotion, crisscrossed through her like the strings of a cat's cradle. She slipped a fingernail in the seam of the wrapping and it fell from the little white box. She lifted the hinged lid and stared down at a charm that dangled from a fine gold chain. Her heart stopped mid-beat. The charm was in the shape of a daisy.

Chapter Twenty-Three

Rand held the invitation in his hand, brought to him by a messenger from Uncle William's office staff. The square linen card stock was heavy in his hand. If he were honest, it was more than the invite that weighed on him.

He looked at the clock on his desk. Cameron hadn't called yet. He had tried her cell phone a few minutes ago and the call still went straight to voice mail. What on earth were they doing for two full hours? His anger surprised him—not so much that he felt it, but the reason for it.

He knew William's tactics. He imagined the wily fossil grilling Cameron in his signature diabolical way, with his craggy smile and his sugar-coated proddings. He hoped Cameron had fared well—that the old guy hadn't been too tough on her—and that's what had him confused.

The envelope was foil-lined, the text, although digital, appeared crafted by someone's hand. He read the words again. Such a beautiful display for nothing more than a pack of lies. The invitation seemed, for some reason, a travesty of its own.

His secretary, Celia, offered her typical soft rap on the door, opening it just enough for her head to poke in. "Rand, someone's here to see you."

He looked up, recognizing her tone. Whoever was here had put a question mark on Celia's tongue and it clung to her sentence like glue.

"Who is it?"

Celia came into the room and softly closed the door behind her. She was a stout woman, God only

193

knew how old, but old. Yet, she was perfect. She never called in sick, didn't question his whereabouts, and basically covered his ass. "Okay, what?" Rand said. "You've got that look."

"It's a rather, um, interesting-looking young man. He doesn't have an appointment, but he seems anxious to speak with you. And, by the way, he's holding one of those invitations, too."

Rand looked down at the stiff card in his grip. His mouth went dry. He hadn't realized that the invites had gone out to everyone already. Florence had wasted no time, but of course she wouldn't. The old gal was propelled by a relentless machine, and Cameron was his target today.

"He says his name is Adam Cameron," Celia said. "And when he said his name he slapped that invitation on my desk." She held a hand to her breast. "Can you imagine?"

"Send him in."

She seemed surprised, but nodded and left, leaving the door ajar. In a moment, the tall young man strode into the room. He looked different today. Adam was missing some of his silver-studded accoutrements. And instead of being dressed completely in black, he wore pea-green army fatigues and a plain tan, offensive-logo-free tee-shirt. His sky-blue eyes, uncannily akin to his mother's, were narrowed as he stared at Rand. The kid had the invitation in his fist.

"Hello, Adam. This is a pleasant surprise," Rand lied.

Adam let out a bark-like sound. "Look," he snarled, using the paper in his hand to stab at the air between them. "Some bullshit's going on around here and I want some answers."

Rand's breath caught. He eyed the card on his desk and quickly scanned the wording. It was simple, standard engagement party lingo. What was the kid's problem?

"Adam, have a seat. Clearly you're bothered about something. Why don't you take a minute, and then explain what it is."

"I don't want to sit down," he said like a belligerent little boy. Rand was glad that his dealings with him would be short-lived.

"Who the hell is Cameron Day? And, why was my invitation made out to Adam Day? My mother's been acting all weird and now this. It was one thing that you decided to call her by her last name, but now she's got an entirely different name? And so do I? I want an explanation and I think it should come from you."

Rand looked back down at the text again. *Shit.* He didn't know how he was going to explain it in any feasible way to this irate head banger wearing G.I. Joe's outfit.

****

There was just so long Daisy could stare down at the shiny object displayed in the little box in her hands. She looked up at William, an ancient-looking Cheshire cat with the satisfaction of having eaten a slew of canaries written on his insufferable face.

"Thank you," she offered, deciding in that instant to simply play along, take it as far as the rope would let her before she choked. "It's lovely."

"And appropriate, isn't it?"

"Appropriate?"

"The daisy is a symbol of innocence. Did you know that, my dear?"

"Uh, no. No, I didn't know that."

"I thought that was perhaps why your parents gave you the name."

So, there it is, Daisy thought. She was at rope's end. She placed the little box on the table in front of her and folded her hands on the surface. "And I thought you were giving me a thank you gift just for

195

sharing my afternoon with you." She gave a little laugh. "I actually started to feel sympathy for you, thought perhaps I've misunderstood you, William. Turns out, I've underestimated you."

"I'm sure Randolph has warned you not to."

"Yes."

He smiled. "That was honest. That's a start anyway."

She waited for him to continue. She felt as if she was before a judge and jury, and she needed to exercise her right to remain silent. She wished she could run out the door.

"Why don't you continue with the truth, Miss Cameron? Start at the beginning."

"You need to discuss this with your nephew. Not me."

"I beg to differ," he said. Clearly the man enjoyed the parlay as if it was a chess game and she a cornered pawn. "Although Rand has plenty to lose in this, my guess is that you do as well. You are not the sort of woman to involve yourself in whatever scheme he's concocted without something very big at stake. Am I right?"

Tears sprung into her eyes, and she swatted at them. "Yes."

"Tell me. What did he promise you?"

"You need to talk with Rand."

"Either you tell me or I will confront him today—right after I call my attorney to go ahead with my will change."

The idea of Rand losing everything to this cold-hearted patriarch unnerved her, let alone her single purpose for being involved in this mess. Indecision clawed at her, choking her breath. She wet her lips, set her jaw, and resigned.

"Rand promised to fund my son's college tuition. I am unable to afford it. He—my son—wants to attend a very good, but very expensive, art school."

"Is he good?"

"I beg your pardon?"

"Is this son of yours a good artist?"

"Yes. But, leave my son out of this. He knows nothing."

"I believe he would have to be quite the artist in order for you to agree to Rand's offer."

She stared him down, the muscles in her shoulders aching in their clench.

"Then he shall go."

"I don't understand."

"I have an offer of my own, Miss Cameron. I'd like to offer that we keep this information between us—for now. If you agree to continue to play along then I shall insure that you receive the funds to send your boy to the college he deserves to attend."

"And then what happens with Rand?"

"My dear, I'm going to watch it unfold. Give that son of a bitch a taste of his own medicine." Although William's words were harsh Daisy detected folly in his tone. She didn't know if the man were simply enjoying the prospect of sticking it to Rand or if there was affection there in his implication. She didn't know anything anymore. Except that she wanted out of here.

"So in the end Rand loses and I still get my end of the bargain?"

"Would that bother you?"

"Yes."

"Why should it?"

"Because..." She stopped. It was a good question. *Why indeed?* "I don't know."

He uttered a low, sardonic sound and shook his head.

"I haven't made up my mind yet about the outcome," he said finally. "For now, I just want to watch Rand jump through some hoops. Indulge an old man his pleasure, Miss Cameron. What is your son's full name?"

"Why do you want to know?"

"So that I can contact my attorney as soon as our visit is over. I want him to set aside the amount of money for college. All you have to do now is continue to play the game you signed up for and give me the boy's name to put on the codicil.

Daisy swallowed hard, took a breath, and stood from her chair. "My son's innocent. Put my name in the damned statement, since you get such a charge out of knowing its Daisy Cameron.

"If you don't agree, Cameron...you lose now and so does my nephew. All bets, as they say, are off."

She let out the air she had locked in her lungs. "You must not involve my son, Mr. Press. Do I have your word?" The question sounded lame to her own ears. Based on what she knew of his behavior, how on earth could she count on the man's word?

"Just the name, Daisy. To make things nice and legal."

"My son's name is Adam Aster Cameron."

The old man smiled. Daisy turned to leave. "What does the Aster stand for?"

"An aster is a strong, perennial flower that can withstand adversity." She lifted her chin to him. "My family honored me with my name for a special reason and I wanted my son to know the same honor.

"I'm leaving now."

"A lovely sentiment, Cameron," he called. "I shall continue to refer to you as Cameron. But, obviously, the codicil will name you and your son by your real names."

She nodded and took a step further away.

"Don't forget your gift, my dear. I went to great length to have it ready for today."

She gave him a long look. She didn't want the damned thing.

"Or I could give it to Rand to deliver to you. Would you like that better?"

Daisy snatched the box into her grasp.

"Wear it to the engagement party, dear Daisy flower, to signify you've agreed to my stipulations.

She clutched the gift box in her hand and gave the man one last look. She wanted to tell him to keep his filthy money. The same words she'd uttered to another cruel beast eighteen years ago.

In spite of the urge to blast him and salvage some dignity, she knew it would cost Rand his inheritance. She couldn't dirty her hands with that deed. All she wanted at the moment was to scream the truth, any truth, just to purge the bile from all this deception.

"By the way," she said with a sudden surge of energy, a burst of satisfaction that came out of nowhere but felt good. "I'm not the one that made that damned mocha cake. I couldn't bake to save my life. But even if I could, I wouldn't bake for you. That's not part of the deal."

He noiselessly clapped his gnarled hands and a string of scratchy chuckles erupted from his mouth. "Dear Daisy, I know you don't bake cakes. You serve them."

"Not to you, I don't."

She strode away, the hollow sounds of her footsteps droning in her head and echoing in the cavern of her heart.

Chapter Twenty-Four

"What are you talking about, Adam?" Rand said. He kept his tone casual, bored even.

He waved the invitation at him. "This," he spat, and proceeded to recite the text aloud, finishing with a repeat of his mother's bogus name. "Cameron Day! What the hell, man. What is this?"

"I can explain if you'll calm down a minute." There was just so long Rand could stall with his bluff. He had nothing. *What the hell am I going to tell this kid to keep him quiet?*

"I'm listening."

"It's a long story," Rand said. He almost laughed. *Yeah,* he thought, *it'll be a long story as soon as I pull it out of thin air.* "By the way, aren't you supposed to be in school or something?"

"It's after three. When I got home some guy delivered this. After I puked, I came right over here."

"Did you really vomit?" Rand said, disgusted.

"No. But, I wanted to."

"Listen, are you hungry?"

"What? No. You're hedging. Tell me why my mother's using a phony name."

"Adam, I promise there's a logical explanation for this, but you've got to give me a chance to tell it to you. Frankly, you're...your agitation is disturbing. Are you always this volatile?"

Rand was good at turning the table on an adversary. It was how he dealt with difficult people, and this kid of Cameron's was both difficult and annoying. Yet, he had to smooth the boy's feathers before he flew right back to his mother and blew this whole thing apart.

"No," Adam said, his tone calmer. It was just what Rand hoped to achieve, but wondered if it could be just a lull before his storm. "I'm not. But, you have no idea how upset I am."

Adam took a deep breath and then started to rant, arms flailing around as if he was being attacked by a swarm of angry bees. "One day my mother and I are just going along like always and then you show up out of nowhere and she's engaged. You're some big, rich dude and she's telling me I have to go out and get formal wear or something to go to this uppity dinner at your uncle's palace. And, oh yeah, p.s., our names have been changed."

"I certainly understand how this must seem."

"Yeah. Like totally messed up."

"But, I can explain."

"Like I said in the beginning, man. I'm listening."

"First things first, Adam. I, uh, was just on my way out to get a bite to eat. Come with me and we'll talk about it."

"I don't want to talk about it. I don't want food. I've got stuff to do anyway, so just tell me now."

Rand pushed a button on his phone. "Celia, I'm heading out for a bite. The rest of my afternoon's open isn't it?"

"Yes," she said.

"Okay, pack up early today if you want. I'll see you in the morning."

"Thank you."

He pulled his car keys from the top desk drawer, with his index finger in the ring, and flipped the fob into his palm. He walked around the desk and continued right past a rather stunned-looking Adam. "You coming or not?"

"Wait," he protested. "You're leaving? Just like that?"

"You hear that?" Rand asked although there truly was nothing to hear. "That's my stomach grumbling. Come on. You like hotdogs?"

"Hotdogs?" The kid sounded startled that the word had come from Rand's lips.

"Yes. You know, those cylindrical objects made with ambiguous ingredients that just happen to be great with mustard? You coming?"

****

On the drive back to her office Daisy could not calm her nerves. She didn't know what she was going to tell Rand but she did know she felt like crap. He certainly would want the details of today's luncheon, that is, the audience with the "king" of the Press clan.

It was as though she needed a shower. Her skin felt grimy. Just a short time ago she was a woman who could at least pride herself in being true and being truthful. She had been someone with a shred of hope that all people had a soft side somewhere. She could almost laugh.

She had really thought Uncle William was extending himself with a thank you gift for having given her time to meeting with him today. She looked over at the passenger seat where the little white box poked out from her open purse.

Although she'd like to toss it off a bridge, she didn't dare. Who knew what the old man was capable of? Keeping the little gold daisy pendant was something she had better do. After all, she needed to don the object on the night of the engagement party—a noose for her accuser's display.

Her throat felt tight, her air choked.

Back inside the cool interior of the Brookside Café Daisy relished the familiar surroundings. Mr. Carbone sat on a stool at the counter in his signature red and black plaid flannel shirt. He told another of his tall tales to a rapt Candy, an expert at pleasing her customers. Candy looked up when she heard the door and broke into a welcoming grin. That made Daisy's eyes prick with a sad tear.

"Hey, girl. How was lunch with Thurston Howell, III?"

Daisy laughed at her friend's reference to the eccentric millionaire character on *Gilligan's Island*. William was eccentric, all right, but after today's experience she'd more liken him to Hannibal Lector rather than a lovable guy on an old sitcom.

"It was very nice," she said. The words tasted like a wood chip on her tongue. "Hi, Mr. Carbone."

"Hello, there, Daisy. I understand congratulations are in order."

"Um, yes. Thank you."

"There's a surprise for you." Candy's lips curved into a happy smirk. "Up in your office."

The best surprise she'd like to find up there in her office would be a time machine to transport her back to the day before this whole thing happened. She was pretty sure that was not what she'd find.

"Thanks, Candy. I better get upstairs. I've got a ton of work to do."

She climbed the stairs with leaden feet marveling at how she used to think money woes weighed her down. Now she carried an anvil in her heart.

Sitting on her desk was a bouquet of flowers— daisies. Her heart stammered as she approached the over-sized arrangement as though it might explode. There had to be two, maybe three dozen white daisies surrounded by a fringe of fern.

Daisy lifted the little card from its envelope and stared at the words with stunned eyes. "Thank you for lunch today, my dear. Enjoy the daisies, a sweet genuine flower that seems to personify you so precisely. Always, Uncle William."

****

They walked from Rand's office down a few short blocks to the center of Morristown. Rand's favorite street vendor, "Top Dog," was positioned each day in the same spot on the southern leg of the town square. Luckily, at this late hour of the afternoon, Emilio was still there.

He and Adam hadn't spoken during their entire walk, but Rand could sense the seething in the rigidity of the boy's body. His hard footfalls had been more like stomps. He turned to the kid as they stood in line at the vendor's window.

"Best dogs on the planet."

Adam shrugged, arms folded across his chest.

This was not going to be easy and Rand still had nothing. He was better than this. Giving this kid some line of bull to shut him up was what he excelled at. It was doubly annoying that his brain wouldn't cooperate.

"Emilio!" Rand sounded of good cheer he didn't possess. "We'll take two of the foot-longs."

"How are you today, Mr. Press? This is a late one for you, huh?"

"Yes. Busy day," Rand said. He turned to the sullen Adam standing at his side. "Mustard?"

The kid hesitated, made a face. "Okay. Yeah. Mustard."

"You want a drink?"

"I guess," Adam shrugged.

"Two waters, Emilio."

They found an unoccupied bench in the park. Rand ate his hotdog slowly knowing that the moment he was done the questions would start. He noticed out of the corner of his eye that Adam was wolfing his, taking huge bites in between big swigs from his water bottle. Seriously, the kid could win one of those ridiculous hotdog-eating contests Rand had seen highlighted on the evening news from time to time.

In a blink the paper sleeve Adam cradled in his hand was empty with exception of a smear of Gulden's spicy brown. Rand had two bites left, if he took dainty bites, which felt ridiculous, especially when he knew that there were no answers to be found in his empty hotdog holder.

Just then a young woman walked into their path, dragging a tearful little girl by the hand. The little girl held firmly to the string of a helium balloon that, because of their fast pace, trailed behind her at an angle.

"Patricia, Mommy's not mad at you. I told you that," the woman said. She crouched down in front of the little girl and wiped her little face with a tissue she pulled from a pocket. "There now, honey. It's okay."

"But you yelled," the little voice said. The girl's mouth pulled down in an exaggerated pout. "You yell when you're mad, Mommy."

"I know, I know. I'm sorry. But, Patty, you have to remember what I told you. It's very, very important. You must never tell a stranger your name."

"Okay."

"Honey, even if someone seems nice, you can only tell them your name if they know our secret password. You remember that, don't you?"

The girl nodded.

"Sometimes people seem nice and they're not. Remember the talk we had with Daddy?"

"Yes."

"Okay, honey. You are Mommy's good girl."

The scene was familiar, one Rand recalled from when he himself was a little boy and had come home with a puppy. A man on the street had approached him and had given him a baby mutt from a box of four. Rand's mother had been livid. Not for the new mouth to feed, but for the fact that her son had stopped on his way home from school and had an exchange with a complete stranger.

The memory warmed him with its nostalgia, but more importantly, it gave Rand an idea. He swallowed the last of his hotdog and turned to his surly lunch partner.

Chapter Twenty-Five

Daisy did her best to immerse herself into the stacks of receipts and invoices that crowded her desk. Each time visions of today's lunch fiasco came to mind she tried to distract herself by looking away from her work and stretching her neck, but then her eyes would fall on the over-sized spray of daisies in the fluted vase.

She had put them near the window, away from her direct line of vision, yet they had a radar of their own. And each time she looked at the tender white petals ringed around their yolk-yellow centers, she felt ill. William Press had her all figured out—which made one of them.

"I'm heading home," Candy called in from Daisy's office doorway.

Daisy lifted her gaze to her friend. Candy looked tired. Perhaps it had been another of those crazy days when a busload of seniors heading to Atlantic City had made their midday pit stop here. There were times in the past when on unusually busy days like that Ima would implore her to abandon her paperwork and help with the crowd downstairs. Daisy wondered what Mr. Press would think if he strolled in and found her serving toasted corn muffins to a group of sweet old ladies.

"I'm going to be here a while," Daisy offered. "You look beat. Go home and put your feet up."

"Yeah, right. Little Bruno's scout den is coming over tonight."

"You're kidding."

"Nope. Each father had to take a merit badge

and help the boys earn it. Bruno took athletics. The kids are coming over to jump and run and tear up my yard."

"Sounds fun."

"Sounds noisy," Candy lamented. "I need a nap."

"I hear you," Daisy said. She was exhausted from this day.

"So, how did lunch go? Good?" Candy asked, leaning now in the door jam.

"Yes. Good."

"Nice flowers. Rand?"

"Uncle William sent them. You know, to thank me for having lunch."

"Well la-de-dah."

"Yeah," Daisy said.

"You all right, honey?" Candy asked.

"Me? Sure. I'm tired too, I guess."

"We got the invitation today for the engagement party. Bruno called and said some guy delivered it this afternoon. He's waiting for me to get home so I can be the one to open the envelope."

"You guys can make it, right?"

"Make it? Honey, we wouldn't miss it for the world".

Daisy's heart did its thud that lately had become routine. She wondered if it would ever remember how to beat freely again.

****

"Okay," Adam began. "We ate. So, what's the story? Why did I get an invitation to my own mother's engagement party with fake names?"

"It's a matter of privacy, Adam," Rand said, his voice as light as his heart. "To keep your mother's identity from leaking to the media."

"I don't follow."

"My family is rather well-known. For the time being we thought it would be best for your mother's identity to be obscure enough so that anyone looking

208

for a story would be deterred. It's just temporary."

Adam made a face. "You couldn't tell me this in your office? I had to follow you down here and waste like an hour for that? Why didn't you just say this in the first place?"

Because I only now thought of it, shot through Rand's mind. He stood from the bench and tossed the empty bottle in a nearby trashcan. "And, it wasn't a waste of an hour. You had the chance to experience the best hot dog in Morristown."

Adam stood now, too, and tossed his empty water bottle, throwing it like a torpedo into the can. "Okay, well, thanks for the lunch," he said.

"Something about this doesn't feel right. I've felt this way all along. I guess I'm just worried about my mom. She's all I've got. You know?"

"That's why we took this unorthodox step to keep her protected from anyone who might be interested in causing some, shall we say, unpleasantness."

"Does somebody have stuff on you and your family? Are you like in the mob or something?"

Rand laughed out loud. "Do I look like a mobster to you?"

"People aren't always what they seem."

Rand felt a tug inside his chest. He looked at Adam, the bright blue of the boy's eyes filled with concern. His look was one of defiance. *Maybe the kid looks and dresses like a wannabe loser, but he sure as hell loves his mother.*

"I'm starting to realize that," Rand said.

"Look, I have to go now. I'm going to be late and, you know, I'm in enough trouble with Mom."

"Okay," Rand said. Suddenly he felt awkward. "Wait a second. You don't have a car, right?"

"Uh, no," the kid laughed sarcastically, "Neither does my mother thanks to me. Remember?"

"How'd you get to Morristown from Hanover

Heights?"

"My girlfriend dropped me off."

"How are you getting back?"

"I hadn't thought that far. I was so mad when I got that damned invitation, I couldn't think straight." He shrugged and looked at his watch. "I'll text Elizabeth and see if she can pick me up after she's done with her guitar lesson."

"Look, Adam, tell you what. I'll drive you home."

"That's okay."

"It's no trouble. I feel responsible for taking you away from whatever you had planned for the afternoon."

Adam shrugged again. "All I was going to do was get in a little fishing before Mom came home. I'm grounded for-like-ever."

"Fishing? Where do you fish?"

"In the pond down off Edmond Lane."

"Yeah? What's it stocked with?"

"Striped bass, yellow perch," Adam said absently.

"You have an extra pole?" Rand asked, surprising himself.

"Why?" Adam said. His voice rang with disbelief.

"Maybe I'll join you."

"You fish?"

"Sure," Rand said. "Well, at least I used to."

"I wouldn't take you for someone that likes fishing."

"A wise man once told me that 'people aren't always what they seem.'"

For the first time that afternoon the kid's mouth broke into a smile. A smirk really, but it was a definite improvement. "Well, it's kind of late now and I have to be home before five or else I'll be in even worse trouble. What time is it?"

"Don't concern yourself with that, man," Rand said. "You're with me. What can happen?"

Chapter Twenty-Six

Rand was surprised to see that the kid emerged from the hallway carrying, indeed, two fishing poles. They were ordinary, inexpensive certainly, but appeared to be well cared for.

"Excellent," Rand offered as Adam strode into the kitchen, rushing past him.

"I don't have a lot of time, though," he said.

"No problem."

"I'm going to grab some boiled ham for bait," Adam said. "Wait, can you get my tackle box? It's on the floor of my closet. Right in there." He pointed to a doorway down the hall.

Obligingly, Rand went to the room. His eyes scanned the artwork on the walls and he had to admit the kid really could draw. He liked the piece displayed on the wall above the bed, old weathered-looking hands holding a fresh young daisy.

Adam, he decided, would do well in a fine art school, no doubt. Somehow it made Rand feel satisfied, as though his scheme was contributing to the betterment of someone else's raw talent. The thought gave him a warm charge like a pat on his own back.

He found the tackle box, which was heavy, its contents rattling as he carried it. In no time they were back in Rand's car and headed to Edmond's Pond.

It was a small body of water just a few steps from the blacktop lot at the town's park. Beyond the pond was a baseball diamond where a cluster of boys played man-on-man football. The playground area was vacant, the swings blowing listlessly in a cooling breeze. No one else was fishing, so Rand and Adam were alone at the water's edge.

Adam placed the black plastic box on the flat stone ledge and started to work. Rand watched. It had been years since he'd done this. He tried to think back to a time. He remembered that one time he and his father had caught a bucket-load of fish, a totally unheard of take for the two of them, and they had carted their cache home covered in the ice they had dumped out of their cooler.

They had delivered the fish to Rand's mother. His heart had been filled with pride. What a shock it had been when she started to cry.

"Mom, why are you crying?" the ten-year-old Rand had asked. Fear rushed to his senses.

"Oh, honey, for crying out loud. They're just fish," Rand's dad soothed.

"I'm just happy, that's all. It's so nice to see my men together like this, happy and suntanned."

His dad had put the bucket on the ground then and pulled his wife into his arms. He whispered in her ear, indiscernible mumblings Rand hadn't been able to decipher, but whatever he'd said had made her smile against his shoulder. Her pretty eyes, happy again, focused on her on-looking son.

"You're a pro at this, aren't you?" Rand asked, snapping himself back to the present as he eyed the items in the top tray. He put his cell phone down into an empty tray section and touched a finger to the assortment of lures and weights.

"Nah," Adam said. He fiddled with the yellow fish-shaped lure at the end of his line. "I've been collecting this stuff all my life. It's nothing fancy."

"Well, it's been a long time since I did this and all I can seem to remember is putting a worm on the hook and casting the line," Rand said. He closed the box's lid and flipped the latch.

"Um, that could be a problem," Adam said.

"Why?"

"I think you just closed your cell phone in there."

"Yes, it's new and I don't want to risk getting it wet."

"The key's home in my room."

"Oh boy," Rand said. He shrugged. "Hopefully nobody will be looking for me. Okay, let's see about catching us something."

"Need me to help you with that?" Adam offered as Rand manipulated a chunk of the boiled ham onto the hook.

"Maybe," Rand said with a laugh. "Wait, there. How's that?"

"Good, let's do it. But remember, I have to be home by five, or I'm dead."

"Not to worry," Rand said.

They cast their lines and waited in silence. Rand wondered what the boy was thinking, if he was mulling the load of crap he'd given him about why his mother was suddenly going by a new name.

They exchanged a look. Adam's eyes narrowed with question. "So, what's the plan?" he asked.

"Plan?" Rand snapped to attention. He hoped the kid wouldn't start probing him for more details. He didn't have any beyond getting his fortune. He needed to steer him from more third-degree. "Funny, Adam, I was just about to ask you the same thing."

"Me? Why?"

Rand shrugged, nonchalantly, wiggling his pole to stir the water around his lure. "Pratt. Are they having an orientation soon?"

Adam made a face, reeled in his line, and recast it. "I'm not sure."

"Not sure? The way your mother talks you'd think your bags were already packed. She's quite proud of you. This means a lot to her."

"Tell me about it," Adam said, his tone subdued.

213

"You are looking forward to going, aren't you?"

Adam shrugged. "Sure."

"Here's a tip, kid. If you're trying to convince somebody that you're enthused about something, you've got to put more effort into it. You having second thoughts?" Rand felt a little stab of alarm. *What if the kid doesn't even want to go to Pratt? Shit. Would that be a deal breaker if Cameron learned that news?*

"Did you go straight to college when you graduated high school?" Adam asked.

"Immediately," Rand said. He remembered the way Uncle William had made the decision for him to go to their family's alma mater, Rhode Island's Brown University. He also recalled that the head of admissions and William were good friends and that may have aided his acceptance, although Rand was never able to determine so. "I went to Brown."

"Did you like it?"

"Sure," Rand said. He thought that was a funny question. No one had ever asked him that before. He had known what awaited him at the end of his four years, and that position of rank in the Press conglomerate was one fine carrot.

"Did you always know that's what you wanted to do? I mean, my mom always wanted her college degree and, well, I came along, the surprise baby, and she wound up quitting. I think that's why it means so much to her that I go to school."

"Does it mean that much to you, Adam?"

"*She* means that much to me."

"That's not what I asked, though. Do you have something else in mind?"

Adam shrugged again then looked at Rand full-faced, his blue eyes wide and bright. "Europe. Well, France. I'd like to go to Paris for a while, live among the artists, try my hand at sketching in Montmartre.

"But, I haven't actually said anything to my

mother, so please don't mention it. It's just a dream anyway, not going to happen."

Rand felt a pulling sensation in his chest. He suddenly remembered what that felt like, having a dream, a real dream. But, that desire had died and been replaced by a new quest. Fortune became his drug and Uncle William had administered his first hit.

And, now, his fishing partner was at a bend in his own road. If he took the route to Paris, Rand's plan could collapse.

Suddenly an image of Cameron's face flashed into his mind—the gentleness in her eyes when she spoke about Adam, the gleam of pride. His heart flopped over on itself. *Keep your eye on the prize, man,* he admonished silently.

"Do you love her?"

The words snapped Rand out of his reverie. "I'm sorry, what?"

"Do you love my mother?" Adam recited the words as though speaking to a foreigner without a grasp on his English.

"Where'd that question come from?" Rand said. He forced a laugh. "That's usually the criteria for an engagement, isn't it?"

The boy looked at him long, held his gaze as though in a vice. "I shouldn't have said anything to you without first leveling with her. If you care about her feelings, then please let me be the one to talk with her about this. Okay?"

"Your secret is safe with me, Adam," Rand said. An uncomfortable jab poked at his insides "Don't worry. I won't say a thing to your mother."

The park's automatic lighting system kicked in at dusk. Strobes lit the parking lot and the areas around the pond. Adam became aware that the boys that had been on the ball field were gone. Rand's Jaguar was the lone car in the lot—until the police car pulled up next to it.

"Oh, man," Adam said. He pulled his line from the water.

Rand followed suit. "Don't worry about this. I'll handle it."

The officer lumbered out of the vehicle, a sour look on his face. He approached and halted his footsteps at the edge of the blacktop, as though crossing onto the grassed area would give him some sort of electrical shock. Rand noticed his black boots were polished and shiny.

"You men know this park closes at dusk?" he said. His hands were on his hips. His eyes narrowed and fixed on Rand.

"No, sir," Rand said. He used his bullshit-sweet-as-honey-tone. "I assumed the lights meant it was still open for business."

The officer pointed to a sign affixed high on a post which clearly stated in big red letters that the park was closed at dusk each day.

Rand offered his signature embarrassed laugh, tucked his chin and then looked at the oaf in blue using a wide-eyed innocence that he had perfected in junior high. "Didn't even see that. We're sorry. We'll just pack up and be on our way."

"Do you have a license to fish in the state of New Jersey?"

"Adam," Rand turned to his partner. "Show the officer your license."

"I see his," he said. He pointed to the document encased in a plastic protector that dangled from the kid's belt loop. "I'd like to see yours, sir."

"I don't have one," Rand said. He remained pleasant although he had stopped *feeling* pleasant. "I'm just here as a guest fisherman."

"You must have a license to fish in the fresh water areas of New Jersey," Robo-cop stated in a mechanical sounding voice. Rand wasn't a fan.

"Look," Rand said. He smiled falsely and squinted at the man's badge. "Officer..."

"Glower. Sergeant Glower. Can I see some identification please?"

"Absolutely," Rand said. He reached into his pocket, hoping his name would ring a bell with this guy. But, his pants pocket was empty, as were the others he jammed his hand into.

This was ridiculous. Rand always had his wallet. Maybe it was in his car. "It's in my car, I'm sure," he said. He darted to his vehicle. He checked the seats, between and under them. His damned wallet was gone.

He racked his brain, then remembered the last time he had seen it was at the hotdog cart in Morristown. Somehow it must have fallen from his pocket when he was on that bench in the park. He turned back to the cop. "Sergeant Glower, I seem to have a problem here. My name is Randolph Press, that's J. Randolph Press, Jr. My family's firm is in Morristown, Press Industries on the square. My, er, friend here and I were in the park in town having a hotdog from a vendor there. I must have left my wallet behind."

"Do you have your vehicle registration in the car?"

"No. I never keep it there in case of, you know, theft."

"Insurance certificate?"

"Yes, certainly," Rand said. He sat awkwardly in the driver's seat of his car and reached over the gearshift to open the glove box. He pulled the insurance card from the leather cover and handed it to the officer. The sergeant held it close to his face, nearly touching his fat nose, and scanned the document with a scrutinizing stare.

"J. Randolph Press, Jr., huh?"

"Yes, sir," Rand said with a smile. He was sure

the man recognized the name and the prominence that it signified. "I just hope I find that wallet of mine. When we leave here I'm going to head over there and look for it."

"Not in this car you're not," he said. He handed the card back to him. "You have no license to operate this vehicle and you don't have a registration in your possession. You have been fishing with no license in a park that's been clearly identified as closed. Mr. Press, you've got bigger problems than the location of your wallet."

Adam stared wide-eyed at Rand. "Should we call my mom?"

"What's your name son?"

"Adam Cameron."

"Do you have a driver's license?"

"Yes," he said. He reached into his back pocket and retrieved his wallet. He withdrew the laminated document and handed it to the officer.

Sergeant Glower took it with him into his squad car and, Rand guessed, was running it to see if the boy had been in any trouble. He watched the man eye his Jag's plate, figured he was going to run it to see if there was anything on him. Luckily, Rand knew he was squeaky clean. But, the kid, well that was another issue.

"Rand," Adam whispered with tight lips. "Is it all right for me to call my mother or should I wait until this guy comes back?"

"You better wait. I don't want us to piss him off any more than he is."

"Shit."

"Yeah, shit. And we didn't even catch a single damned fish."

Adam laughed then and Rand turned to meet his gaze. For some crazy reason he laughed, too. The absurdity of this whole scene suddenly seemed like a clip from *Dumb and Dumber*.

Sergeant Glower returned standing with his feet again strategically placed on the pavement. He, apparently, saw no humor in any of this and now, neither did Rand.

"Adam, how do you know Mr. Press?" the cop asked when he handed back Adam's license.

"He's...he's engaged to my mother."

"Your mother's name?"

"Daisy Cameron," he said. Rand detected a note of sarcasm.

Suddenly Rand's phone rang from inside the closed tackle box. The sergeant took a step closer, leaving the comfort of the pavement to stand on the grassy area closer to the ringing box. "What's that all about?"

"By mistake I locked my cell phone in there. I didn't realize Adam left the key at home."

"Do you have a cell phone with you, son?" he asked. When Adam nodded, he added, "It would be a good idea if you called your mother."

Adam pulled out his phone and began to dial. The officer turned his attention to Rand. "I'm going back to write up your violations while we wait for the boy's mother."

"Well, this will be a first for me, Officer," Rand said. Indignity crawled up his spine.

The officer pointed with his fat hotdog of a finger to the rectangular piece of cardboard jammed into the drink cup holder of the Jaguar's console. "Is that right, Mr. Press?"

Rand looked in through the window of his car and spotted the damned parking ticket he'd found on his dashboard last Saturday. "That's just a parking ticket," he said.

"Uh-huh." The officer's mouth was a sinister slash. He headed back to his squad car.

"Stay calm," Rand whispered to Adam. "This will be okay."

"Shit."

"Now what?"

"My phone's dead. I forgot to charge it."

"Jeez. When this guy comes back we'll let him call your mother for us."

"I'm *so* dead," Adam said.

"It'll be okay."

Adam laughed. "Man, you've got a lot to learn about my mom. She's not only going to kill me. You're pretty dead, too."

****

At five-thirty Daisy was seeing red. Based on the drumming in her ears, her blood pressure had to be spiked. She had been home for a half hour and there was no sign of Adam.

She continued to fix dinner, heating up leftover meatballs and sauce, and putting on a pot of water to boil the spaghetti. She over-salted the water with sharp jerky jabs of the shaker. Taking the pot from the flame, she dumped the water in the sink and refilled it, starting over again. She slammed it on the burner, the contents pitching toward the rim of the pot.

She was giving him fifteen, no, ten more minutes. Then she was going to get into that lousy rental car that she had been forced to drive, thanks to him, and she would comb the planet until she could find him—just for the satisfaction of killing him.

Her chest heaved with exaggerated breath. In no time whatsoever, her responsible, caring, thoughtful son had turned into an alien. The image of Adam and that Elizabeth cowering in her good, saved-for-company bath towels only served to enrage her further. She and the bubbling liquid on the stove were at full boil.

She took the long strands of pasta from its box and gripped the bundle in both hands like a handlebar. She held it over the water, feeling the steam on her hands. With a surge of satisfaction she snapped the skinny sticks in half and dropped them into the pot. She gave the pasta a mighty stir with a wooden spoon.

She looked at the clock. Okay, she couldn't go looking for him now that the spaghetti was on the stove and that angered her more. But, as soon as it was cooked, the second it sat in the colander, she was heading out.

At six o'clock she was still home. Thankfully, her common sense had kicked in and she realized that her nerves were too on edge for her to be behind the wheel of a car.

Staying home was agony. Dinner was ruined. She had thrown out the gummy spaghetti that had wadded into a ball of string, although she had entertained saving the gluey mass to serve to her son for his supper. The pot of sauce and meatballs sat on a cold burner.

There was no one left to call. She had run through the list of Adam's closest friends, hating having had to do so. She didn't want anybody else to worry about where he might be and she also didn't like having to admit that she didn't know where he was. It pissed her off, actually, but not as much as it scared her.

She felt ill-equipped for dealing with this type of scenario. This was so atypical of Adam's behavior. She couldn't wrap her brain around the changes in him.

Daisy was no fool. She knew that this kind of pendulum swing could be indicative of drug use. She'd read the pamphlets, had seen the television programs. Under normal circumstances, she would have bet what little money she had that her son wouldn't go near an illegal substance. But, things had changed. He often smelled of smoke, and Rand

M. Kate Quinn

had even asked if she suspected the boy was smoking something other than tobacco.

And the girl he had taken up with—what was that Elizabeth into? After all, what did Daisy know about her except that she'd been naked with her son? She groaned out loud.

She yearned to call Candy but didn't want to involve her in this. Ever since she'd become part of Rand's scheme, there was a distance caused in her relationship with her best friend. Actually, these days she felt a perpetual disconnect with her whole life. Right now she couldn't find her son and she was all alone in dealing with it.

Daisy surprised herself when she dialed Rand, of all people. His secretary said he had left the office earlier in the afternoon, not saying where he was going. His cell phone just rang and rang. It had been stupid to reach out to him, anyway.

She had no choice now but to call Adam's shower buddy, Elizabeth. Adam's friend, Paulie had given her the girl's full name and phone number.

As much as she dreaded it, she dialed. Elizabeth answered on the first ring. "Adam?" she asked, her young voice anxious.

"No, Elizabeth. This is Adam's mother, Mrs. Cameron."

"Oh," she said. "When I saw the number come up, I thought... Is Adam home?"

"No, that's why I'm calling. You haven't seen or heard from him?"

"No. Are you worried? I'm worried," the girl said. "His phone's off."

"I know. I'm concerned," Daisy offered.

"I shouldn't have driven him to Morristown."

"What?"

"This afternoon he asked me to drive him to your, um, Mr. Press's office."

"What? Why?" Daisy asked, really loud.

"He was upset and…"

"Upset about what, Elizabeth?"

"An invitation some guy delivered to your house when Adam got home from school. I wasn't there with him, Mrs. Cameron," the girl was quick to add. "I was still at school. He was mad about something on the invitation. He said his name was wrong."

Well, that didn't make sense. Adam was missing because he couldn't deal with a typographical error? "Elizabeth," Daisy said slowly, thinking now that perhaps she wasn't dealing with a rocket scientist. "Adam needed a ride to Mr. Press's office because there was a misspelling on the invitation?"

"No," Elizabeth corrected. "It wasn't spelled wrong. It said his name was Adam Day. And the invitation said your name was Cameron Day."

Daisy continued to hold the receiver to her face but did not speak into it. Her breath caught in her throat. *Damn this. Damn it all! This whole thing has made a mess out of everything, and for what?*

William Press is onto us anyway. We're both probably going to wind up worse than we started. Now Adam is nowhere to be found.

"I'm sorry, Mrs. Cameron," Elizabeth said in a hushed tone. "Can I help somehow?"

"No," she said. "Thank you, Elizabeth. If you hear from him though, please ask him to call me immediately. Will you do that?"

"Sure, yes, of course."

"Thank you."

"Mrs. Cameron. When you hear from him could you, um, let me know? I'm really worried."

"Yes, I will," she said. She hung up the phone.

Daisy paced around the room, and then went back into Adam's bedroom again to look for a clue she might have missed earlier. Everything was the same, familiar. She opened the drawer to his nightstand, fished around in the mess of clutter, but saw nothing out of the ordinary. She looked under the bed, in his sock drawer, in his closet. And it was then that she saw something she hadn't seen before—a wallet.

The leather was smooth in her palm, fine stitching, embossed with a designer logo. This did not belong to her son. She opened the wallet and staring back at her was J. Randolph Press, Jr., posed with his insufferable pomposity in the headshot of his driver's license.

She tried to piece together what little information she had. Somehow Rand had been here with Adam and each of them had their cell phones shut off. A trickle of panic dripped into her veins, pumping along and sending fear to her heart. This was trouble.

The doorbell rang, jolting her. She dashed to open it with her breath held. She found Elizabeth standing dressed in black-and-red-checked flannel pants that drooped from her frame, puddling at her moccasined feet. Her black sweatshirt was turned inside out. Her nose ring glistened in the entryway's light, winking at Daisy.

"Is it okay that I came over?" the girl asked timidly. She fiddled with the shoulder strap of her nylon purse. "My mom let me come even though I'm, you know, grounded."

"Come in," Daisy breathed with a sigh. *Why not? She thought. Maybe the girl could shed some light on Adam's state of mind these days.*

"I have to call her and let her know I'm here," Elizabeth added, as she stepped into the room. "It's like jail."

Elizabeth pulled a cell phone out of her purse and stabbed at the little keyboard. She held it up to her multi-studded ear and twirled a lock of her brown hair with her other hand. Now that Daisy saw it in a dry state, it was actually a pretty cinnamon color.

"Mom? I'm here. No. I don't know. No." She blew out a long sigh. "Okay." She jutted the phone at Daisy. "She wants to talk to you."

Daisy held the instrument to her ear. "Hello?"

"I'm sorry to bother you," a woman's voice said. "I'm Elizabeth's mother, Dorian Lucent. We're keeping a tight rein on our daughter these days and I'm just making sure of her whereabouts."

"I understand perfectly," Daisy said.

"You still haven't heard from Adam, Mrs. Cameron?" the woman asked.

"Please, call me Daisy. No, I haven't heard from him."

"Is it all right that Elizabeth is there? She was driving me nuts over here. I told her one hour. After that she has to come straight home. If that's okay by you."

Daisy eyed the girl who now had moved deeper into the room, standing near the sofa, having already tossed her purse onto the cushion.

"It's okay," Daisy said.

"I hope you hear from him soon. Adam's a nice boy."

The statement surprised Daisy. The woman apparently had occasion to know her son to some degree, at least enough to make such an assessment. *How? When?* Her thoughts reeled.

"Thank you, Dorian."

"Have Elizabeth call when you hear from him?"

"Yes," Daisy said. "Thank you." She handed the phone to Elizabeth.

Daisy watched as the girl listened, still twisting a cinnamon-colored lock. She uttered a sequence of three "okay's" followed by a short "bye" and flipped the phone closed.

"She thinks I'm twelve," Elizabeth said. She sounded annoyed, but her eyes looked kind and

225

gentle.

"Mothers worry," Daisy said.

"Tell me about it," she said.

Daisy stared at the girl. "Would you like something to drink?"

Elizabeth shrugged but followed Daisy when she headed toward the kitchen.

"Something smells good," the girl said.

"Are you hungry?" Daisy asked, wondering why she had made the offer. Maybe it was the mother instinct or the diner mentality.

Daisy didn't feel like talking or eating or anything that involved energy. Suddenly she had none. She was tired of everything, sick of lies and the effects of them. That's what she was, she concluded. She was sick and tired.

Elizabeth shrugged her narrow shoulders. "I can't eat," she said. "No thanks."

Daisy poured water from a pitcher she kept in the fridge, handed a full glass to Elizabeth, and then poured one for herself. She leaned against the opposite counter and the two sipped water in silence. Daisy did her best to keep her eyes from scrutinizing this stranger who seemed to know her son better than she did these days.

"He was mad," Elizabeth suddenly said as though in response to a question. Daisy looked up at her. "Really mad. I'm still confused about why. I know they put the wrong name on his invitation and I tried to tell him that it was just a mistake, but he wasn't hearing it. He said that he was going to 'get to the bottom of this.'" Elizabeth had lowered her voice in an attempt to sound like Adam.

She gave a little, embarrassed laugh. "He's usually so easy-going. It's not like him."

"No," Daisy said. Her throat was tight. "It's not. Can you tell me anything that might help me understand?"

"I know he's worried that, you know, you might be moving too fast with your, uh, plans." She took another sip from her glass, then looked up to meet Daisy's gaze. "Too much change, I guess."

Daisy felt like laughing. *Too fast, huh? At least I'm still bathing alone.* She downed the remaining liquid in her glass, set it on the counter, and then checked her watch for the umpteenth time.

"What time is it?" Elizabeth asked.

"Almost seven," Daisy said. Just saying it aloud sent a zing of panic through her veins. *Where the hell is he?*

"Where the hell is he?" Elizabeth asked as though reading Daisy's thought. She slapped a hand to her mouth. "Sorry," she said.

Daisy waved away the girl's apology for the use of the word *hell*. After all, Daisy figured maybe she should get used to it, considering it seemed more and more as if she'd taken residence there. Yup, she'd gone to hell.

"Um, by the way, I just want to say that I'm sorry for, you know, the other day. My parents are furious at me for skipping my afternoon classes. They don't know, you know, the details."

She shrugged then continued. "So, I have detention at school which is jail and then I go home and can't go out or call my friends, which is more jail."

"Sounds as though you have good parents, Elizabeth. You'll thank them someday."

"Well, I'm never going to treat my kids like criminals," Elizabeth said.

"Tell me that again in twenty years," Daisy said. A wry smile formed on her lips.

"Maybe I'll get the chance. You know—to tell you that in twenty years. That is, I don't know, if Adam and I last that long," the girl said. She suddenly sounded soft and shy.

Catching the flush that pinked the girl's cheeks made Daisy's heart squeeze. Elizabeth was in love. This wasn't just some kid with an excuse to use her "get out of jail free card" to come over here. This was someone that genuinely cared about Adam, loved him even.

"Elizabeth, I'm going to try calling Rand again."

The look on the girl's face changed, as though a cloud had passed over her head. *Was it the mention of Rand that caused it?*

"How upset *is* Adam about my engagement, Elizabeth? Will you tell me?"

She blinked her eyes, hesitated. "He's not happy about it. I guess he's not sure about Mr. Press."

"Does he dislike him?"

She shrugged those narrow shoulders again. "I think Adam's not happy about *life* these days."

"What makes you say that?" Daisy's heart hammered, banging against the walls of her ribs.

"We're seniors. We're supposed to know what we want and how to get it and, well, it gets frustrating, I guess."

"Frustrating how?"

"Maybe you better talk to Adam about that."

"Yes," Daisy said. "You're right, Elizabeth. Adam and I do need to discuss this on our own."

She couldn't help but admire the girl for her loyalty to Adam. There was definitely something Daisy and her son needed to get out into the open, and it hurt to know this ring-nosed Elizabeth knew more about him than she did.

Daisy grabbed the handset, unsure of who she'd call—Candy maybe, the police, the Pentagon, hell, somebody... But it rang in her hand before she could decide. She hit the "on" button so fast and so hard she was momentarily afraid that she may have disconnected the call. Elizabeth darted close at the sound of the ring.

Before she could speak Daisy heard a muffled word. The voice was Adam's and it sounded as if he had just said "shit!"

"Adam?" *Is he really swearing into the phone? Really?*

"Mom?"

"Yes. Where are you?" she demanded, sounding mad—not scared, like she felt. Suddenly, relief washed over her, and her voice caught in her throat.

"I'm at Edmond's Pond. We have a little problem."

"We? Who is 'we'?"

"Rand. I'm here with Rand. We were fishing and..."

"You went fishing? *Fishing?* Are you seriously telling me that I've been home trying to call you—and him, too for that matter, neither of you has your phone on—and while I'm here about to call the police, you two were *fishing?*"

"Well, you don't need to call the police. They're here."

"They are? Why are the police there?"

"It's kind of a long story and, um, the officer wants to leave but is waiting for us to get a ride. Can you pick us up?"

"Rand doesn't have his car?"

"Yes, but he lost his wallet and has no license or registration on him so he can't drive."

"Is Rand right there?"

"Yes."

"Please give him the phone." Daisy said through clenched teeth. She glanced at Elizabeth who appeared leery—perhaps because of Daisy's venomous tone. And, that was just too bad. Nothing would quell her anger now.

She heard a muffling sound while the phone exchanged hands and, if she wasn't mistaken, she thought she heard that word again. Now Rand had said "shit."

"Hello," Rand said jovially.

"What do you think you're doing?" she spat. Daisy felt Elizabeth's stare penetrating her skin like lasers. "Tell me *now* what this is all about. I mean it."

"Yes, I'll explain everything in vivid detail, darling. I promise. For now, though, would you kindly come pick us up so the officer can be on his way?"

She hated his drippy, sweet tone. She nearly barked her reply. "I'll be right there."

When the call ended, Daisy noticed that Elizabeth was on her cell phone talking softly. She heard bits of what was being said and knew that the girl had called her mother to let her know Adam had made contact.

"Elizabeth, I'm sure you heard. Adam is fine. I have to run over to Edmond's Pond to pick them up, him and Rand."

"I know, I heard." Daisy saw the glisten of tears in the girl's soft brown eyes. Her mouth quivered. "Can you, um, tell Adam, that I, you know, that I'm glad he's okay?"

"Elizabeth..." Daisy said. She looked at the doe-eyed kid, feeling the air deflate from her lungs. "Would you like to come with me?"

"Really?" she said. It sounded more like a squeal. She flipped open her phone and called her mother. When the call ended, Elizabeth turned to her with a brighter look on her face than Daisy had yet seen. "My mom said it's okay but I have to go home right after."

"Let's hurry then."

They grabbed their purses and dashed out the door with Daisy muttering one word. "Shit."

Chapter Twenty-Seven

Daisy pulled up next to the police car, then immediately strode over to Adam. He looked stunned to see Elizabeth trudging along beside her.

"Hi, Mom," he said. He embraced her loosely. "I'm sorry about this."

"We'll talk about it when we get home," she said. She kept her tone even for the sake of the policeman.

Rand pulled Daisy into his arms, and she turned to granite at his touch. She knew the officer's eyes had to be on them, and maybe his trained eye noticed the less-than-loving response coming from her, but she didn't care. Rand was lucky she didn't haul off and whack him one. She yanked free.

"Darling...what a mix-up. None of this would have happened if I hadn't misplaced my wallet. I think I may have left it at a hotdog vendor on the square in town."

She pulled the brown leather wallet from her purse. "It was on the floor in Adam's room." She tossed it at him harder than she should have, but the way it slapped at his chest made her happy. By this time, Elizabeth had plastered herself against Adam whose arms where wrapped around her torso like a stole. They were whispering.

The officer, his smirked mouth forming a gash in his fleshy face, finalized the ordeal by issuing a stack of tickets that he ceremoniously dealt into Rand's palm like a hand of poker.

On the ride home she periodically took glimpses through her rearview mirror of the silent young couple in the back seat. She did not play the radio, nor offer conversation. That would wait until they got home. Rand followed closely behind as though his car was tethered to her bumper.

The four of them marched up the sidewalk to Daisy's front door in single file and entered the apartment without a word.

"Did you say that you needed to call your mother when you were ready to head home, Elizabeth?" Daisy asked. She was ready for them both to leave, needing to speak to her son alone.

"Yes," she said in a barely audible whisper. "I guess I better call her now."

"Yes," Daisy said.

Adam followed the girl to the door. While they were alone for the moment, Daisy leaned close to Rand and whispered to him in what came out as a hiss. "This is unacceptable."

"I'd like to explain. This is not Adam's fault, by the way. I am totally to blame."

"What right do you have to drag my son out fishing when you know he's already in trouble? Rules may not apply to you, Mr. Press, but they apply to the people in this house."

"I'm sorry. We lost track of time."

"Why didn't one of you at least have the courtesy of calling me?"

"My phone got locked in the tackle box."

"Then why didn't *you* call?" She directed this question to Adam when he re-entered the room after walking Elizabeth to her car.

"I forgot to charge my phone."

"This is so irresponsible. You're both pathetic."

"Yes, we are," Rand said. "And we are both heartily sorry. We're sorry, *and* we're starving."

"Is that dinner I smell?" Adam asked tentatively.

"Chicken noodle casserole?" Rand asked like a kid that had heard the ice cream man's bell.

Daisy looked at the two men in her living room, wondering which one she should slug first. If she didn't know better she'd think the two of them were in some sort of cahoots. "Meatballs!" She was glad the word came out more as testament to their behavior rather than a revelation of what sat in the pot on her stove.

"Hey, that'll do," Rand said. He rubbed his hands together.

"Mom makes the best sauce," Adam said. He led the way into the kitchen with Rand following close behind.

Daisy watched as they retreated, leaving her alone in the living room. Her head spun.

****

They ate in heavy silence, Daisy biting at her sandwich like an assault. She had no appetite but at least the mouthfuls kept her from screaming. Incredulously, Adam and Rand exchanged occasional bits of dialogue, making futile attempts to draw her into the conversation.

"Mom, did you know Rand used to fish? Like, when he was a kid?"

"He mentioned it, yes."

"And did you know that he has a boat? It's thirty-eight feet long. Right? Thirty-eight?" Adam turned to Rand for confirmation.

"Yes, it's a Sea Ray. But, like I told you, Adam, technically the boat belongs to my Uncle William."

"Still," Adam said. "That's awesome."

Hell was a funny place, Daisy decided. *It made for the strangest of dinner partners.* The out-of-body feeling persisted as she passed the parmesan, sipped her Diet Coke, and licked a dot of tomato sauce from her fingertip.

"We'll go out on it sometime soon," Rand offered. "How about that, darling, would you like that?"

If I can jump overboard, sure. She shook the

thought from her head. After all, she was still in this stupid game. She had to maintain the façade of a woman newly engaged. She had allowed herself an appropriate amount of time to vent her rage at the man without blowing the falsehood of their partnership.

Adam, it appeared, had turned a corner with Rand, which would make things easier, for sure. However, it only made Daisy sicker for the whole mess.

"Now that we've eaten, tell me how we got here. Start at the beginning." She folded her arms in front of her on the tabletop.

"We—" Rand began. But Daisy raised her hand at him.

"No," she said. "Adam, I want to hear this from you."

"Okay," Adam said. He raked his fingers across his spiky hair, making the points poke up straighter with his effort. "When I got home from school some guy dropped off the invitation to your engagement party. When I saw that your name was Cameron Day and mine was Adam Day I kind of flipped out.

"I mean, you know Mom, this whole thing's been like out of nowhere. Like all of a sudden you're engaged and your name's changed? Then mine, too? That's messed up."

She was speechless. She understood her son's frustration, but she had no plausible explanation for the name issue other than the fact that she'd sold her soul to the devil. Her common sense had been the down payment.

"Darling," Rand said. He caressed her forearm. "I explained the reason to him."

Daisy blinked. *That's nice. Would you mind filling me in on that one?*

"I called Elizabeth," Adam continued, "and asked her to give me a ride to Morristown. I decided to confront Rand myself."

"Then we went for lunch at a hotdog cart in town and I explained how for the time being we decided it would be in the best interest of your privacy if we kept your true identity from the media. I impressed upon him how the media could turn our lives into a local circus and none of us wants that. Right, darling?"

"Uh-huh, right," Daisy said. She didn't know why she should feel surprised. Really, Rand's coming up with that line of bull was just another of his talents, being the big fat liar that he was.

"It made sense to me," Adam said. He shrugged. "I get it now. It's ridiculous, but I see how it could be a problem."

Rand started to chuckle. "He asked me if I was in the mob."

Then Adam started to laugh along with him. Daisy looked wide-eyed from one to the other as though she was watching a movie on a screen. All she could think was that if anyone walked in on the scene they'd think they were witnessing one little happy family. The fact that it was a fake one was nearly laughable in itself. Only, she didn't feel like laughing.

"And then you decided to go fishing? Even though you're grounded?"

"I know," Adam said. "I intended to be home before five."

"In time for me to get home and not know you'd gone—have I got that right?"

"Sort of," Adam said softly. "I didn't think it would be any big deal. I mean, I was just going to go over to Edmond's Pond for a little while. It's a good place to, you know, think."

"Grounded is grounded, Adam," she said. "What's gotten into you?"

"I don't know," he said.

Daisy saw clouds move into the blue sky of his eyes. Something was weighing on him, but the anvil of guilt pressed on her heart.

"Do you want to talk about it, Adam?"

His gaze went to Rand, then Daisy. "I've got homework to do."

"Okay," she said.

Adam stood from the table. He extended a hand toward Rand and the two clasped into a quick handshake.

"We'll go out on the boat sometime soon, okay?" Rand said.

"That'd be great. Maybe I could bring Elizabeth along."

Daisy saw Rand's face fall, ever so slightly. She had come to know that insufferable look of disapproval. She thought of the way Elizabeth must have appeared to him when he first laid eyes on her—the clownish getup, the ring in her nose, the heavy eyeliner, maroon lipstick.

"Yes," Daisy said. She felt a twinge of pleasure. "Absolutely. And, please bring her to the engagement party, too."

Rand's eyes bugged out like shiny green hockey pucks. This tickled Daisy to high heaven.

****

What was she doing? Rand thought. If he didn't know better he'd think she was deliberately trying to sabotage their effort. Now she'd invited Adam's girlfriend—what was her name? Elvira?—to the engagement party. Was she nuts? Uncle will get one look at the two of them and think it's a Halloween party.

"Darling, walk me to my car?" Rand asked, sweet as pie, after Adam had retreated to his room.

"Sure," she said with as much sugar in her tone as a cube of salt.

When they were out into the night air, cool and

clear, she started before he had time to speak.

"I have to hand it to you, Rand. You're the best liar I've ever known. And trust me, I've known some of the best."

"I'd say thank you, but I know you mean to insult me."

"You'd almost think you actually like Adam. Bravo."

"News flash, Cameron darling, I do. He's a good kid—smart and loyal. I like him very much."

Just saying it made Rand realize how true the words were. Adam *was* a nice kid. He still didn't understand the need to pierce his body and don chunks of metal on his fingers, but aside from that the kid was all right.

Cameron's stare shone with surprise, but why not? He was kind of surprised himself.

"Well, I saw that look in your eyes when I told Adam he could bring Elizabeth to the engagement party."

"What look?"

"That regal disdain of yours."

"Well, come on, Cameron, think about it. You told me that it wasn't easy to convince Adam to dress more conservatively for the party. Now, you're going to make sure the girl does the same? Why add another thing to concern ourselves with?"

"I'm sure it won't be a problem." Cameron sighed.

They had reached his car. He instantly touched his hand to the door handle then stopped and turned toward her. "I didn't mean to get Adam in any more trouble. I figured it would be a good idea to spend some time with him, to get him to cool his anger. You should have seen him when he showed up at my office." Rand shook his head. "That was one angry boy."

"Wouldn't you be?" Cameron asked, placing her

hands on her hips. She looked down at her feet then back up at him. "This is not worth it."

"No turning back, darling," Rand said. "A full ride to his top choice college is worth it, wouldn't you say?" The words felt like gauze on his tongue. Now that he knew Adam's doubts about Pratt he detested using the ploy.

"Yes," she said. "I want my son happy. But, he doesn't seem happy these days. Something's up with him. I don't know. I think it's more than this engagement."

"It's growing pains, Cameron," he offered, unable to meet her eyes. "You remember what it was like to be eighteen, right? Talk with him."

Her eyes had started to tear and Rand had heard a catch in her throat. Something had begun to melt inside of him, and that was worrisome. He liked the kid, liked the impromptu dinner in the cramped kitchen, and most assuredly he liked the woman.

He watched her mouth pinch on one side, a gesture of dismay he'd come to know in such a short time. For the life of him, Rand couldn't fathom what it was he was feeling. All he knew was that this woman with the flyaway curls and the sadness in her crystal blue eyes was a magnet. And his metal heart was being tugged. Worrisome.

She gazed into his eyes, bit her lower lip. "I'll be glad when this is behind us. I need to get back to normal."

She smelled good, a crazy mix of scents he couldn't identify, home cooking and autumn, maybe. He inhaled with pleasure. A gusty breeze flittered over them, and he reached to brush an errant strand of her hair from her eyes. She didn't move.

"Cameron..."

Her nearness was killing him. He felt her energy, even though their bodies did not touch. It was heady and dangerous in its appeal. None of this was in their bargain. But here it was. Alive.

Her lips parted. The tip of her tongue darted over them quickly. She felt it, too. He could tell. He saw the flicker in her eyes, the embers of desire, there for him and the world to acknowledge. This woman scared the hell out of him.

"My..." she said. She paused and took a step away from him. His hand fell to his side. "My son believed your rationale about the name change." She reached up to push that same lock of burnished gold that tumbled again over her brow. "You really made him think the paparazzi are trolling around looking for the scoop on me?"

Suddenly Adam called "Mom!" from the open front door yards away.

"What is it, Adam?" she asked.

"Mrs. Martino just called. She was on the internet. You're in the news."

****

The three of them huddled at the kitchen counter, Adam's laptop open in front of them. They stared at an image of Rand and Daisy leaving his Jaguar. She could tell by her outfit that the photo was taken on the night of her birthday party. The caption, in a large bold font, read "Press Playboy to Wed."

Daisy scanned the text. It mentioned Rand's string of breakups with women whose names she'd never heard, except for Jada Jeffries. And it named his fiancée as *Cameron Day, an unknown*.

"It's no big deal, darling," Rand said. "Nice likeness, though." He pointed his finger to the image of her face. "That's one attractive *unknown*."

"Ha-ha," Daisy said. She turned from the screen.

"You weren't kidding," Adam said. "Your engagement *is* news around here."

"What I want to know is who took this picture? Was somebody hiding in the bushes or something?"

239

she asked.

"Probably," Rand said.

"Are photographers going to be at the engagement party?" Adam asked.

"No way," Rand assured them. "Uncle's house is like Fort Knox. Nobody's getting in there."

Daisy hoped Rand was right.

Chapter Twenty-Eight

Daisy wore the sapphire-toned, cap-sleeved sheath that Candy said had the "wow factor." It was the only dress in the boutique on which the two had agreed. While Candy had suggested she try on the selections with plunging necklines and slits up the thigh, Daisy had somehow managed to walk out with a suitable purchase.

Now, ready for the event, she shook in her two-inch heels. The gold chain around her neck felt like a noose, the dangling golden daisy charm, its knot. She had done her best to banish the sickness she felt going into this evening, but her temples throbbed with the tightrope performance ahead of her.

William Press already knew the truth, but Rand still believed their sham was in place. The way she played it tonight would determine everything—all, or nothing. Now, she was determined that Rand would receive his inheritance.

The old man had soured her with his cold objective and just the thought of acting in front of him tonight made her want to scream. There was no wonder why his only living heir had gone to this extreme.

When Rand showed up at her door, her insides knotted like twine. She didn't worry that Rand was onto her nervousness. His eyes were glued to her dress.

"Dear God, woman, you're stunning!" He said this with such sincerity that Daisy was taken aback. Heat flooded her face.

"Thank you," she managed. *It's just a*

241

compliment, girl. A line from the script. Don't get rattled now.

But she couldn't help it. Rand was in a finely-tailored suit that obviously was cut to his exact proportions. Daisy swallowed hard. He was stunning, too, come to think of it. But there was no way she'd verbalize that. Caution stirred inside her, fueled by his affect. "You look nice," she said, as nonchalantly as she could.

"Ready?"

"As I'll ever be," she said. Her stomach had turned into a Slinky, spilling over on itself back and forth exactly like the coiled toy.

"Where's Adam?"

"He and Elizabeth went on their own."

"Then, shall we?"

****

Rand couldn't keep his eyes off her, even as he drove. His every nerve ending was aware of her seated beside him. Her perfume beckoned him like a fresh cut meadow; summoning with the scents of cedar, sandalwood, and wild flowers. *Dear God, get a grip, man.*

But that dress on her. He stole another glance. He caught the way the fabric hugged her thigh, the hem hit her at just the right length. There would be no problem tonight convincing a roomful of his uncle's cronies that this was the woman of his dreams.

He looked again, at her face this time. She was amazing. What he appreciated most was that she didn't have that classic Barbie-doll perfect face. Her eyes were perhaps too far apart if truth be told, and her nose was a little crooked, her mouth was wider than it was lush. But, together her features made for a uniquely beautiful woman.

"Before we get there, I just want to say thank you, Cameron. I mean, I know the turmoil this ordeal has caused and I appreciate your efforts."

"Well, it's not as though I don't have a vested interest, Rand, but thanks for that. I appreciate it."

That was another thing. He liked her, *really* liked her. When this was all over he would regret the end of their liaison. But, there was no sense thinking about that now. Tonight was the most important piece of their puzzle and he needed to concentrate on that.

His eye caught the glint of her necklace and when he saw the charm that adorned the smooth milky space that peeked at her neckline, he startled. "Are you wearing a gold daisy?"

Her hand immediately went to it. She pinched it between two fingers and tucked it in behind the fabric of her dress.

"Do you think it's wise to call attention to a daisy this evening?" he asked.

"I'll keep it hidden."

"Is it important that you wear it?"

He heard her sigh loudly. "Very."

****

When she and Rand pulled up to the mansion, Daisy was surprised to see valet attendants awaiting their arrival. They were early, as William had requested. God only knew if the old guy had another bomb to drop. Daisy's gut continued to roil.

The interior of the house was dressed in a multitude of white roses, displayed in crystal vases scattered throughout. Florence, dressed in a bead-trimmed dress, looked bright-eyed and eager for their reaction to the festive decorations.

"Flo, you've outdone yourself," Rand said. He kissed the older woman's cheek. "And, you look ravishing."

"Oh, go on, you," she said. She tapped his arm. She turned her attention to Daisy. "Cameron, dear, you're breathtaking."

Maybe that's why I can't breathe, Daisy thought. She and Florence shared an embrace. The pressure of the woman's arms around her felt tighter than casual, more familiar, and Daisy was ashamed.

They were ushered in to peek at the dining room. The massive table was set for twenty. *Twenty!* She counted the chairs again. Who the heck was coming here tonight?

"It's lovely," she managed. "But, wow, I didn't realize how many guests there'd be."

"Oh, William's included all his important associates. Rand, he's quite proud of your turnaround. And, I think he's smitten with your Cameron."

Yeah, right, Daisy thought, recalling their luncheon conversation. She'd come to understand that setting her up for this evening was his type of fun. Something other than panic and fear tumbled inside her. Anger had joined in, and it was sharp, its points jabbing at her. The gold charm burned against her skin. She'd be damned if she'd fall apart in front of that old geezer. Daisy took a deep breath and released it.

"Where is our host?" she asked.

"Right here." His voice came from behind them.

They all turned in the direction of the doorway. William Press stood in a dark suit, his craggy face alight.

"Uncle, the house looks terrific," Rand said. They approached the patriarch and the men shook hands.

"Credit goes to Florence," he croaked. "She's an amazement. As are you, Cameron. You are indeed amazing."

Daisy accepted his bony hand into her own. He squeezed her tight in his clutch. Meeting his eyes, she saw challenge in the rheumy orbs. Daisy smiled at him and pulled free.

"Thank you for hosting us, Uncle William. You're looking well this evening."

"Oh, I'm better now that you're here. I've been waiting for you. Rand, would you mind if your beloved and I had a private moment? I'd like to show Cameron the library."

"I told you," Florence said in a staged whisper. "He's smitten."

"That's fine, Uncle, but don't be long."

Daisy and Rand exchanged a look. His green eyes beamed with encouragement. As she took William's arm Daisy did her best to return a look that told Rand she would be fine. And they walked away.

Inside the double-doored enclave of the library, Daisy could not help but marvel at the numerous volumes aligned along the shelves. The wall above the fireplace was adorned with photographs and artwork, arranged in a series of rows. It was a room like no other she'd seen in the Press mansion. This room was warm and inviting.

"How lovely," she said, glad for the chance to tell the truth. "What a terrific room."

"It's Rand's favorite, too. Ever since he was a boy."

They stepped closer to the fireplace. Daisy saw that the photographs were of members of the Press family. She recognized the family traits, saw that Rand's emerald eyes were a gift of his lineage. She pointed to a photograph of a handsome young man, a pretty woman tucked close to his side, a little boy in shorts at her hem.

"That's him," William said.

"He looks like his dad."

"Yes. And, if life had taken a different path, Randolph would have been just like him."

"I don't follow."

"Randolph's father, my brother, was a dreamer.

He did everything he could to break free of our heritage. And his wife, Lord, she was a bohemian. Completely unrefined." He waved his hand in the air as if chasing away a gnat.

Daisy spotted a frame that displayed a red-painted handprint of a child. She looked closer and saw the inscription etched in a childish scrawl—*"To Uncle William, Love, Johnny."*

"Who's Johnny?"

"Why, your fiancé, my dear. His mother refused to call him Randolph, and she had balked at having to continue the family name. Said a child should be his own person, or some such nonsense. So, she called the boy Johnny. Can you imagine? That, of course, was dropped after she perished."

Daisy felt her muscles pull around her torso like a girdle. She did not want the old prig to read his affect on her. She turned away, letting her gaze travel along the rows of books lining the dark wooden shelves.

Collectibles were placed here and there amidst the volumes of classics and reference journals. She stepped closer. There were bronzed figurines— statuary depicting life frozen in molds of metal. *Of course he'd have such collectibles*, Daisy decided, *isn't that what he did with Rand?* William Press had cast the twelve-year-old John into an heir according to his specifications.

She wondered what the young Rand's boyhood had been like here in this lifeless mansion. On the top shelf, far from reach, she spotted a ceramic jar, speckled brown like a fawn, its uneven mouth causing its lid to gap. Around its neck was a chain that held an oval-shaped plaque. She was unable to read the word inscribed from such a distance.

"What is it that's got your attention?" he asked.

"That jar on the top shelf," Daisy said. She looked toward the old man. "It looks handmade." In

246

her heart she knew that it had to be one of Rand's mother's creations, the type that Rand had told her William detested. "I like it."

He clucked his tongue. "Dear girl, of all the antiquity and precious artifacts in this room, you comment on an amateur's feat of clay?"

"It's the only object here that has any life in it," she said. She felt a spark inside her chest. She craned her neck, cocked her head. "What is it?"

"Who knows," he said. He jabbed his hand in the air like a chop of a blade. "I had that sort of bric-a-brac disposed of long ago, but I suppose Randolph convinced Florence to keep that one." He pursed his lips into what looked like a wrinkled bud. "Sentimental nonsense."

Anger pecked at her like a hungry vulture. Her eyes went back to the photo over the fireplace, to the small boy smiling for the camera. She turned her gaze to William.

"We should join Rand and Florence," she said. The clench in her jaw hurt.

"I haven't yet told you the reason I've brought you here."

"I'm listening."

"You don't like me, Daisy Cameron. Do you?"

"No, sir, I do not."

He chuckled like an old crone. "That's fine. I wanted this opportunity to tell you how delighted I am to see that you are wearing my gift. I know that indicates you've decided to accept my terms in this charade.

"Based on what I've come to know about you, I'd say that it was a tough decision. I refer to your sense of nobility. A noble pauper, soon to reap her reward. A quarter of a million dollars is a nice price tag, wouldn't you agree?"

"Can we go now?"

"But, be warned, Ms. Cameron. The night is

young. Your deal with my nephew is far from sealed. One thing you can trust in this sordid plan is that you cannot trust what a Press man will do."

"I wouldn't categorize Rand with what you're capable of, William. I have a feeling you're in a class all on your own. And, while we're here having this little pow-wow, let me just tell you, that I think what you're doing to your only blood relative is despicable. He counted on you to be his family when his parents were taken from him. And, you've reduced your relationship to a matter of dollars and cents. I pity Rand, but I pity you more."

"You're falling for him," the old man accused, with a crack of laughter.

Her breath caught in her chest. But, it was the appearance of Candy, draped in her fancy red party dress, frozen in the doorway that made Daisy's jaw drop.

Chapter Twenty-Nine

"I'm sorry," Candy's voice sounded hollow. "I didn't mean to interrupt."

"Oh, not at all. We're done here. Aren't we, my dear?" William asked, merry-toned. "You mustn't keep your fiancé waiting."

"Yes." Daisy's eyes were on Candy whose face was pinched with concern.

They made their way toward the living room, each woman at one of William's elbows. He offered niceties, particularly to Candy, complimenting her on her dress and welcoming her into his home. Daisy knew in her heart the man was full of crap and that he probably detested Candy's fire-engine red ensemble with the stiletto heels.

Candy gave him her broadest toothiest grin and laughed mildly at his attempts at humor. It was how she acted if a customer at the Brookside was obnoxious. William Press did not fool Candy Martino.

"Won't my business associates take one look at me and think I've hit the jackpot?" he said with an unctuous chuckle. "Escorting not one, but two beautiful women."

Daisy cringed as they inched down the long corridor. The living room was abuzz with guests milling about while tuxedoed wait staff passed offerings of pastry puffs and bits of seafood perched on top of soda crackers. Others carried silver trays of drinks in all varieties.

Candy accepted a flute of champagne from a server and helped herself to a second one, handing it

249

to Daisy. "Can we chat?" she whispered. She sipped from her glass. "Where's the ladies room in this mausoleum?"

"Not now, Candy."

Candy ignored her request, grabbed the attention of a waiter, and asked him for the location of the restroom. She consulted the rhinestone-studded watch on her wrist. "Dinner's in an hour. I'll meet you down the hall to the left, last door straight ahead in a half hour. You hear me? Seven-thirty."

"Candy..."

Her friend narrowed her gaze, her shiny red mouth narrowed into a line of determination. Daisy weighed her options like a paratrooper perched at the plane's open door. "Fine."

Candy went to join her Sunday's-finest-clad family, clustered with Ima and Pete at the opposite side of the room.

"Good evening," William croaked, and the room was at attention. "Thank you all for joining me in this most joyous celebration of my nephew's good fortune of somehow convincing this lovely woman to be his bride." He gazed appreciatively at Daisy.

The bullshit in his eyes was so apparent she would have laughed if she weren't so appalled. "Randolph, come claim your betrothed before I convince her to marry me instead."

Polite laughter tittered among the onlookers, and Daisy's insides jabbed as if she'd swallowed shards of glass. Then Rand appeared before them, all smiles and brightness, so real no one could guess he was a man on stage.

"I saw her first, Uncle," Rand boomed, playing to the crowd. He wrapped his arm around her shoulders and gave her a squeeze. Then, without warning, he planted a kiss onto her lips, lingering there longer than was necessary to convince the roomful of guests that he was a man in love.

Daisy's mind reeled with questions, as though watching the scene from above. Why did she respond? What did it matter that his lips were warm and lush and that they tasted like wine? And, better yet, why the hell was she kissing him back?

She pulled away and realized the guests, many of them her friends as well as her son, applauded with approval. But not Candy. Her narrow gaze peered at Daisy over the rim of her champagne flute. And, Daisy's momentary sensual awareness of the man next to her dissipated into thin air.

Daisy felt as if she was floating in a rain cloud. Her skin was cold and the air she breathed brewed with the promise of an oncoming storm. Numbly, she greeted Adam. She snapped back to life at the sight of him, handsome in his sports jacket.

"Mom," he said. He kissed her cheek. "You okay? You look as if you've seen a ghost."

"I'm fine. Just a bit of the jitters. You look great, honey."

"Thanks," he said with an appreciative smile. "Have you seen Elizabeth?"

Just then the girl appeared beside him. Daisy was surprised to see her in a sleeveless, full-waisted dress, albeit black, but a tasteful choice. Her hair was pulled up at the sides and cascaded down her back in a shimmery brown sheet.

"Elizabeth, you look lovely."

"Thank you. So, do you. You look awesome."

"You're all grown up. Both of you."

"Thanks, but these shoes are killing me already," Elizabeth confided. She circled her ankle around on the pivot of a high heel. "I'm afraid I'm going to fall off these things and break something.

Then Candy and her clan were upon them, everyone embracing, commenting on each other's fancy getups, the lavish surroundings. Candy's eyes continued to be locked on her.

"Holy smokes, this is a princess's castle," Gina gushed. They all laughed.

"Oh, look, bacon-wrapped scallops," Bruno said. "Candy, want one?" Her husband, dolled up in a suit and tie—looking about as comfortable in the outfit as a wrestler in a tutu—went to retrieve the tidbit for his wife.

Daisy and Rand made their way around the room greeting their guests. Rand kept his hand at her back, or on her arm, as they chatted with each person.

Encircled by William's business associates they were bombarded with questions about the details of their relationship's evolution. Daisy felt as though she and Rand were defendants and this trio of barrel-chested, vested, pocket-watched old men was their jury.

Candy appeared at their periphery and introductions went around the circle, breaking the interrogation. Although that was a relief, dread washed over Daisy. It was time.

The two comrades excused themselves from the conversation and made their way toward the hallway. "Brought you this," Candy said. She handed off one of the two champagne flutes she held. "You're going to need it."

The clicking of their heels sounded in unison, occupying the silence between them. They entered the room at the end of the hall and Candy closed the door behind them.

Candy sat on top of the toilet seat, crossed her leg and took a swig from her glass as though it was a beer and not imported champagne. "Okay, I'm ready. What the hell are you doing?"

"I'm not sure what you mean."

"Cut the crap. I stood in that doorway long enough to know this is all a bunch of bullshit and the old guy's got something he's holding over your head. I'd love for you to tell me I'm so full of this bubbly stuff that I couldn't possibly have heard that you're pretending—making fools of all of us, including yourself—for a shitload of money."

Candy bolted from her seat, her voice loud and shrill, filled with rage. "Tell me you haven't done this."

Daisy instinctively took a step away and her hands shook as they gripped the delicate stem of her glass. An ache filled her throat with the urge to cry. There in the small, tiled room there was nowhere to hide. Not anymore.

All of the energy it had taken to participate in the charade, all the angst she'd suppressed during every day of it, the worry and the what-ifs came crashing down on her in an avalanche of self-loathing. It filled her heart and her soul with the black ink of what she knew would be the reward for her deeds—emptiness.

"Honey, honey…don't," she heard her friend say. She allowed herself to be enfolded into Candy's warm, strong embrace. Daisy hadn't realized the crashing sounds that rang in her ears had been her own sobs. "Dear God, how did this happen? Daisy, tell me. Why?"

"For Adam," she said, sobering. She pulled away from Candy's hold. She tugged a series of tissues from a brass holder and held them to her eyes.

"It was stupid. I know that. But, I knew I'd never be able to afford to send him away to that big art school. And, this was my chance to make sure he could go."

"How'd you get roped into this?"

"William threatened to change his will if Rand didn't have intentions to get married before his birthday in January. So, Rand offered to pay for Adam's college if I agreed to play the part of his fiancée."

"Daisy, no offense, kid, but you're nuts if you think Adam would want you to fake an engagement for his sake."

"No one was supposed to find out."

"Well, that old uncle of Rand's figured it out, didn't he? Why didn't he just go to Rand and tell him he knows?"

"Because, apparently, it's more fun for him this way." The words disgusted her. "The only chance Rand has of inheriting the estate is if I keep my mouth shut until William decides to let him know he's onto us. And even then, it's no guarantee."

"No wonder Rand dated the queen of soap operas. This whole mess sounds just like one." Candy downed the rest of her champagne. "Be careful you don't find yourself in the bottom of a well flopped on top of your twin sister.

"So, what now, Daisy? You're going to actually marry the guy?"

"No. Don't be absurd."

Candy laughed. "Oh, far be it from *me* to act *absurd*. She put her hands on Daisy's shoulders. "I have another question. This affection we're all seeing between you two has just been all part of the game? The kissing, the obvious romance, the goo-goo looks?"

"Candy, stop."

She turned to face the mirror above the sink and her own image startled her. The line between reality and fantasy had blurred in the fog of the charade. Fear beamed back at her from the haunted eyes in the reflection.

"Daisy?" Candy said.

"Candy, I'm in so much trouble. How do I undo this?"

"You tell me."

Daisy took a deep breath, dried her eyes, and downed her remaining champagne. "The truth.

Time's up."

"Wait. You're going to go out there and make some grand confession to all those people enjoying their evening? You want them to choke on their coconut shrimp bites?"

"No, we have to get through the rest of this dinner. But, then I'll tell Rand what I have to do. I'm going to apologize to everybody and hope they don't all hate me—especially Adam. Candy, what if Adam hates me for this?"

Candy reached for Daisy's hand and squeezed it. "Don't underestimate that kid. He's got a good heart. Just like his mother."

"Thank you, Candy," Daisy said. She turned again to the mirror. "I'm a mess. Look at me. How am I going to go back in that room?"

"Look," Candy said. "Take a few minutes. Dry your eyes, splash some water on your face, then come back to the party. I'll head back and stall anyone looking for you."

"I don't know what I'd do without you. I owe you," Daisy said. She offered an anemic grin. "Just name it."

"How about *you* deal with Gina after she finds out she's not going to be a flower girl after all?" Candy blew Daisy a kiss, winked a well-made-up eye at her, and left the room.

After a few minutes, Daisy got the notion that someone soon might seek the use of the restroom. She gave one last glance to her image, still too puffy and blotchy, and retreated from the room. Making her way down the corridor, she wondered where she could linger, unnoticed, for a few minutes before rejoining the circus in the dining room.

The door to the library was open and she slipped inside, closing the heavy wooden door behind her. The air was still. The only light came from the subdued hue of a table lamp. She went to the bookshelves and eyed the titles as her gaze moved along the rows. She again spied the speckled jug on the top shelf.

What would Rand do when he learned her decision to reveal the sham? Could he hold her liable in any way? Would he? Would he hate her for it? Why did she care? The questions pummeled her thoughts. She didn't hear the door open, nor see the figure enter the room.

Chapter Thirty

"So, here you are," Rand said.

The look on her face froze him in place. She had been crying, even in the dim light he could see that. He carefully, silently closed the door behind him and went to her.

"What's wrong?" He felt a tug at his insides.

"I just needed a minute," she said. She avoided his gaze. She stared up toward the ceiling, an errant tear dribbled down from the corner of her eye.

"Cameron," he said. The name hit a nerve. "Daisy."

She turned to look at him, surprise in her eyes— surprise and sadness. "You called me Daisy."

"I know," he said. He felt a smile take ownership of his mouth. "We're alone. Didn't you request that we suspend the use of Cameron when we lacked an audience?"

"Yes," she said softly, "I guess I did."

"Is all this too much for you? Is that it?"

"Something like that," she said. She turned away and glanced upward again.

He followed her gaze and saw the object. At first, the oddly-shaped container did not register and his eyes flitted right past it. But then, recognition slapped him like an open hand. It was the little plaque that dangled around its neck like a locket that disquieted him. It was too dark in the room to read the one word etched on it, but he didn't have to see the letters to know what they said—"Wishes".

He realized that Daisy was looking at him now, studying his obvious reaction. "How'd that get

257

there?" he asked, as if she'd know.

"Your uncle said it's been there for years. He said it belongs to you."

"Yes."

"One of your mother's pieces?"

"Yes," he answered, in spite of the knot that had formed in his throat.

The memory of the jar slammed him like a blast of cold air, and he was powerless to stop it. He saw himself as a twelve-year-old, clinging to that clay pot his mother had made for him. "For collecting his wishes," she'd said. But, then she'd died and so did his desire to contain his yearnings—with the exception of one.

He remembered now the day he'd put the jar up on that high perch—how he'd waited for his uncle to go off some place, leaving him there alone. Yes, Rand remembered the jar and he knew what was in it.

He wheeled the wooden ladder over on its casters, his mind unwilling to listen to the caution that throbbed in his head. He ascended the oak steps, gripping the rails. At the top he pulled the jug into his grasp. The lid tilted precariously.

Standing again with Daisy—now with the jar in his hands—he felt silly. What good would it do him to peer inside? If he kept the lid on it he could avoid any questions. He should have left it alone. But he was no better than Pandora.

Daisy touched the lid, wrapped her fingertips around the nub. "A little lopsided, but it's nice," she said. She cocked her head. "What's it say?"

Rand jerked his hand in an effort to hide the plaque from her view but what he accomplished was for the lid to fall off entirely and bounce onto the thick carpet at their feet.

Unavoidably, they both peeked into the crooked mouth, their foreheads nearly touching.

"Is that money?" she asked.

"It is," he said. He reached inside to withdraw the wadded bills. He couldn't remember how much it was, but he did know why he'd put it there.

Rand unfolded the wrinkled bills. "Thirty-seven."

"Was this your piggy bank, or something?" she asked. A gentle smile formed on her lips. She looked closer, then read the plague aloud. "Wishes," she said. "Is that what you've always wished for, Rand? Money?"

Before he could think, Rand told her the story. Even hearing the words coming from his own mouth couldn't convince him that he was really saying them out loud. Nor could he stop himself.

"My mother gave this to me just before she and Dad were killed in the accident." He fingered the dangling disk. "Wishes," he said warmly. "My mother was like that."

He felt a catch in his throat. Too much emotion hurt his insides like too much dinner. "I used to love this room, still do, come to think of it."

"It's nice," she agreed. "Less stuffy."

He nodded at her. "It's got character.

"When I moved in with Uncle William I used to come in here to be by myself, to think. After my parents died I decided on a wish."

He looked up to see her eyes glued to him, penetrating blue pools of compassion that should have halted his speech, but didn't. "I wanted to save up enough money on my own to take a trip." He laughed at the absurdity of his boyish plan. It was an empty sound, lacking mirth.

"Where did you want to go?"

"To Dalton, Florida," he said. "It's a little town in Lee County."

"Isn't that where your parents went to work with Habitat for Humanity?"

He nodded. "I thought if I went there and saw

259

what they built, touched the wood maybe, I'd be able to feel them." He shrugged. "Maybe meet the people who had known them."

He shrugged again and breathed deeply to dispel the effect of her sincere gaze. "I was just a kid."

Daisy was silent, looking down at her hands. He watched as her thumb manipulated her engagement ring, making it turn around on her finger.

"I have something to tell you, Rand," she said. She raised her tear-filled eyes to him.

She's going to bolt, he thought. *She's done.* He knew in that instant that he would do nothing to dissuade her. He braced himself for the announcement. "I'm listening."

"I'm afraid the jig, as they say, is up." She smirked. "Your uncle knows everything."

"What?" He felt his heart bang in his chest and his blood race.

She nodded, her mouth pulled into a grimace that trembled. "And, Candy, too."

"Wait, what's she got to do with it?"

"She overheard your uncle talking with me about what he knows—and his warning to me."

Rand's jaw ached from the tight clench. *Shit.* "Warning? Daisy." He gave her shoulder a squeeze. "Start from the beginning."

She blew out a long breath, wet her lips and began. "Your uncle invited me to lunch that day to lower the boom." She reached into her neckline and withdrew the gold charm that had hung discreetly behind the fabric of her dress. "He gave me this."

"He gave you that daisy?"

"He told me if I still wanted the money you and I agreed to then I had to keep playing along with our hoax. He told me to wear this tonight as a confirmation that I agreed."

"So, let's see if I've got this, Daisy. He knows

we're just pretending to be engaged, he's stringing me along to get his jollies, and in the end you get your money. And, what, I'm disinherited? I'm left without a cent?" Disappointment slugged him like a fist.

He didn't know what was worse, the evidence of his uncle's heartlessness or Daisy's agreement to the deal.

What else could he expect from this woman? Theirs was a business agreement and Uncle was just making her an ironclad deal.

Looking at her dewy eyes and her mouth pulled into a frown, he hated the entire mess, all of it.

The little ceramic pot in his hand all but laughed at him for the new, even more illogical wish that had brazenly shot through his thoughts like a comet.

"Not exactly," she said, her voice soft, barely audible.

He snickered, shaking loose the thought that teased him moments ago. "You're right, Miss Cameron. I'm not left without a cent, am I? I do have, let's see," he looked again at the crumbled bills. "Yes, I have thirty-seven dollars."

He put the money back into the jug and placed it on the lamp table. "I guess we should go out there and play as though we mean it. Correct?"

"No," she said. She touched his arm. "Wait."

They exchanged a long look and he waited for her to speak.

"Your uncle said if I play along there's still a chance that you'll still get your inheritance. Without my cooperation you'd have been cut from the will immediately."

"What happens to you if he learns you've told me?"

"I get nothing," she whispered.

Rand felt the floor pitch, as though a fault line

had rumbled beneath his feet. The dichotomy of his feelings made him dizzy.

"Daisy, I..." he said. A lump formed in his throat. "I'm sorry I put you in this situation.

"Now my best friend knows the truth. It's a mess." A tear dribbled down her cheek. "And I'm afraid Adam's going to hate me."

"What do you want to do?" Rand asked.

"I don't want you to be disinherited. It's not fair and your uncle is acting rotten, no offense. But I also don't want my son to find out and have it crush him.

"I don't give a damn about the money anymore," her voice quivered but her tone was emphatic. "I don't want one cent."

Rand's mind reeled. He pictured himself losing out on Uncle's fortune, saw his future without all the bells and whistles that made him a Press and defined who he was. What would he do?

How would he be able to look himself in the mirror? There were no poor Presses. He'd be the first. Rand almost laughed. He could actually go down in history, make *Page Six* again perhaps, as the only one of the Press dynasty to have nothing to his name. Nothing.

He turned his gaze to Daisy, her chin tilted up to him, her eyes glistening with tears. Either way he was a loser. He saw that now. However this ended he'd still wind up with an image in a mirror he wouldn't be able to stand looking at.

There was only one true thing in this mess. Daisy Cameron and her son were a real family. God help him, he knew he couldn't participate in its unraveling. *Shit*.

He took her hand. "Let's go play truth or dare."

"What?" she asked. "What do you mean?"

"Game over, Daisy. Let's go find Adam first and we'll tell him together, and then we'll tell our guests."

"But, what about you? You'll be cut out of his will for certain."

"I'll figure something out. I always do."

"Wait," she said. "I can't. Not tonight. I can't make some big announcement like that. Your uncle will be furious. Maybe there's a chance we can speak to him privately and reason with him."

Rand laughed. He wished he had a fraction of her belief in goodness, just a fraction. "No chance, Daisy."

"Let's try. Let's get through this party. Candy won't breathe a word. I trust her.

"Tomorrow we'll talk with Adam, and then William. Maybe that way there's a chance we can salvage my son's faith in me and your inheritance, too."

"Okay." He had no hope. "But it's wishful thinking, Daisy."

"Maybe," she said with a wry smile. "But, your mother's jar is for wishes, isn't it?"

He smiled at her, his brave accomplice. He touched a knuckle under her chin, tilted her head up toward him. "So, back into the fray for tonight?"

"For tonight."

He kissed her and Daisy Cameron let him. Her lips were salty, the remnants of a tear perhaps. He gently tugged at her lower lip claiming the saltiness, relieving her of its taste. The salt of her tears belonged to him and he knew it.

The kiss ended and their eyes locked for a long moment. "Practicing for when we're back out there fooling people?" Daisy asked, her voice a whisper.

"I'm the only fool, Daisy."

"Cameron," she said. "For the rest of tonight I'm Cameron."

And they left to join the others.

Chapter Thirty-One

Dinner was announced as Daisy and Rand rejoined their guests. At the long, elaborately set table conversations were polite and superficial enough for Daisy to relax the overall clench of her entire body.

Beside her Rand was attentive, a model fiancé. He'd even reached to her lap to hold her hand and give it a squeeze, massaging his thumb over her skin. It felt genuine. Maybe it was the wine, or the way he looked in his dark suit, or the scent of the man, but whatever it was, she liked it.

She decided that she'd actually miss some parts of this nightmare. Feeling the sting of her abject thought, she decided to just savor the moment and forget about all the anguish that had brought her there.

Tomorrow would arrive soon enough. She squeezed Rand's hand. The rest of the evening would be the calm before the storm of tomorrow's truth.

But then the door chimes sounded.

Two young waiters darted to join Florence at the dining room's entry and Daisy saw the urgency in their mannerisms, the rapidity of their mouths' movements as they whispered.

One of the valet attendants joined the threesome, his arms flailing. And then she heard the escalated vocals of a female.

A young woman, accompanied by a broad, muscular man in a tight white shirt, charged into the room. Her frosted hair, fashioned into an up-do, looked as though it had fallen prey to a windstorm. Tendrils of starchy hair flapped alongside the woman's head. Her lipstick was smeared beyond her mouth, giving her an exaggerated grimace.

"I understand congratulations are in order," she said. Her voice was thick as if her tongue was swollen. Daisy recognized her now. That deep alto voice had a hint of a southern accent masked by efforts to lose it. Dear God, this was Jada Jeffries—and she was drunk.

"Oh my God," Candy said. She knocked over a goblet sending rivulets of water travelling through the table settings like the rush of a flooded river. Ima and Pete dabbed at the currents with their linen napkins. Gina and Little Bruno pitched in with theirs, silverware clinking to the floor in the process.

Daisy, stunned by the intrusion, hadn't realized that she continued to grip Rand's hand as though it were a life preserver. She saw startle in Rand's green eyes. She felt as if her heart had fallen from her chest like the water goblet that crashed to the hardwood floor.

****

Rand stood from the table and tossed his napkin onto his plate. He cleared his throat, determined to quell the potential disaster.

He should have known that article in the papers would reach Jada somehow. One of her little lap dogs had surely brought it to her attention and gotten her riled up all over again.

He needed to stop this now before it served to unravel his scheme right there and then. "Jada," he said louder than he intended. "Please, join us. Everyone, I'm sure you know who this is. Meet my dear friend, Jada Jeffries."

"Mommy, isn't that Isabella from *Bridge's Crossing?*" Gina asked. Candy shushed her.

"Hey, Mom, can we get her autograph? I could sell it on eBay," Little Bruno piped in. His father leaned down to him and silenced the boy with a stern look.

Rand gazed at Daisy who remained seated, her face pale and stoic. He needed to pull her into his effort. *Shit.* "Darling,"—his tone was sugary in spite of the tightness in his throat—"come meet Jada." He extended his hand to Daisy.

Like a zombie, she lifted a slack hand and allowed him to guide her from the chair. She grabbed hold of her wine glass, and allowed Rand to usher her toward the disheveled television star.

Jada seemed glad now to be settled in at center stage in his uncle's home. Getting her out of there would be tough.

"Uh..." Daisy said, the utterance sounding like an expression of pain. She gulped at her wine. "Yes, of course, I know who this is. Hello, Jada. It's a pleasure to meet you."

"Is it?" Jada spat. She wobbled on unsteady legs clad in burgundy leather, rocking on the spiky heels of zebra print boots. "Is it *nice* to meet me?"

Jada laughed and burped simultaneously. "Well, good...because I'm here to save your ass. From him." She pointed a long, cherry red-painted finger nail at Rand. "Your fiancé is the biggest louse I've ever met. You hear me, Rand? Admit what you are."

Rand rushed at Jada, not knowing what he'd do once he grabbed hold of her shoulders. Shake her quiet, maybe? She pushed at him. He'd forgotten how feisty she could be, despite her diminutive size. He toppled backward.

Jada swatted her hard leather clutch at him like a blindfolded player whacking at a piñata. Losing her balance, she fell on him. She kept chanting the same word. "Liar!" she screamed. "Liar!"

Rand stretched a hand out from his side, a feeble attempt to remain standing. Daisy grabbed him and tried to hold on. In one swift thud, the three of them fell to the floor.

****

Daisy's head was hurting. The cacophony in the room made it worse. Everyone had gathered around, hands reaching to offer assistance, voices calling their names.

When she was on her feet again, Daisy saw that the bulky man that had come in with Jada was now in the anteroom talking with two police officers. She heard Rand groan and saw that his eyes were fixed on the scene in the doorway. Jada Jefferies had been escorted to a chair by William Press's pinstripe-suited cohorts who doted over her like school boys.

"What the hell is going on?" Candy asked, closing in on Daisy.

Adam was with her, crowded so closely she could barely breathe. "Mom, are you all right? What's she so pissed about?" Adam said. "She like hauled off and hit Rand, pummeled him."

"She can pack a wallop, that's for sure," Bruno chimed in. "Thank God nobody got hurt. That floor's hard."

Daisy's head was sore. She rubbed a finger across her forehead.

"Mom, do you need me to take you home?" Adam asked.

"No," she said. "I'm fine."

"Darling," Rand said. "Are you sure you're okay?" His arm was around her waist, his voice filled with concern. "I'm so sorry."

"Randolph," Florence called from the periphery of guests ringing them. "The policemen would like a word with you."

He looked into Daisy's eyes and touched a finger to her chin. Although her head throbbed, her heart hurt more.

The alarm she saw in his emerald eyes had touched her. Though she knew it was more playacting, she realized in that instant she wanted it to be real. She did. She wanted him to care. Right there, right now, in that moment. She wanted J. Randolph Press, Jr.'s affection and concern, really and truly. That fact hit her like a bucket of ice water. Her own joke was *on her,* and no one was laughing.

****

As Rand headed to confront the policemen he felt a hand on his arm. Adam stood beside him with his face contorted in anger.

"You know what's interesting?" he said, his tone coated in sarcasm like a slick of varnish. "My mom's known you for like no time and already police have been on the scene twice. Is this what it's going to be like from now on?"

"Adam, I'm sorry. I should have known the news would have made its way to Jada's attention. I should have been prepared."

"Is she *unstable* or something?"

"Just angry, I think...and maybe a little drunk."

"Why's she calling you a liar?"

"Because when she and I broke up I told her I'd never get married."

"That's interesting."

"Well, that was before I met your mother." Suddenly the truth in his statement popped in his mind.

Rand looked back at Daisy, surrounded by Candy and her family, and the couple she worked for. She was making a valiant attempt to reassure them that she was fine. He could tell by her gestures and the curve of her smile.

What he knew came to the front of his mind, throbbing like a knock on a door. Daisy Cameron had compromised all that she was for her single most important purpose—this overprotective boy that loved her like crazy. What would Adam do when tomorrow came and the truth came out? Rand felt a stab in his center.

The high-strung Jada Jeffries might be drunk, but she did know a louse when she saw one. It sucked to admit it. A foreign thread tugged at his heart, wound itself around his pulsating life source and held fast. Rand was ashamed.

Jada's goon seemed quite concerned with the threat of trespassing that the police had dangled in front of him. He was glad enough when Rand convinced the officers that should he and Jada just leave, there would be nothing they needed to stick around for.

Jada wasn't as easily convinced. Her chest heaved like a fighter waiting for the next round. Jada Jefferies had always needed the last word, so Rand gave her the opportunity with the hope that it would satisfy her enough to leave.

He went and crouched down in front of the chair she was sitting in. She held a glass half-full of water. Her eyes bored into him like x-rays. "Jada, can I get you some more water?" he asked gently.

With her mouth pursed, she waved the glass in front of his face, as if he was a moron for not noticing she already had water.

"Is there anything else you need?" he continued.

"Yes," she said. "I need for you to explain to me how it is that you publicly humiliated me by telling the whole frigging world that the reason you broke it off with me was because I wanted marriage and you, Mr. King of the Bachelors, did me a *favor* by *sparing* me having to wait for a proposal that would never come."

She emitted a harsh crack of laughter, and then snorted through her nose. "'J. Randolph Press, Jr. is not the marrying kind. He'll never get married. *Ever.*' Isn't that what you said? Isn't it?"

"Jada—"

"No!" She held up a hand. "Answer me. Isn't it

what you said?"

"Yes, it is. I'm sorry."

"So, you meet this country pumpkin. Is that what they call them? Pumpkins?"

"Bumpkin."

She spewed a string of cackles. "Yeah, country bumpkin. You decide now that you're going to marry a nobody country *bumpkin?* And you blast that all over the goddamned news so that I look even more like a discard!"

He reached for her hand and she let him hold it. He petted it as if it was a bunny in his palm. Her eyes softened. Her mouth twitched. He wasn't sure if she was going to yell some more...or toss her cookies.

"You never loved me," she said in a pathetic whine punctuated by a sob.

"Jada, I never meant to hurt you."

"Well you did. You frigging did." She started to cry, wracking sobs with quivering shoulders.

Rand pulled her into an embrace and patted her back, feeling the hardness of the water glass wedged between them. The water glass did not jab near as sharply as the narrow-eyed look Daisy gave him when he glanced her way.

****

Daisy's head continued to throb and now she felt a rush of blood to her cheeks. She felt sweaty and clammy. She was confused as to why anger pulsed in her veins. Seeing Rand genuflecting at the foot of that crazed woman whom he then embraced made Daisy mad enough to spit. This made no sense.

She rubbed her temple in a circular motion, pressing two fingers to the soft hollow there. Thoughts tumbled and zigzagged through her head like laser beams in a light show. Her eyes hurt from the bright streams flashing in her head.

She watched Rand comforting Jada, then wondered what they'd been like as lovers. Images appeared in her mind like a movie—the two entwined in each other's arms, naked, having crazy Hollywood-type sex...whatever that was.

She banished the image, closing her eyes and squeezing them tight. What popped in next was the memory of Rand's kiss and the look he'd given her that made her heart melt, convincing her that she wanted something real from him.

She hated all of it and cradled her head in her hands like a bowling ball, wishing it to cease torturing her.

"Mom?" Adam came up to her and touched his forehead to hers. He whispered softly. "What's the matter? Are you feeling sick?"

Just then Florence came over with a glass of water. "Would you like some water, dear?" Daisy shook her head. She didn't want water and she didn't want to think. The best she could hope for was that she'd pass out and wake up in Kansas.

"Adam, help me, would you? I'm going to bring your mother upstairs to lie down for a bit."

"No, no, no..." Daisy said.

"Mom, maybe that's a good idea," Adam said. He held her tightly under her arm.

"What's going on?" Rand appeared beside her. "Darling, are you all right?"

"I'm fine," she said. She finally let go of her head. When she looked up at him, she saw that blasted concern again in his countenance. It seemed too real to be fake. She saw the caring that she didn't even know she'd been missing and, apparently, longing for. Suddenly she was exhausted.

"I'm going to have her rest a bit in one of the guest suites," Florence said. Together she and Adam held Daisy and ambled toward the staircase. They ascended slowly and when they reached the top, Daisy looked down the sweep of stairs and saw Rand with his green, green eyes on her.

****

When Jada's sedan actually rolled down the driveway, Rand felt his chest muscles release. He had more to contend with. The evening's mess was far from cleaned up, nice and tidy. Already his uncle was eyeing him and he could feel the old guy's scrutiny.

Though Rand had managed to calm down their guests, the party was abruptly over. As each attendee said good night, they all voiced their concerns for his fiancée. His Cameron was a woman loved. She may not have a penny to her name, but she was far richer than he'd ever be.

Florence convinced Uncle William to retire to his room. Rand found himself alone with Adam and his date.

"Elizabeth has to be home," Adam said. "But, I don't want to leave my mom here. I want to make sure she's okay."

"Adam, you go on. Florence says your mom's sleeping. I'll check on her. When she awakens I'll bring her home. Don't worry."

"I'd feel more comfortable waiting."

"It's okay, Adam, I can drive home by myself." Elizabeth held onto his hand and nuzzled close to his side. "I'm a big girl."

"I just don't think we should wake your mom yet. It's been a rough night," Rand said.

"I know," Adam conceded. "Okay, I'll wait for her at home. But, please call me if anything—"

"I will, Adam," Rand said. "I'll have her call you the minute she wakes up."

After Adam and Elizabeth left, Rand wandered into the library and poured himself a brandy. He sat back on the tufted leather sofa and closed his eyes. He sipped the potent liquid, savoring the tingle in his mouth. The feeling continued down his throat, soothing him in its path.

The events of the evening cascaded through his thoughts. Throughout each image he saw Daisy's face and her reactions.

He remembered her response to his kiss. Either she was getting good at this lying stuff or she was feeling something for him. Could that be? And, if so, was it a hindrance, a bother for him? His mind wondered, but his heart said no. Conjuring a response from Daisy Cameron was no bother. But, since when did he listen to anything his heart had to say? When had it started talking to him again? *Shit.*

"Randolph?" Florence's voice interrupted his thoughts, and he was glad for it.

Rand sat up from the cushion and turned in her direction. "Is she awake?" he asked.

"Last I looked she was resting," Florence smiled. "Go up and check on her. I'm sure she'd like that."

If Florence only knew just how wrong that statement was. Daisy Cameron would be about as glad to see him as she would to wake up with the flu. But, he needed to demonstrate a fiancé's expected reaction. He needed to go up to her room.

Chapter Thirty-Two

Daisy opened her eyes. She blinked at the shadows around her and couldn't focus in the darkness. There was a dresser on the one wall and a looming wardrobe on the other. A chenille throw had been draped over her. She shrugged it off. As she stood from the bed, she felt a twinge of dizziness.

She made her way across the room, feeling along the way, holding on first to the bedpost, and then the edge of the dresser. She opened the door and was grateful the hall light was subdued.

She saw a light at the end of the corridor and walked toward it. The door to William Press's bedroom was ajar, soft string music wafted gently out to greet her. She inched close and peered inside.

William was sitting up in bed, reading glasses low on his nose. In his lap was a small leather-bound book. She turned to go, but heard his voice bellow out with a gravelly directive. "Young lady, come here."

Daisy stood frozen, her feet unwilling to allow her to run the other way.

"For God's sake, enter the room," he said.

She stepped into the suite hovering close to the door. "I was just—"

He waved a bony arm. "Can't hear what you're saying, woman. Come closer."

Daisy took tentative steps toward William's massive bed. Her heart thudded. She was unprepared for this. There was no script available. She and Rand had agreed to talk to William tomorrow, together, to perhaps appeal to him to keep

Rand in his will. She didn't want to blow the chance tonight by saying anything foolish.

"There," he said. He pointed to the chair near the bed. "Sit there."

Daisy sat down on the edge of the chair, clasping her hands on her lap. "I saw your light and wanted to, you know, make sure you were all right."

"How nice of you, my dear," he said with all the warmth of the big bad wolf. "And how are you faring? How shall I address you, by the way? Shall I keep up the pretense and continue to call you Cameron?"

"My name is Daisy."

"Good. Daisy it is. So, tell me a bedtime story, Daisy."

"I'm all out of stories, William."

"Nonsense. I know...tell me how you came to be named 'Daisy.' At our luncheon you were emphatic that your name was something that meant a great deal to you. Tell me about that." He settled deeper into his pillows as though he were waiting for a fairy tale to be read to him.

"It's late," she said. She placed her hands on the arms of the chair.

"Please," he said. "Indulge an old man."

She released her grasp on the wooden arms and took a deep breath. Her name was personal, and the last thing she wanted to do was share the story with this ogre. But, for tonight she needed to keep the old guy happy so that tomorrow he might have it in him to grant Rand his due.

"I was two months premature," she began. "And it was touch and go for a while. My parents took turns sitting vigil by the incubator day in and day out waiting for my eyes to open." Daisy shrugged, embarrassed by the intimacy of her words. "When I did, my parents decided to name me Daisy because, according to Chaucer, it means 'the eye of the day.'"

William didn't comment and for a moment Daisy wondered if he had nodded off. She leaned closer to see if his eyes were closed. If so, she could get up and go. He looked right at her with piercing orbs, his reading glasses having been removed from his face.

"The eye of the day," he mused.

"Yes."

"Touching," he said. He cocked his head to one side. "You were well-loved, Daisy. Weren't you?"

She nodded, feeling a lump forming in her throat. *Yes,* she thought. *I was loved.*

Suddenly she thought of Rand and how he, too, had been loved by his parents. But then he'd been thrust to endure years with this cold man. *Did William ever know love,* she wondered?

"I should think that anyone lucky enough to be named with such sentiment should feel honored. It is no wonder you are so proud to be Daisy."

She did not comment, being confused by the genuine tone with which he spoke. It was late and perhaps he was just tired, but he sounded melancholy.

"Randolph's parents called him John."

"You told me that, yes."

"I decided it was too common a name. So, I insisted he be Randolph. More prestigious. But, when you're an old man in poor health you second guess your decisions, Daisy. And, now...I wonder what life would be if things had gone differently."

"My parents always said there's no sense in wondering 'what if.' All you have is what's now."

"Wise people, your parents."

"Yes."

"Come here, Daisy." His gnarled hand reached toward her. "It's time to say good night."

Obediently, she rose from her chair and stepped close to the bed. His eyes shone with a brightness that belonged to someone younger. She felt awkward standing there.

"You're a good woman, Daisy Cameron."

"Thank you, William."

"Now go."

"Good night, William," she said.

She padded back to the room down the hall and felt her way to the bed. Fingering the lamp on the stand and searching for its switch, she pulled the chain.

The room—now that she could see it—was well-appointed, dressed in heather and cream satin stripes. She found her purse beside the bed and retrieved her cell phone. She pushed the speed dial. Adam picked up immediately.

"Mom?"

"Yes, honey. You're still up?"

"Of course I'm still up. Mom, how are you feeling? You okay?"

"I'm fine. Actually, I feel silly. Maybe three glasses of champagne is too many. Write that down."

He didn't laugh at her attempt at humor. She heard his breath on the line. "I'll have Rand run me home in a little while. You go ahead and go to sleep. Okay?"

"Okay," he said, sounding doubtful.

"Please get some sleep, Adam," Daisy whispered with eyes closed, after the call had ended. "I need you rested, so tomorrow when you hear what I've done you'll forgive me."

"He'll understand," came a voice that made her eyes snap open.

Rand stood in the doorway, minus his suit jacket and tie. His white dress shirt was open at the neck. Momentarily, Daisy was startled at the appeal of his naturally tan skin against both the starchy fabric and the shock of ebony hair falling on his forehead.

She slipped her phone into her clutch and held it to her chest like a breastplate. His name whooshed from her lips, riding on a breath. "Rand."

He moved toward the bed with slow, cautious steps, as though not to awaken her. She was awake all right. She swallowed hard, gripping her faux alligator purse closer to her body.

"I came by a few minutes ago and you weren't here." His voice was smooth. Daisy detected a hint of something sweet on his breath—a liqueur, maybe brandy.

"I was going to come downstairs, but I saw your uncle's light on and heard music. For some reason I went to peek in on him."

"Oh, boy," he said. He sat beside her on the bed. She felt the aftershock of the mattress yield to his body. It was nothing compared to the quake that jiggled her insides.

She noticed his gaze on her purse and wondered how he'd perceive the way she held it. The last thing she wanted was for him to guess the physical reaction that sprouted from her nerve endings like buds in springtime. She had only recently let herself in on that sorry fact. She released the clutch, tossing it aside like a nuisance.

"Was he asleep?"

"No," she confessed. "And he saw me. Made me come in and talk with him."

"How did that go?" Rand surprised her with the evenness of his tone.

She'd done so many things lately that deserved scorn that she couldn't dig out from under the urge to apologize. "I don't know what possessed me to do that, Rand. I sure didn't expect William to notice me."

"Well, you're tough not to notice," he said. His mouth curved into a half smile. He reached to cover one of her hands. "Tell me what he had to say."

"It was odd, actually. He was subdued. Asked me why I was named Daisy. I told him the story and he got very quiet. Then he told me about your name being John."

"Did he?" Rand's brow furrowed and a crease appeared on his forehead. "That's odd."

"I don't know him at all, Rand, but he seemed...I don't know, wistful maybe."

Rand laughed then, releasing the seam that had pinched his brow. "In all my life no one has ever referred to William Press as 'wistful.'"

She didn't respond. Embarrassment bathed her in warmth. She was reading everybody and everything wrong these days. Ever since this big, tall, trust-fund megalomaniac with the emerald-colored eyes had crossed the threshold of the Brookside Café.

After tomorrow she'd be free to pick up the pieces after their confrontation with Adam, and then William Press.

In spite of herself, she studied Rand's face—even as his eyes bore into hers. The furrow was back in his brow. If truth be told, she'd miss him—even though putting this entire mess behind her was her only hope to regain her self-respect, let alone maintain Adam's faith in her.

She found herself studying Rand as if memorizing him, embedding his image in the recesses of her mind, a buried thought for another day. Some day when this was all over and normalcy dwelled in her heart again, she'd indulge in conjuring that face. It was a good face.

Rand squeezed her hand. "Hey, I wasn't teasing you, Daisy. It's just that you see things that some of us don't. I mean, Uncle...wistful. Maybe we'd all be better off if we could all see more good in people."

He chuckled softly. "When I'm around you I sometimes even forget I'm an ass."

"Pompous ass."

He laughed. "Yes, pompous ass."

She didn't stop the thought that her mind unabashedly delivered to her lips. "You're better than you think you are."

His lips parted and Daisy was sure he was about to speak. Her heart thundered in her chest, in her ears, throughout her veins. But, Rand did not utter a word. Instead he cradled her face in his hands and slowly, carefully, lowered his head, touching his lips to hers in a kiss as soft as silk.

He pulled away from the kiss, their mouths separated by no more than a whisper. "You make me wish for things I've never yearned for, Daisy."

She could not respond for fear of releasing a sob that ached in her throat. Rand was not the only one with new yearnings. Hers betrayed the remnants of her common sense. Wasn't it just moments ago that she wished this man had never crossed her path? But, that was *then*.

"Right now,"—her breath locked in her lungs, and blood raced shamelessly with an abandon new to her—"all I want is you."

Rand's kiss claimed her, his arms pulled her to him. Together they fell back on the bed, limbs entwined. Need and want wove them together, casting them as one. They were a single pulse of fire, unquenchable and undeniable. Their flame devoured any thoughts of tomorrow and what it would bring.

Much later—God only knew what time it was— Daisy lay against his smooth, naked chest, feeling the beat of his heart against her cheek. She would not allow the caution that knocked on the door of her brain to enter.

Her mind was locked tonight. There was no room for thinking. *Just feel,* she told herself. *Feel him and remember this always.*

Even as they dozed, the knocking persisted, getting louder and louder. When Rand stirred beside her, she snapped alert and realized it was genuine rapping on the wooden bedroom door that she was hearing. The two sat upright, and listened.

"Randolph!" Florence's voice on the other side of the door was loud, urgent. "Randolph, please open the door! It's William. Hurry! The ambulance is on its way."

Chapter Thirty-Three

The green-tiled corridor was dimly lit and smelled of antiseptic. Rand had followed the ambulance, a silent wide-eyed Daisy beside him in the small interior of his car. Each time he stole a glance of her face he saw the blink of her eyes, the only evidence that she hadn't turned to stone. He whispered her name and she shook her head "no."

Rand's mind reeled as they waited their turn in line at the check-in of Memorial Hospital's Emergency Room. The couple ahead of him, each sitting on a plastic chair at the in-take desk, responded in low voices to questions asked by the nurse. His clenched chest muscles hurt, his throat was dry. He wondered, *is this it?* After all the schemes and all the pretenses, was this it for Uncle William?

Rand's mind veered to the image of the other time he'd faced death. He saw William presiding over the arrangements, all but holding court at the funeral home. He saw the two shiny caskets, side by side, surrounded by an orchard of flowers. Rand squeezed his eyes closed, pinched two fingers at the bridge of his nose, and massaged the memories away.

He felt Daisy's touch on his arm and turned to her. "It's your turn," she said softly.

Rand refocused and saw that the couple had vacated the chairs and the nurse behind the counter was looking at him with a scowl.

He identified himself, wallet opened under her scrutiny. She clicked her keyboard, staring at her screen. Rand watched her eyes as they moved from right to left as she read whatever text appeared there. His jaw ached.

"Mr. Press, I'll be back in a moment," she said. She padded away on squeaky rubber soles, disappearing through a doorway.

When she returned, she wore an anemic smile, one Rand had seen a long time ago. It was the kind that offered sympathy, one that said this tired-eyed nurse already knew something rotten that he was about to learn.

"You can go in. Through those double doors," she said. She pointed to an entry with a sign that read, "No Admittance."

"Are you family?" she asked Daisy.

Daisy looked to Rand. They held a long gaze and he wondered what was going through her head. Was she family? The question rendered him mute. All he could do was look at her.

"Rand, go," she said. She gave him a nudge. "I'll wait here."

****

William Press looked like a cadaver on the gurney, his pallor as gray as dishwater. Florence sat on a short stool beside the bed, the rims of her eyes red, her face lined with worry. She had insisted on riding to the hospital in the ambulance and the EMT's didn't dare tell her no.

"Any news?" Rand asked in a hushed tone. "Is he sleeping?"

"No news yet. They've got him on a heart monitor. We're waiting for his cardiologist to get here," she said, her voice weary.

"Is that you, boy?" he heard William say in a muffled voice that sounded like his mouth was stuffed with cotton.

"Uncle?" Rand said. He stepped closer.

"Yes, I hear you, Randolph," he said. His voice

was low, weak. "What took you so long?"

"I followed you here, but the waiting room's busy. You know how that goes. How are you feeling? You look okay."

"There's no time for bullshit, Randolph," he said, his lips pursed. "I'm thirsty. Get me some water."

Rand looked to Florence who shook her head emphatically "no."

"I think we need to wait until your doctor gets here," Rand said.

Florence stood from the stool. "Randolph, I'll go check at the desk to see if William can have ice chips. I'll be back in a few minutes."

Florence disappeared through the curtain that surrounded William's cubicle. The only sound in the room was the steady beeping coming from the monitor that intermittently flashed numbers and graphs.

"Is she gone?" William asked.

"Florence? Yes."

"Okay, listen to me, boy. Sit down. Go on, sit."

Rand lowered himself onto the ridiculously low stool, feeling like a small child next to the sheet-draped man.

"Before I go—"

"Uncle Will—"

"Hush," the old man sputtered. "Before I go, you have to know something."

"I'm listening."

"We've behaved like fools, you and I."

"We can talk later. You should rest—"

"I've discovered something, boy." William made a sound, an unnerving wheeze. "You're not like me, are you? All these years I've worked to mold you into someone else. Almost worked, too, boy, didn't it?" He attempted a chuckle and coughed a string of rasps.

"You are not my son."

"Uncle—"

"You are the son of John Randolph Press and the woman he loved enough to defy his heritage. Your mother was *his* fortune."

Rand did not speak. He watched the place where the two halves of the curtain met, willing the fabric to part with the arrival of either Florence or the cardiologist. William's words were agony and he didn't want to hear another syllable. Rand stood from the stool.

"Don't forget that J in front of your name," the old man spewed. "It's who you are, too. And, the J comes first. Remember that. And, well, I guess what I wanted to say, to put it simply, is that I'm sorry."

Rand's chest locked as though a metal sheath had clamped around his torso. He could barely pull air into his lungs. He eyed the curtain. Was William delusional now? Had he actually said he was *sorry?*

"I'm sorry." He said it again.

"For what?"

"For steering you wrong."

"Well, Uncle, fear not. I'm on my right path, now, aren't I?" The words felt like metal in his mouth. It made no sense to continue the ruse of his impending marriage. William knew it was a lie, and suddenly Rand felt strangled by the falsity.

He stepped closer to his uncle and leaned down so the man could see his face. "Uncle, listen. I know you've learned the truth about my so-called engagement. It's all my doing. I coerced a nice, naïve woman to play along with my scheme. Please don't take it out on her. Daisy's only guilty of loving her son so much that she'd partner with the likes of me."

The old man smiled, his lips pale and bloodless. "You're right, son. You *are* on the right path now."

****

By the time they escorted Florence back to William's house it was nearly three in the morning.

Sitting beside Rand in his car, Daisy fought to

keep her eyes open. Every time she closed them she saw images that bothered her. She and Rand in their embrace, their bodies melded. There was the image of Rand's face when he came out from the emergency room to check on her. The sadness in his eyes, the way his face brightened when he spotted her in the chair by the wall.

It all swirled in her mind like a drizzle of icing over warm cake. When she tried to dispel the thoughts by staring out into the night, her peripheral vision saw him at the wheel. He was everywhere.

They turned into her parking lot and Rand pulled into a spot near her door. He turned off the engine, faced her, and swung an arm up over the back of his seat. With his other hand he ran fingers over his hair.

Gazing directly at her, he said, "I guess time will tell."

"You'll keep me posted?" she asked softly.

"Of course. I told him, Daisy."

"You did?" She felt a panic stirring in her system. "What did you say? Oh, God, what did he say?"

"I told him the whole plan was my fault," Rand said slowly, his tone sullen. "The man's on his last legs, and he's still onto me." He shook his head and his mouth turned up in a weary, half-smile. "One down, one to go. We have to tell Adam."

"Tomorrow," she said. "We'll tell Adam tomorrow."

****

Daisy found Adam asleep on the couch, the television tuned to an old episode of Seinfeld. She gingerly reached for the remote and clicked off the power button. She slipped a throw over his long frame and switched off the table lamp.

Finally in her own bed, she felt the kind of

fatigue that comes from heavy physical work, as if she'd dug a garden or raked leaves from off a football field.

She ached from the inside out. Misery took a great toll. That's what she was, she'd decided. She was miserable. *Well, that's what happens when you start believing your own lies.* And, there was no blaming Rand for their bedroom antics, that was for sure. She remembered her words to him. *I want you.* If she weren't so totally exhausted she'd groan. The best she could hope for was that sleep would come soon.

Chapter Thirty-Four

Daisy woke to Adam nudging her. Opening her eyes, she saw bright daylight streaming into her room. She squinted. "Hi, honey. What time is it?"

"Noon."

She sat upright.

"How's Rand's uncle?" Adam asked. He handed her a ceramic mug steaming with coffee.

"Bless you, child," she said. She took the cup and with two hands guided it to her mouth. She took a deep pull of the aromatic liquid. "William's in ICU. He was stable when we left."

"Think he'll be okay? I mean it would be awful if he didn't make it to your wedding."

"I don't know," she said. She placed the mug on the nightstand. "Adam, I need to talk with you about something important." Suddenly, she decided she couldn't wait another minute to confess. God only knew what Adam's reaction would be—and Rand had enough to contend with.

"Mom, what is it?"

"The truth is that Rand and I are not engaged."

"Wait. You broke up?"

"No," she shook her head. God, this was tougher than she thought it would be.

The diamond on her hand winked at her. "It's all been a lie, Adam. A scheme, actually. Rand found out that his uncle was going to cut him from his will unless he got married and he asked me to play the part."

"What?" Adam shot up from the bed. His face contorted with confusion. "Are you kidding me?"

"I know, I know. It sounds insane. But, Rand offered me a lot of money to pretend to be his fiancée."

"If I ever see that asshole again I'll punch his lights out. Mom, have you lost your mind?"

My mind, my soul, and now my heart, apparently. "It would have been enough money to send you to Pratt."

"Oh for God's sake," Adam said. He started to pace alongside the bed. "Now you're going to put this on me? Seriously?

"I don't even want to go to Pratt, so the joke's on you, Mom."

"What do you mean you 'don't want to go to Pratt'? Pratt's your dream school."

"No, Mom, it's *your* dream, not mine. You gave up listening to me about what I want a long time ago." He stormed out of the room.

Daisy jumped out of bed and darted after him. "Wait a second!" She sounded angrier than she intended. "Hold up. You're a talented, brilliant artist. It's my job to make sure you get the best possible opportunities in life."

"And you think it's best for me that you to sell yourself to the highest bidder?"

"Do not disrespect me, Adam."

"You've already disrespected yourself, Mom." He yanked his leather jacket from the back of a chair and exited the apartment, slamming the front door behind him.

Daisy thought to follow him, but stopped herself. It would only make things worse. She was sure of it. Her mind raced. She picked up the phone and dialed Candy's number. "Can you come over?" she asked, and then began to sob.

In next to no time Candy was at her door. Worry was all over her as though someone had poured a bucket of it on her head. "Daisy-girl, what is it? Tell me."

Daisy knew she probably sounded and looked hysterical there in her baggy pajamas, her hair not having yet seen a comb. She didn't care. When Candy wrapped a strong arm around her shoulders she let her friend guide her to the living room sofa. "Okay, take it easy, and start from the beginning."

Candy listened, her eyes intent, as Daisy went over the details of William's emergency and now Adam's reaction to the truth. By the time Daisy was done, her friend noticed she'd shredded a fistful of tissues into a mass of fat flakes that peppered her lap.

"First off, where do you think Adam went?" Candy's tone was steady.

Daisy shrugged. "Elizabeth's I guess."

"Fine, let him cool his jets. He's just stunned, that's all. Give him some time to let the news settle."

"You didn't hear him, Candy. He's never been that mad. The rage in his eyes—well I'll never forget it." She felt tears coming back, blurring her vision. She blinked them away and swallowed hard.

"I'm still reeling about him saying he doesn't want to go to Pratt. Since when? I mean, isn't that all he's talked about since he got into high school?"

"Sweetie, listen. Since this is truth or consequences we're playing these days, let me say this—I don't think I've ever heard Adam say he wanted that school."

When Daisy opened her jaw to protest, Candy waved her silent. "Tell me why it's so important that he go."

"Because," she replied, fingering the shards of torn-up tissue in her hands. "He's a talented, smart kid and nobody's..." She stopped herself.

The memory of her conversation with the vice principal popped into her thoughts like a prank snake exploding from a tin can. Oddly, the serpent had a face like David's father's when he'd tried to buy her off.

"Finish the sentence," Candy coaxed. "And nobody's what?"

"Nobody's going to see him as less worthy." A lump lodged in her throat. She stared at Candy whose mouth appeared like a seam on her face, lips tucked in tightly.

"Can I ask you something, Daisy-girl?"

Daisy didn't say yes, but she didn't say no either. She waited.

"Do you think this hell-bent push for your kid to go to some fancy school says you believe in him, or that he *needs it* for you to believe in him?"

"Of course I believe in him, Candy."

"I know that, sweetie-pie. Now, find out if he does."

Daisy released a long breath sending the bits of tissue scattering to the floor. "I wish my troubles would blow away as easily," she said. She reached to gather the scraps into her hands.

"You'll be fine," Candy said. She pitched in to pick up the pieces. "You pulverized these things.

"Have you heard from Rand yet about how his uncle's doing?"

"No."

"What's going to happen now, Daisy? With you and the gazillionaire?"

She shrugged. "It's over. The truth's out so there's no point."

"You okay with that?"

Daisy had no answer. She wasn't "okay" with anything, nothing at all. She closed her eyes. How many times had she wished that Rand had never crossed her path, wished she could go back to the day when he walked into the café and lock the door before he entered?

Well, now, with luck, she'd have the chance to

retrieve her old life. So, why wasn't she *okay*? "I slept with him," she blurted flatly as though she was telling her friend the weather forecast.

"Oh, boy. Well, that complicates things, doesn't it?" Candy said with a smirk.

"Not really. I'm an idiot, so it's just more confirmation of that fact."

Daisy stood from the couch and carried her wad of tissue pieces to the kitchen to throw them in the trash. Candy hopped up and followed her. "Hey, not so fast, you," she said. "So, how was it? You know, was it good? Disappointing?"

"I wish it were disappointing," Daisy said. She leaned against the counter. "That way it would be easier to forget."

"Good then, huh?"

Daisy couldn't let herself relive the details, not yet anyway. Someday—maybe when she was a couple hundred years old, at least—she'd revisit the scenario, detail for detail, touch for touch. But for now the memories would only drive her mad.

"Yes," she said. "Very."

"So, why can't you and he just pick up from here? Go on dates or something."

"Well, for one, my son told me if he ever sees Rand again he's going to beat the crap out of him. Besides, this was an agreement that went awry. I need to concentrate on getting my life back."

"Have you told Ima and Pete yet?"

"No," she sighed. "But, when I show up for work tomorrow and ask for my Saturdays back, maybe that'll make them forgive me quicker."

Candy pulled Daisy into an easy embrace. "Sweetie-pie, there's nothing to forgive on any count. We all love you."

****

After Candy left, Daisy flopped onto the couch and closed her eyes, but her thoughts would not turn off. Somehow she had to make it right with Adam.

Had it been her pushing the idea of going to that art school on him? What did he really want? She didn't know now, and it hurt to admit that.

The phone rang and she thought about ignoring it. She reached for the receiver just in case it was Adam calling her.

"Hello?"

"Mrs. Cameron? It's Elizabeth."

"Yes?" Daisy sat up straight. The girl's voice was low and she could hardly hear her. "Is Adam with you?"

"No, yes, I mean, he's here, but he's in the bathroom. I wanted to call you quickly and let you know he's okay. He told me what happened."

"Thank you," Daisy said. She felt an ache behind her eyes. "I appreciate it, Elizabeth. Is he all right?"

"Yes, just upset. Don't tell him I called, though, okay?"

"Okay."

The line went dead before Daisy could thank the girl again.

Adam was with his girlfriend, and for whatever reason she'd called to reassure his mother about him. She was thankful for that much, at least. Daisy realized that she actually liked this Goth-girl.

In a little while, gratefully, she slept. It was a deep, dreamless slumber that Daisy needed like medicine.

When the doorbell rang, it jolted her awake. On an instant surge of adrenaline, she trotted to the door with Adam in mind.

It was Rand. He looked tired and sad. "Hi," he said.

She opened the door wider for him to enter. She was a rumpled, pathetic mess. But what did it matter really? She raked her fingers through the tangles of her hair to no avail. A mess was a mess.

"How's William?" she asked.

"He made it through the night all right. I'm on my way back over to the hospital. I stopped by so we can have *the talk* with Adam." He looked around the room. "Is he here?"

"No," she said. "He's hiding out at Elizabeth's."

"Hiding out?"

"I told him the truth." The words came out flat, defeated.

"How'd he take it?" Rand stepped further into the room.

"Not well." Daisy was too spent to go over it again. "He's mad as hell at me...and he hates your guts." Tears of exhaustion sprang to her eyes. Rand's look of concern melted her heart into a pulsing liquid.

Saying goodbye to this man would be bad enough. Forgetting him would be impossible. She pulled the ring off her finger and extended it toward him. "I believe this belongs to you."

Rand accepted it into his palm but didn't close his fingers around it. "I'm sorry I wasn't here with you when you told him. I couldn't sleep and wound up back at the hospital."

"Rand, it doesn't matter, anyway. I need to have a talk with my son. Actually I need to *listen* to him.

"Turns out he doesn't want to go to Pratt, and apparently never did. He was just appeasing me. Go figure, huh?" She made a pathetic attempt at chuckling. It sounded more like a squeaky hinge.

"So, the fact that our deal's a bust is of no consequence. I don't need the money after all."

"Would you like me to talk with him?"

"No," she said too quickly. "It might make it worse. But, thanks."

"Maybe not. He shared his hesitancy about Pratt and the whole Europe thing with me when we were fishing, so..."

"What? You knew all along?" Rage sprang alive in her veins, a fiery ball of emotion, frustration and disappointment feeding it like a lit torch. "*What* Europe thing?"

Rand sighed. "He's mad now, but when he comes back I'm sure he'll explain. He wants to delay school for a while and go to Paris."

She still couldn't believe that her son had leveled with Rand, of all people, and not her. Elizabeth must know too, of course. *I'm the only one in the dark.*

"Why didn't you tell me?"

"He asked me not to."

She detested his cool demeanor and wanted to slap him. "Let me ask you something, Mr. Press, were you honoring your word to Adam or making sure I'd still play along with our farce?"

"Listen, Daisy..." he said. When he stepped near she jumped backward as though accosted by flames.

"No. You're a liar and you seduced me."

"Are you serious?" he asked with an incredulous tone. "You've got one skewed memory, darling."

"You knew full well that I was in this for one reason and you were aware that my whole involvement was for naught. And do not call me 'darling.'"

"Wait..."

She ignored the softening of his voice.

She'd never felt so mad in her life. Her shaking hands scared her. She'd been duped before. And now, thanks to this big ass, the entire bottom of her world had plummeted straight to hell.

"Please leave."

Rand's cell phone sounded and he reached into his jacket pocket to retrieve it. His voice resumed its bold resonance. "Press," he barked into the device.

She watched his face as he listened intently, his eyes narrowed. "I'll be there momentarily." He switched off the phone and looked into Daisy's eyes. "He's failing."

Her hands flew to her chest but she did not speak.

In an instant Rand was gone.

Chapter Thirty-Five

The sun was setting. Its last rays of light shone cool and dim in through the blinds. Daisy had dozed on and off for who knew how long. At last, she forced herself upright. She sat on the couch amid wads of used tissues looking as though she'd lost a snowball fight.

She craned her neck toward Adam's bedroom, admonishing herself instantly. *What do I think, for God's sake, that he'd miraculously appeared out of thin air when I wasn't looking?* That thought fell flat at the sight of his open door. She knew he hadn't come home, but the confirmation still stung.

Standing from the couch, her stomach pitched precariously. *When's the last time I ate anything?* she wondered. First, though, she needed tea.

She shuffled into the kitchen and put on a pot of water. She pulled out her stash of teas, fingering through the tin containers. The one named Persephone's Tea caught her eye, especially the figure of the woman on the label. She squinted to read the text. Persephone was the goddess that symbolized the natural process, the seasons of life.

Daisy popped the tin's lid, inhaled the pungent aroma. She consulted the label again. "A blend of organics—dandelion root, burdock, grape root, milk thistle seed. This tea is ideal for those in transition, those under stress." She sprinkled the leafy mix into the mesh infuser.

The jangle of keys and fiddling sound at the front door stalled her heart. She listened intently.

After an agonizingly long moment Adam stood

at the entrance of the kitchen, himself disheveled, his backpack slung over one shoulder. In his hand he held a wax paper bag from a donut shop and the day's newspaper.

"Hi," he said.

"Hi," she said.

"Mom, I..." He took one step toward his mother and she flew to him. Daisy wrapped her son in her arms and held him tight.

She didn't care about his harsh words to her the previous day. Nor did it matter that he didn't want to go to Pratt. All that mattered was that he was here with her.

"I'm sorry, Mom." He handed her the bag. "French crullers."

"I am, too, honey," she said.

"Did you eat, Mom?"

"Not yet. I'm making tea." Daisy peeked inside the bag, the aroma of sugar and grease hitting her senses. "My favorite."

"I know," he said. "Eat. I had something at Elizabeth's. She told me she called you last night so I knew you weren't worried about where I was. But, still, I should have called you myself."

She nodded ruefully, then poured tea into a mug. "Want some tea?"

Adam made a face. "It's all yours, Mom."

Daisy sipped the aromatic blend, willing it to do its job of lowering her stress and easing her mind.

"How's Rand doing?"

She shot him a look. "Rand?"

"Yeah, you know, since his uncle died. How is he?"

"I..." She felt her voice catch. Her lips closed and she swallowed hard. "I didn't know William died."

Adam unfolded the newspaper that he held in his hands. The two-inch-high headline was about William Press. The letters were big, black, and final.

Daisy took the publication from Adam's hands.

There was a picture of William from an earlier, younger time. He had been handsome, but not nearly as charismatic as the young Randolph Press standing beside him in the photo. She scanned the article. William had died in his sleep after what they termed "a long illness." The family, it said, had decided upon a private service, closed to the public. "Family and close friends only." That, she knew, excluded her.

"I'll send flowers, or something," she muttered. An ache squeezed her throat tight.

She raised her gaze to meet Adam's. His face was contorted with confusion. "Honey, sit down. It's time we talked."

They sat on either side of the kitchen table. The newspaper folded in the center of the surface made Daisy think of the net on a ping pong table. It was her *serve.*

"My liaison with Randolph Press is done. I don't know what will happen in regard to his uncle's estate. That's none of our business anymore. I just want us to get back to normal."

"But, Mom—"

She held up a hand and took another sip of tea. "Tell me how long you've been thinking about going to Europe. And, yes, Rand told me that part—but only because he thought I knew the whole truth."

Adam leaned forward on the table, hands clasped like a confessor. She noticed that when he began to speak his words were alive—in his eyes as well as his voice.

"Since junior year," he said. "I've been researching it and I'm sure we can do it for almost two months without getting jobs. But our hope is to find something we can do and stay longer, until Christmas maybe."

"Okay," Daisy said. She took a deep breath.

"First of all, by 'we' are you referring to Elizabeth?"

"Yes, of course," he said.

"What's her mother say about it?"

"Well..." Adam ran a hand through his thick hair. "At first she wasn't thrilled about it. But, you know... Elizabeth's promised to enroll in the winter session at the university when we get back. That's, uh, what I thought I'd do, too."

"But, Adam, seriously, wouldn't your work fare better at an art school? Especially one like Pratt?"

He shrugged. "Sure. But, I feel like I have to do this, Mom. It's like this burning quest I have. I don't want to ignore it."

"And how do you two plan to fund this trip?"

"I've been saving," he said with a hint of pride. "We both have."

"Enough to go to Europe?"

"France, actually. Our target is Montmartre, a village inside Paris." His eyes sparkled again. "It's where the great artists lived. Think about it, Mom, I'd live and breathe in the same place as Van Gogh, Dali, Degas.

"And, Normandy, which is nearby, is having an art festival that spans the whole summer. It looks as if it'll be amazing. I have all the information in my room. Do you want to see it?"

"Yes," she conceded. "But, you still haven't told me how you'll pay for it."

He winked and left the room.

While he was gone Daisy's mind raced. Could she do it? Could she really just give in and let him go halfway around the world? She thought about her conversation with Candy, heard her friend's words in her mind. She finished her tea.

Adam walked back into the room with an armful of pamphlets and papers in one hand and a coffee can in the other.

When he dumped out the contents of the can—

300

thick folds of money—Daisy was reminded of Rand's jar that had held the thirty-seven dollars...the unfulfilled wish of a young boy. A lump appeared in her throat.

"Wow," she managed to say as Adam unfolded the money and put it in separate stacks by denomination. "Where'd you get all this?"

"I've been saving since I was thirteen. Twenty-three hundred," he said. "By the time I graduate I should have almost three grand. Elizabeth's got more than that. Her grandmother left her a lump of money and she's going to use part of that."

"Adam, honey, even three grand isn't going to fund a trip like you're talking."

"Ah," he said. His old smile was back on his face. "Look, at this."

They spent time going through the material he had collected. Daisy hadn't known about hostels and the affordability of such youth-housing overseas. The one Adam and Elizabeth had targeted was right in Montmartre and cost twenty dollars a day. She eyed the pamphlet, seeing the list of perks that were included, breakfast, linens, maps, internet and even very affordable bike rentals.

"It looks great, Adam." She had to admit it—she'd never utter another lie as long as she lived.

"I'm really sorry I didn't tell you sooner, Mom. It's just that I knew how upset and disappointed you'd be. I want to make you proud."

Tears misted her eyes for the umpteenth time. "You do, honey," she said. She got up from her seat, went to him, and bent down so that her forehead could touch against his—their age-old custom of union. "You always have."

"Please trust my choices."

"Do you smoke, Adam?" The question surprised her even as it came from her lips.

"Smoke? Where'd that come from?"

"Lately you've smelled of cigarettes. I don't need to tell you why that's not a good choice."

Adam exhaled, shook his head. "I do not smoke. Elizabeth has been smoking. Not a lot, but she had been. She quit as part of our agreement."

"What agreement is that?"

"She agreed to quit smoking and I agreed to level with you about Europe. I was going to do that right after the engagement party."

Daisy's heart swelled in her chest. She touched her forehead to Adam's again, mother and son silent in the moment. One thought passed from her mind to his. Adam was going to Paris.

****

Rand sat alone. He'd spent hours with Florence discussing Uncle's wishes. The man wanted a private funeral. Actually, what was it Flo quoted him as saying? *I will not be the dead ringmaster of a circus!*

A smile crept across Rand's lips. William Press knew what he did and did not want, in life *and* in death.

It was an odd feeling, missing the old guy. William had been dead for only a day and already Rand felt his loss.

There were no Presses left—just him. He had no family now. Rand's head hurt, but he couldn't stop his brain from racking up the list of don't-haves. When it came down to it, he had nothing. And at the top of that list was Daisy.

Uncle's estate was another matter. William had died before Rand learned the man's final decision. It was true that his sham had been exposed and he certainly hadn't fulfilled Uncle's request that he marry. He wasn't counting on the patriarch having had a last-minute change of heart.

Rand remembered their last conversation and the way the failing old man had looked at him when he made that comment about his nephew's being on the right track. He knew the reference was about Daisy.

However, she had made it all too clear that she was done with him. The good thing was that Uncle hadn't lived long enough to know that Rand had screwed that up, too.

****

The funeral was simple, tasteful, and the service was brief. The few invited attendees were business associates, a few of William's domestic hires, and Max Willoughby, his attorney. Rand sat beside Florence in the front row of chairs, the two of them the lone representatives of William's family.

"I loved him," Florence uttered periodically in soft, barely audible whispers. "I did."

Rand held her hand, cool and parched in his grasp. Her gray eyes glistened with the tears of longing. He tightened his hold and pressed his shoulder against hers. "He loved you, too, Flo," he assured her, to which she nodded with a closed-eyed little smile.

Rand had never heard the words from William's lips, but he knew his uncle had loved Florence. Rand gave the woman a long glance. Did Uncle ever say those words to her? Had he ever actually professed his love? He wished so.

The burial service at the cemetery was closed to everyone except for Florence, Rand, and for some reason, Max Willoughby. It irked him that Max was included in Uncle's request. All Rand could think of when he saw the little weasel was how he must be gloating over the outcome of William's will. He carried the knowledge as though he had a golden nugget in his pocket.

The minister was a stranger to Rand and he doubted William had known him, either. Pastor Francis Geary ministered at the local Presbyterian

Church, the one with which the Press family had been long affiliated. Rand hadn't been to a service in years, and he surmised William's relationship with the parish resorted to an annual tithe that kept the Press name in prominence.

The minister's words were hollow to Rand's ears. What did this stranger know of his Uncle? Rand felt a zing of protectiveness toward William's memory.

He glanced at Florence who stood at the graveside clutching one white rose between her hands like an offering. His heart tugged. He slid his gaze over to Max Willoughby and was surprised to discover that the little man was crying.

Tears cascaded down Max's skinny, concave cheek and he intermittently swiped at them with two fingers. When Max turned toward Rand, his mouth quivered to an anemic grin. Too abashed to look away, Rand nodded his head as though to approve the man's distress.

Afterward they lunched back at the mansion, an intimate setting in the dining room where just days ago the debacle of the engagement party had taken place.

Florence, for the first time Rand could remember, took her seat for the full meal as a member of the family. He had been accustomed to her darting in and out of the kitchen during all the times he'd dined here. But, today Florence was a family member. Sadness washed over him. It was a pity that William's death marked the woman's feeling of belonging. Some things happened too late.

"It was a nice funeral," Max said as he was about to leave. He had extended his hand to Rand for a firm handshake. "Just as William would have wanted it. You did a fine job, Randolph."

"Max," Rand said. He felt an odd rush of sympathy. "Thank you for coming. I know how long you and Uncle had known each other."

Max nodded. "He was a good man, Randolph." He chuckled awkwardly. "I do realize how tough he could be, but he was good to me. We were good to each other. I'm going to miss him." Rand saw the glint of tears spring back into the little man's eyes.

"Max," he said. "I'm sorry for the way I talked with you that day in your office. You and I haven't always seen eye to eye over the years, but I do apologize for being so brusque."

"Thank you," Max said. "I appreciate that. I'll be contacting you regarding the reading of the will, Randolph."

Later Rand found himself alone in the library of William's mansion. He liked the dusky darkness. He poured himself a cognac and, sat on the leather sofa.

He had nearly forgotten about the reading of Uncle's will until Max mentioned it, and now that was all he could think about. What would he do now if the outcome were to render him a pauper? His gaze travelled to the top shelf of the bookshelf. He wished he knew.

What he did know was that he wanted to speak with Adam, even though Daisy had told him not to. He wanted to make sure the boy knew that his mother was not to blame for any of this mess of lies.

He had programmed the kid's number into his blackberry after their fishing expedition just in case he ever needed it. And now he did. He dialed the number.

Adam was silent after Rand identified himself. "Adam, listen, I know you're not happy with me, but..."

"I'm sorry about your uncle," Adam said. The youth's words threw Rand for a loop.

"Thank you," Rand said.

"Mom said the funeral was today and that it was private."

Rand's heart did a spastic jiggle at the reference

305

to Daisy. "Yes."

"She, um, she said you two, you know, called it quits."

"Yes, your mom's glad to be done with me and the whole ordeal I put her through. That's why I'm calling, Adam. Please don't be mad at her. Her intentions were honorable. I wish I could say the same for mine."

"You don't have to worry. She and I are good."

"I'm glad," Rand said. He racked his brain for something else to say, for a reason to stay on the line. He came up empty. "Well, Adam, I guess that's it then. Take care of yourself...and your mom, too."

When the call ended Rand downed his drink and poured another.

****

On Saturday Daisy gave herself plenty of time before she had to be at work. She showered and dressed way ahead of schedule. It was her first day back waitressing on the weekend and she felt lucky that Ima and Pete had taken her confession so magnanimously.

She wanted to feel free of the baggage of her ordeal, but it was always there, in her mind and in her heart. Maybe over time she could count on forgetting the pain of her foolish decision. But she had no hope of forgetting the man who had wooed her into it. The memory of J. Randolph Press, Jr. was etched well inside her.

Oddly, after she and Adam had had their talk, she didn't expect to feel anything more than relief. But she did. She felt the absence of Rand.

"Going to work already?"

She startled from her thoughts to find Adam standing in his bedroom's doorway, clad in a tee-shirt and plaid flannel pajama pants.

"Why are you up so early?" she asked. "It's six-thirty."

"It's early for you, too, isn't it?"

"Yes," she said. "I'm making a stop at the cemetery before I go to work." She reached for a container of flowers she had placed on the table. "I'm bringing this to plant at William's grave."

"What is it?" he asked, walking over to her, touching a finger to the red and white blooms.

"They're called Sweet Williams," she said. She still couldn't believe she'd actually found them at the nursery when she stopped by yesterday. "He, William I mean, he marveled at how nice it was that grandma and grandpa named me Daisy because of its meaning."

"That's nice, Mom." Adam said. "By the way, Rand called me."

Her heart stammered. "When?"

"Yesterday. He wanted to make sure that I wasn't mad at you."

Daisy swallowed hard and her chest clenched tight. "How...how is he doing?"

Adam shrugged. "He said he's doing okay. But to tell you the truth he didn't sound great. I kind of felt sorry for him."

"I thought you said that if you ever laid eyes on him you'd kick his butt?"

Adam smiled sheepishly. "We say stupid things when we're pissed. But we say even worse stuff when we're scared."

Daisy grabbed the potted flowering plant, her trowel, and her cotton garden gloves. She headed toward the door before her son's words could sink too deeply into her thoughts.

She drove through the iron gates and travelled the winding path toward the grave as a caretaker in the office had directed.

The overturned dirt was easy to manipulate and the trowel's blade quickly sunk into it. She loosened the plant from its pot, tenderly freed the tangled

307

roots, and eased it into the hole she had dug. With gloved hands she patted the soil around the plant.

She took an empty soda bottle she'd found in her car to the water spigot at the end of the row of headstones. Filling it with cold tap water, she carried it back to the site. As she wet the soil she gazed at the large, intricately carved headstone, already etched with William's name and date of birth. Missing, of course, was the date of his death. Soon, she assumed, someone would come to add that to the stone.

"These are Sweet William," she said aloud as though having a conversation with him. "The actual name is"—she fiddled with the spike that had been in the pot, reading from it—"'Dianthus Barbatus. The name Sweet William comes from Saint William of York or William of Marlborough, Duke of Cumberland.' Men of status and power." She felt a smile curve on her lips. "So, you're in good company, William."

Daisy drove to work with a dichotomy of emotions. She felt a sense of closure combined with a sense of starting anew. In truth, she was free to be her old self again, to take up her former life. Yet, she didn't feel like *that* person now.

As she crossed over the Algonquin Bridge she saw the rooftop of the Brookside Café ahead of her, awaiting her arrival.

Chapter Thirty-Six

Rand had gotten the call. He had an appointment at Max Willoughby's office for the reading of the will, the lowering of the boom.

He steered his Jag toward the Morristown office wondering what the news would be and what he would do about it. He still didn't know. It was as though his brain would not go there, not allow him to process the scenarios of win or loss.

The thing his brain did do was continue to torture him. He'd spent so many years with memories comfortably locked away, all but forgotten.

Ever since he'd concocted the plan to fool William, what had happened was pathetic, if not laughable. He could very well be left with nothing but those recovered memories now compounded by new ones.

How he managed to create a pretend life and now mourn its demise was beyond his comprehension. But, that was the sad fact.

Uncle, what was your dying thought of me? He could not make the thought stop. He somehow wanted that answer more than he wanted the one Max Willoughby would give him in just a little while.

He checked the clock on the dashboard. He had plenty of time before the meeting. On a whim, he turned down Ridgedale Avenue and headed toward Gate of Heaven Cemetery.

As he trudged along the lineup of headstones, a sea of granite, he found the row marked "30" by a wrought iron stake in the ground. Uncle William's final resting place.

The first headstone in William's row said "Nash." Rand paused in front of it. The man's name had been Anthony Nash and, according to his stone, had died ten years ago. Rand hadn't known him. And, now his was the name Rand would look for whenever he visited William.

He noticed the plant right away. Beside it was a white plastic stick jabbed into the still-moist soil. Rand plucked the stick and shook the crumbs of dirt from its end. He knew immediately it had been her. He felt a stab in his center. Daisy had planted this squat little plant known as "Sweet William." He was sure of it.

"Well, Uncle, I've made a mess of it, haven't I?" he said.

"I'm on my way to meet Max at his office. I stopped here to tell you that no matter what you decided on your estate, I'm still your nephew. You still raised me when I lost my family. So, I'll survive your decision."

Rand felt his throat tighten. "And no matter what, you and I are Presses. I won't forget."

He jabbed the little plastic stick back into the dirt and returned to his car. He drove back through the labyrinth of paved paths toward the iron gate confident the drive to Max Willoughby's office would take him but a few minutes.

When he exited the cemetery, however, Rand turned left instead of right, and headed for the Algonquin Bridge.

Chapter Thirty-Seven

Daisy refilled Mr. Carbone's coffee cup and plopped two creamers on the counter in front of him. "Can I get you anything else?" she asked.

The man shook his head and reached for his wallet. "I have to head out, Daisy." He unfolded the leather pouch and flipped a couple bills from it. "It's a honey dew day, darling." He gave her a big grin. "Margaret's got a list. Honey, do this and honey, do that."

She laughed and shook her head, scooping the generous tip from the counter. She had missed the familiar banter with customers like this affable man. She saw him blow a kiss to Candy after she rang him up at the register. She'd missed working side-by-side with Candy, too. To anyone who didn't know better, Daisy Cameron had gotten just what she wanted.

"You know what you need?" Candy asked, coming up beside her.

"No, but I'm sure you do," Daisy said, unable to keep from smiling. She loved her outspoken friend like a sister and that was something that hadn't changed since her hiatus to never-never land. "And I also have no doubt you're going to tell me."

"No, never mind." She huffed and walked away, injured. Daisy knew it was an act.

So, she played along for old time's sake.

"Oh, come on, Candy, don't pout," she coaxed. "Tell me what you're thinking. What do I need?"

Candy smirked, gave Daisy a wide-eyed look. "I've got a better idea. How about you let *him* tell

311

you?" She motioned her head in the direction of the front door.

Daisy turned her gaze to the entrance and saw the Jaguar pulling into a parking space. She watched Rand emerge from the vehicle, stride to the door, and push it open. Her heart clenched like a fist and seemed to fly into her throat.

She tried to busy herself unloading a tray of coffee mugs and placing them on the shelf behind the counter. She willed her hands to stop shaking.

Rand walked back to the far stool and straddled it. "Coffee, please."

Daisy turned to her friend with pleading eyes. Candy shook her head with an emphatic message of "no way."

Daisy brought him a mug of coffee and a couple of creamers. There was no avoiding it. She looked him in the eye.

His eyes were brilliant emeralds, deep green pools absent of the spark of arrogance that she had first seen in them. Now she read something warm, something that did not repel her, but rather wooed her like a hypnotist's watch.

"How are you?" he asked.

"I'm fine. Rand,"—she cleared her throat but what she wanted to do was clear her head—"I'm so sorry about William. I hope he didn't suffer in the end."

"Thank you. He didn't, as far as I know. I miss him."

She nodded and wet her lips.

"I'm taking a few days and going down to Dalton, Florida." He smiled ruefully. "Better late than never."

"Yes." The word "never" rang in her ears. Late was indeed, better.

"Daisy, I came here to say something to you," he said. "About William's will..."

"Rand," she interrupted. "I meant it when I said I didn't want anything."

"That's not what I want to say," Rand said. He reached across the counter and pulled her hand into his. Her knees threatened to buckle.

She let him hold her hand, relishing the feel of his palm against hers, the warmth of his skin. Her heart whirred.

"I'm listening," Daisy was shocked by her ability to speak, but suddenly she needed to hear whatever he had to say. Otherwise she would never forgive herself.

"Daisy, I'm on my way to Uncle's attorney's office for the reading of the will. I still don't know if I'm a rich man or a poor man.

"But, I do know that all I can think about is you. At this point I don't know what I have to offer you besides my heart." He stood from the stool and leaned across the counter, cradling her face in his hands. "But what's in this heart is true," his voice caught. "Will you have me, Daisy?"

She blinked at the tears flooding her eyes. They spilled down her cheeks. Rand caught them with his thumbs. "I want *us*, Daisy. I want you and me...and chicken noodle casserole...and fishing with Adam and—"

"Yes," she said. She was laughing and crying all at once. She loved him. *That* was the truth.

"Then, I already know my fate, sweet Daisy. I am the richest man on Earth."

A word about the author...

M. Kate Quinn draws on her quirky sense of humor, hopelessly romantic nature, highly developed sense of family and friendship, and her love for a good story while writing her novels.

She is particularly proud of her Perennials Series that began with Summer Iris (released by The Wild Rose Press in July, 2010) and the heroines that she says possess the same hopes, fears, and ultimately the same courage that lives in all of us.

M. Kate Quinn, a life-long native of New Jersey, born and raised in the Cedar Knolls section of Hanover Township, now makes her home near the beach in Ocean County.

She and her husband (the man she attributes to her belief in soul mates) have a combined total of six—yes, that's six—children and two beautiful granddaughters.

The king of their castle is a magnificent, apricot-colored Siberian cat named Sammy.

CPSIA information can be obtained at www.ICGtesting.com
Printed in the USA
BVOW020548060212

282143BV00003B/2/P